SOMEWHERE
IN THE
DARK

ALSO AVAILABLE BY R. J. JACOBS

And Then You Were Gone

SOMEWHERE IN THE DARK

A Novel

R. J. Jacobs

CROOKED LANE

NEW YORK

Published in the United States by Crooked Lane Books, an imprint of The Quick Brown Fox & Company LLC.

Crooked Lane Books and its logo are trademarks of The Quick Brown Fox & Company LLC.

Library of Congress Catalog-in-Publication data available upon request.

ISBN (hardcover): 978-1-64385-300-0
ISBN (ebook): 978-1-64385-321-5

Cover design by Melanie Sun

Printed in the United States.

www.crookedlanebooks.com

Crooked Lane Books
34 West 27th St., 10th Floor
New York, NY 10001

First Edition: August 2020

10 9 8 7 6 5 4 3 2 1

To my family.

One does not become enlightened by imagining figures of light, but by making the darkness conscious.
—Carl Jung

If this were a movie I'd be the bad guy.
—Johnny Cash

1

’m late.

I know because of the way the sun blares through my window, creeping around the edges of the bath towel I draped over the curtain rod to dampen the dawn. I hardly need a clock during June in Nashville because the days start so early and I'm extremely sensitive to light.

For just a second I remember that all-thinking world from when I was twelve. It's a world I never fully left, a space in my head that goes on forever. I've gotten lost there when I've visited for too long, so I grit my teeth to come back out of it. I have to get up. I have a therapy appointment I need to get to.

I focus on the worn but comfortable sheets brushing my skin and the birds calling to each other outside my window. I throw off my covers and stretch, listening to the *chug-chug* of the air-conditioning window unit. The white plastic fan propped on my dresser whirrs, moving the half-warm air around. Summer came early this year, and already my apartment is baking. My place is tiny enough that when my window unit switches off I can hear bits of what is happening in the apartments on either side of me. Most mornings, I hear the footsteps of the family who lives above me and the arguments of the couple to my right. I can smell the curry-scented cooking of the family to my left—a smell that seems to seep through the walls and cling to the ridges in my popcorn ceiling.

When I do check the time, the muscles in my legs stiffen. I have to hurry or I'll miss my appointment with Ms. Parsons, who I am *mandated* to see once a week for a year.

Outside, a dog is barking. I hear my neighbor's familiar guitar chords changing from C to G to E, and somewhere else a woman practicing scales—up and down and back up again. That's Nashville. It isn't even nine AM, and already there is music in the air. I overheard one of my neighbors, a girl who sounded younger than me, saying once, "This city has an invisible wind that carries ideas all around, everywhere." I like the way she said that, just like I like picturing an invisible *something* that connects us all.

More than half the people who live in my apartment building are musicians, meaning everyone is poor but acts and dresses like they're already famous. When we pass in the hallways, I notice how they smell like expensive shampoo and cigarette smoke. Musicians are mostly skinny and have sex constantly. I know because I hear them—not at night, because that's when they play or have shows. It's usually in the early afternoon, before their restaurant shifts start. Other times, I'll hear them as they sit on their courtyard balconies practicing their songs. I'll hear someone say, "Let's try that again," before restarting the part of the song they're working on. Usually, country songs are about clay dirt and gravel roads, the backs of trucks, folks who have trouble paying bills. The lyrics sound better than my memories. Sometimes at night, I open my window and listen to the harmonies—so beautiful I hardly mind hearing the same phrases practiced over and over. I don't get close—I don't need to. I prefer the distance and listen in the dark.

I know the people in my apartment building, and their habits, but they don't know me. I come and go like a ghost. At night, I keep my front light off, and if I listen to my own music it's only through my headphones. I don't bother anyone and no one bothers me, and that's how I like it. My furniture is a mix of Goodwill purchases and unfinished wood castoffs that I can't decide if I've chosen not to stain or haven't gotten around to yet. My rent is just cheap enough that my state stipend and the little money I make catering cover it. I keep things exactly how I like them, and the landlords leave me alone and never mention my criminal record.

I get up and brush my teeth—the toothpaste has a bitter flavor I've named "sharp blue" in my mind. Then I dig some clothes from my dresser. I'm in such a hurry that when I yank the bottom drawer, the dresser slams back against the wall with a loud thump. The bottom drawer stays locked. Just in case.

Even though I'm late, I rush to vacuum over my footsteps in the carpet like always, then I turn everything off, lock the door, and jog to my car. I run my finger over my apartment key, remembering how key ridges felt like mountain ranges as a kid. I do the same thing with my car key—another mountain range. Getting an apartment, a car—the mountains I've climbed. Not bad, considering where I've been. I hear the rattle of a wind chime, and more distantly, an acoustic guitar. I look back at the door of my building. Sometimes I can't name my own emotions. The feeling I have right now, I don't know how to describe.

Later, after everything's happened, I'll know that particular feeling is called happiness.

I check my car's mileage before I start the engine. The fuel gauge has never worked, so I keep a small notebook in the center console where I jot down the dates of my fill-ups and the approximate length of each trip to keep from hitting empty. I know other people might be troubled by this routine, but I like having a little system of my own. And no one gets in my car but me.

Before I could save enough for a car, I took the bus everywhere I went. Which I hated, because it was slow and inconvenient, but also I loved it in a way because it reminded me that I was resourceful. I always felt like people who grow up with too many advantages never fully develop that ability, and the feeling that it was me against the world sometimes wasn't all bad. Not needing much made me feel strong and independent—I used to stand on the bus with my shoulders pulled slightly back. Of course, getting to where I was going on time was also nice. And so was not having to stand in the rain, or freeze in the winter.

I turn the key and the engine rumbles to life. I start off toward the Community Mental Health Center, my thoughts turning to the high school graduation party I will be working in Belle Meade that night.

Of the work I've done since leaving jail, catering is the best. On the days we get ready for parties, I work by myself, prepping the food. Some of what I make hardly *looks* like food to me, but that's okay because the people we serve it to hardly eat it. For rich people, food isn't about *good*, I've learned, it's about presentation. My boss, Ken, likes me to prep because I can work alone for long stretches of time with my headphones on, and because I am very, very precise with cuts and angles, and when creating a display I am very good with a knife.

Most of *my* favorite food still comes from places like convenience stores and vending machines. I prefer food wrapped in packages. It is *contained*, and when I open it up, I always know what to expect. Two other cooks, Andre and Malik, work with the catering company too. Malik told me that the dishes I make are his favorites, but I suspect from the way he lingers around the kitchen that he is interested in me as more than a friend. My face flushes when he talks to me. I can't tell if he notices. I work quickly and keep my eyes on the cutting board in front of me, usually unable to meet his kind gaze.

I step on the gas, nearly running a red light. I don't want to be late to my session. The air-conditioning hasn't worked in my car in I don't know how long, so I keep the windows down and the wind blows my hair wild. After I park, I brush it quickly, straightening out the tangles. Therapy always makes me reminisce, and I remember admiring my mother's long brown hair when I was very little. I think of the way she smelled like doublemint gum, and the way she bustled around in quick, jerky movements and bit her lips incessantly, until they bled. I remember sores on her face, like chicken pox that never seemed to heal. Her fingers left dark spots where she gripped my arm, like shadows on a ripe banana. I asked about her sometimes after she left, until I didn't anymore.

I place the hairbrush in my glove box and click it shut. The middle of my back is wet from sweat, which feels cool in the slight breeze as I cross the parking lot. I like the familiarity of going to my appointment. Home isn't a place, it's a feeling. That's a saying, but it's true. Some people make you feel at home wherever you are. My social worker, Ms. Parsons, is like that. She took my case as a referral from the state. She'd read my file before we met, and I'm sure saw my picture in the news. I wonder if she knows more about me than she lets on, or if she is just kind enough to not bring up the trouble I got into at the concert every time we meet.

Before I started seeing Ms. Parsons, I assumed our therapy sessions would feel like those foster system check-ins after I had broken rules or when I was changing homes, but she's so nice I actually look forward to seeing her. I can tell her about most of the things I do—about vacuuming my carpet in straight lines, for example, and about getting nervous around new people. But I know better than to share about every part of my catering job or to talk about what I keep in my bottom drawer. I'd never want to put her in a bad position.

I've had a lot of counselors before. When I was very young, I saw a dark-haired man who sat so that the sun was behind him, making it impossible to read his expression. The chair in his office was so soft it felt like constant sinking. He took notes on a paper tablet and nodded when I answered questions. He mostly wanted to talk about my *real* parents, even though I barely remembered them. I was always confused. Once, I asked about where my father actually was, and the man pursed his lips like he tasted something bitter. "No way to know," he told me, his eyes narrowing the way people's do when they are frightened by the truth.

Another counselor wanted to know if I prayed. "This is the South," she said. "People go to church." God was always around, she explained, someone who hears us when we speak from our hearts. God listens when we're scared, and sometimes answers our prayers. Prayers are talking to God. She pointed her index finger toward the ceiling. I tilted my head back and looked up.

I knew better than to tell her about how Shelly and Owen James's songs got me through life when I was locked in the dark. Shelly and Owen James are *legitimately* famous—two of the biggest stars in country music. Everyone knows who they are, but no one knows them the way I do. I can never explain my relationship with the Jameses, not really.

It would make me sound insane.

I'm slightly famous too, in a way. The state took care to hide my identity because I was a minor when I was discovered, but I *did* make the history books. I was the person held in captivity the longest in the state of Tennessee—kept by foster parents in a dark closet for more than a year.

I don't like to talk about that, but sometimes I have to.

I hustle up the stairs of the Community Mental Health Center, which is a weathered old building, loud with echoes and the creaking of heavy doors. As I spin past the glass of an office door, I see the reflected spray of my brown hair and black T-shirt. I'm nineteen now, but I stand under five feet tall because of the "extended period of malnutrition" when I lived in the dark. Ms. Parsons doesn't make me feel bad about being different. I've seen her fifteen times already, and she still doesn't understand me completely, but she *tries* to. She makes me feel . . . *another word for okay* . . . she makes a space that is *comfortable* to talk in, which seems like the most important part of counseling.

Large nature photographs line both sides of the hallway— purple and orange wavy rock formations that look like they could be from another planet. My heart swells as I remember how Ms. Parsons protected me, even after I messed up very badly. It was at the end of our second session. She touched my shoulder—I know she meant it as a gesture of encouragement, like the expression "a pat on the back," but a person's head can know one thing while their muscles know another. I grabbed her wrist the second her finger reached my back, wheeled her around, and had my fist pulled back before either of us understood what had happened. She screamed a little, and I stepped back, panting, and started to cry—crying, telling her I was sorry because even if I was very afraid, I would never hurt her. Ever. She smoothed down the front of her shirt.

We heard banging on her office door and a man calling out, "Amanda! You okay in there?" I put my hands over my ears. Ms. Parsons made a motion toward my face, and I wiped my cheek. A man who I understood was her work-neighbor threw open her door, but Ms. Parsons smiled and said, "Oh my gosh, Bill, I'm so sorry. I tripped and dropped a stack of folders."

The man looked at the floor. There were no folders anywhere.

I tried to slow my breathing, using a technique Ms. Parsons had shown me a week earlier.

She reassured him, "Everything's fine, really. I was just silly. Sorry if I startled you." She nodded toward me and her work-neighbor looked at me like the police had when I did *the thing I regret most*. Ms. Parsons told him, "Sorry for the excitement."

She rubbed her wrist behind her back.

After he left, Ms. Parsons and I sat down again. She leaned forward and folded her hands in her lap. "I didn't mean to startle you, Jessie," she said. "That was just a reflex you had. I want to talk about what happened more next time, if that's okay with you."

When our time ended and I went outside, I felt as if I'd flown high and nearly crashed to the ground. I wanted to be back inside with Ms. Parsons and away from her at the same time.

I know I can't tell Ms. Parsons everything because her "professional responsibilities" mean she would have to let the police know if there was any chance I would harm myself or anyone else.

I understand why.

Ms. Parsons's door is halfway open, but I stand in the hallway until she sees me, shifting back and forth from one foot to the other.

"Jessie," she says, standing up. "Come in." She has a Tennessee accent, like mine, and always greets me like I'm important. Lots of people in Nashville actually have no accent at all because they're mostly from other places now, but I like that Ms. Parsons and I come from the same place. "Do you need a minute? You look like you rushed to get here. Want to use the restroom or grab some water before we start?"

I shake my head. Even with her, I'm slow to talk.

"Well, come on in then, make yourself comfortable."

Her office is crowded with books and smells like the jasmine tea she always drinks. Behind her desk are two large windows. Through them, I see the crawl of traffic on Charlotte Pike. When I feel shy, I watch cars pass and wonder where everyone is going until Ms. Parsons brings my attention back. *The word for showing kindness . . .* Ms. Parsons is always very *gentle* with her questions.

She sits cross-legged in her high-backed chair and holds a steaming cup of tea in her lap. "How are you feeling about the techniques we've talked about so far?" she asks. "For times when you're feeling especially restless? I'm thinking in particular about when you're meeting new people."

She taught me how to rub a rough piece of cloth between my thumb and forefinger to calm down when I feel I may lose control instead of indulging in my normal compulsive behaviors like organizing trinkets on a shelf. Sometimes her strategies work, and sometimes I give in and do what I'd intended to do in the first place. I think for a technique to work, you have to actually want it to, but I know Ms. Parsons really wants me to succeed, so I tell her, "It's going pretty well. I'm staying pretty calm, especially when I do the one with the fabric."

"Sometimes just that little bit of friction keeps us anchored in the moment. From there, the skill really is learning to tolerate a little anxiety. Knowing that feeling anxious doesn't mean you have to act."

I'm not good at *not* acting. Ms. Parsons sets her tea down on the table beside her and lowers her voice. "Jessie, when we meet, we usually focus on how your life is now. But maybe you could tell me about when you started wanting to keep your things in order. Was it when you were by yourself?"

She means when I was inside the closet, but there is no way to *really* talk about that. I've tried and tried before, but unless you've had an experience like it, you can't understand. I get why Ms. Parsons is curious though, because that part of my life is so uncommon.

How do you talk about only being able to imagine the things around you, and never see them? When I lived inside the closet, it was very, very important to keep my things organized so I could find them by feel in the dark. I only had a few possessions, so the world seemed tiny. But the space in my mind became huge. There isn't a good way to describe it.

Ms. Parsons's eyes stay steady and warm as I begin to talk. "Most of the time I didn't know whether it was day or night. I had to put on music to fall asleep. I kept my Discman about four inches, or a palm width, from my headphones. I kept the CD I had another palm width away from that so I always knew where it was. I needed the Discman to keep going, so I arranged the batteries in order of how long I'd had them. When Mr. Clean gave them to me, I marked their sides with my thumbnail. I made another mark each time a week passed. I counted the marks to get the most out of each battery and kept my hand on the Discman when it played to feel it vibrate as the disc spun around inside."

Ms. Parsons already knew I had only one CD in the dark, so I didn't have to tell her that. What I always listened to was Owen and Shelly James's first album.

"When I came back to the regular world, I kept ordering everything around me like I did in the dark. Whenever I moved after that, I arranged my things—my toothbrush, hairbrush, clothes—the same way."

Ms. Parsons touches her fingertips to the corners of her eyes, like she is trying to stop from sneezing. "I see how that helped you keep the world together. It can be hard," she says slowly, "to try new ways of doing things when old ways have worked so well . . ."

There is a knock at Ms. Parsons's door and she looks up. I look up, too. She frowns at me as if giving me a chance to explain it. No one ever interrupts our meetings.

I shrug.

"Just a second, Jessie," she says on the way to the door. "I have to see what this is about."

Through the glass I see a shadow. It looks familiar in a way that makes my heart begin to pound.

2

Ms. Parsons braces one hand against the wall as she cracks the door open.

"Oh, good morning," she says formally, like someone trying not to sound annoyed. "We're actually in the middle of our meeting. Can I talk with you afterward?" I glance over my shoulder, but I'm afraid to turn all the way round to see who she is talking to. I hear the squeaks of shoes and voices echoing in the hallway.

Ms. Parsons clears her throat, then drops the pretense of politeness. "Frankly, I'm not used to spot checks during my sessions. I would've been happy to send an e-mail later. That way, therapy time with my client . . ." I can see Ms. Parsons tapping her index finger against the door frame. "Is this really the only time?" she asks, before mumbling something I can't quite hear.

When she opens the door, my parole officer, Ms. Carr, walks in, her footsteps click-clacking on the hard floor. She wears a maroon dress like someone in a movie might wear to church, so long it almost brushes the ground. Her hair is glossy and stiff with hairspray and is pulled back tightly. She nods once at me, then glances around Ms. Parsons's office as if she's come by just to have a look at the space.

My stomach tightens immediately, maybe because Ms. Carr reminds me of jail. My parole is supervised, meaning Ms. Carr checks in on me at least once a month. She likes to show up unexpectedly. Usually she comes to my apartment, where she mainly glares at me from the hallway. I know that I messed up at the concert—I hurt someone and scared a lot of people—but the hateful way Ms. Carr looks at me always cuts me to the quick. It's as though she hopes to catch me doing something awful—like she wants to prove to the world that I'm fundamentally bad.

I realize that, if she can show up here, there's no reason to think she *wouldn't* show up at my job—a thought that makes me lightheaded. I try to push it from my mind.

Ms. Parsons closes the door behind her and quickly returns to her chair. Her eyes are wide open and pretend-calm, her demeanor very different than it was just a few minutes before. She runs her index finger around the rim of her tea cup. "Ms. Carr wants to join us for part of our session, to hear about the work we've done so far and talk about the work we're planning to do. Is that all right with you?"

"It's fine with me," I say. I don't see how I have any choice.

Ms. Carr opens a tablet in her lap slowly, like she's not in a hurry. She unfolds the reading glasses that dangle around her neck, puts them on, then coughs once into her fist. She jabs the tablet's screen roughly with her index finger and asks Ms. Parsons, "Has Ms. Duval been fully compliant with her treatment so far?"

"Absolutely. Jessie has been on time or early for each of our meetings." She takes a sip of tea as if to show that she plans to keep her answers short.

Ms. Carr gives a tiny nod as her fingertip hovers above the screen. "Do you sense that Ms. Duval is a danger to herself or to others?"

Ms. Parsons's forced smile grows as she shifts forward in her seat. She twists the fabric of her skirt nervously, as if she had misjudged just how uncomfortable answering questions about me, *in front of me*, was going to be. "You know, I actually think we should talk later," she says.

"This is the time that I have," Ms. Carr says back.

Ms. Parsons looks at me and then at the office door. "Jessie, would you mind if Ms. Carr and I spoke privately for a few minutes? That might let us get back to our meeting faster."

If Ms. Parsons is asking, of course I don't mind.

She leads me to a bench just outside her door. "I'll be right inside," she says, loud enough for Ms. Carr to hear. "Hopefully this won't take too long."

Then Ms. Parsons shuts her office door, the one with a glass middle that looks like scalloped oysters. Through it, I can see her shape as she folds her arms and leans against her desk. I can hear their voices when they start to talk—the way concerts sound if I put my fingers in my ears.

People always seem to think I can't hear as well as I can. Maybe the abilities of anyone who is different are underestimated. My hearing is particularly clear, though, because of how sharp my ears became in captivity. Take away one sense and the others strengthen.

Ms. Parsons says, "Well, to answer your question, no. I don't think she's a danger to herself or anyone else. And honestly, you don't even need to ask since I'm sure you understand my responsibility to warn the police and whoever might be at risk if I ever thought Jessie would put someone in danger."

Ms. Carr's voice is equally audible, "I have some responsibilities too. I have a responsibility to the James family and to the citizens of Davidson County."

"You're acting as if we're not talking about someone with special needs," Ms. Parsons says.

Special needs is a phrase I've heard many times before. I've also heard *developmentally delayed, slow, intellectually challenged,* and *retarded.* Each of those makes me think about dreams where you scream but can't be heard.

Ms. Carr says, "With all due respect, I don't think you know whom you're dealing with here. We're talking about someone who is *very* capable of being violent based on her previous behavior. Yes, she has a unique story. And yes, she has some deficits. I'm well aware of both. But this isn't someone who can't take care of herself. Jessie Duval followed a concert tour around the country for months, managing to elude security over and over so she could get close to Shelly and Owen James. She severely injured someone. It took three officers and a stun gun to subdue her. Now, she lives independently with only my once-a-month oversight."

I have to hand it to Ms. Carr there. Most people don't know who they're dealing with when it comes to me. My talking isn't very good, but I'm much more capable than people realize. I don't mind their not knowing. I fold my hands and close my eyes, but then I realize someone could touch me when I'm not expecting it, and that would be very, very bad with Ms. Carr just inside the office door, so I open them again. I try to sit still while noise reverberates around the hallway.

Ms. Carr mumbles a question that I can't quite hear, to which Ms. Parsons answers, "Oh, I'm sure she handles money fine and she's generally really perceptive. But Jessie has some specific difficulties—mainly in productive speech and word recall. She has trouble naming certain things—feelings and other descriptive words, and with saying them out loud. She seems to understand everything said to her, though, and is good with procedures. Like you said, she holds down a job, gets around town just fine. She's had tons of treatment before, been bounced around from one counselor to the next. But I mean to stick with her."

Hearing Ms. Parsons talk about me makes me dizzy in a good way. It's hard to connect what she's said with me.

I see Ms. Carr's shape dip as she looks down at her laptop. "Were these deficits she was born with?"

"We're not sure. I've ordered a neuropsych assessment, but they're scheduling seven months out. She easily has the worst case of childhood neglect I've ever encountered . . . held captive in a place of near-complete sensory deprivation and isolation for over a year. But it's basically impossible to know what portion of Jessie's language deficit and developmental delay is due to a lack of stimulation during that year . . ."

I've heard this said before, but not by Ms. Parsons. I feel my heart quicken again as she says, ". . . what that does to a human? Neglect is the worst form of abuse in my book. When physical abuse happens to a child, they can try to make sense of it, they can grow up and forgive. When a child is neglected, especially in a case as extreme as Jessie's, it's like denying that they are even there at all."

I shiver, wrap my arms around my chest. I remember something I used to say to myself. *I'm not here. This isn't happening.*

Sometimes being alone is best. It is safest, certainly.

Alone and never touched.

I'm small but I've learned how to make myself even smaller. I read a story once where a character could make himself dim. No one could see him, even when he was nearby. That's what I picture myself doing. It's particularly easy in the dark. I usually keep to the backs of rooms, like I did on the James tour. I'd stand against the wall and keep everyone in front of me and feel the music in my back.

Ms. Carr is saying something that Ms. Parsons interrupts.

"*Why* is she fixated on them? Probably because she grew up with no family at all, bouncing between foster homes until what happened, and then the system spit her out. It was probably a lot nicer to live in her imagination, don't you think? Nicer to live in her mind with the Jameses than to be where she was. She has no family, so they became that for her, in her mind."

When Ms. Carr and Ms. Parsons begin to talk about what got me arrested, I hum loudly to block the sound of their voices. A couple of people turn and look at me as they pass by. One shakes her head and glances at Ms. Parsons's closed door.

I don't want to hear about extreme neglect or sensory deprivation. I don't want to be diagnosed anymore. I want to forget about that time in my life—and for the most part, I can. I don't remember much about the actual house where I was kept in the dark except the rough texture of the carpet and that the owners had a dog who barked in a deep, throaty, scary way at weird times. I do remember, before I went in, the couple saying that I had *soiled the bed*. Years later, I sat across from them at an enormous wooden desk in a room with glass walls and a view of downtown Nashville and wondered if they would say it again, but then they didn't say anything at all.

Instead, that same phrase Ms. Parsons used came up during those meetings: sensory deprivation. I didn't understand what it meant at the time, because my senses always worked just fine in the closet. Maybe especially in the closet.

More than a year there.

I slept in blackness, woke, and slept again. There was no sun to make day, so I learned to see in zero light. I forgot thirst. Forgot hunger. I was a shadow, or a vampire, I thought—and it was not a bad thought. I counted strands inside strands of shag carpeting. I learned how to hold my breath so that I could be very, very quiet. I understood voices I wasn't meant to hear. I deciphered tiny noises and distinctions between shades of nothing.

I learned where the door's smooth edge turned jagged and would bite and leave a splinter. I learned how far the wood panels would bend before they started to crackle like fire. I learned to wait and count to myself and to think and think and think, because what else was there to do?

I lived without language, without touch, without time. I knew there were other rooms in the house—and other doors between them—but not in the world where I lived. For me, there was only that one room, and only that one door—just one way in and out of how I lived. And darkness. Always darkness.

I felt footsteps before I heard them. When feet came near the closet door they were loud as thunder. Sometimes, there were voices. Mr. Clean and the woman. If I ever knew his real name I forgot it, but I called him Mr. Clean because he looked like the drawing I'd seen on bottles beneath cabinets, and because he *did* take away my mess. I know the state workers did their best trying to help me to never think about him or the woman again.

It was almost always Mr. Clean who came to the closet. Sometimes the foot thunder faded into silence, and sometimes it grew louder and louder until my door opened, when he would bring food and water bottles. Out went old towels and in came new ones. I had something that people later called a chamber pot. Mr. Clean took and emptied it. He and the woman didn't seem angry, not really. No one hit me. I knew what mean was, and they were not mean in that way. It was more like they forgot about me—except for a once-a-day visit.

When the closet door opened, the light was so blindingly strong it made me afraid of heaven. I shrunk away, always, back into the dark. I had read somewhere that fish at the bottom of the ocean do this. When he came in, my muscles would turn rigid. I would straighten up, try to talk, sometimes embarrassed about how I must have smelled, how I must have looked. I would brush my fingers through the tangles of my hair that remained, that hadn't yet fallen out.

"Good doggie," Mr. Clean would say sometimes. I decided that I would treat dogs better if I ever got out. Mr. Clean tossed in food and gave me a few batteries for my CD player. The front said: D-I-S-C-M-A-N.

"That thing still working?" he asked.

"Yes," I said.

I heard his sighs of . . . *the word for extreme dislike* . . . I heard his sighs of *disgust* as he leaned against the door frame. I would wait to change the batteries when the door outside *my* door closed, when the thunder had all gone away. I could do it without looking, my fingers finding the tiny plastic grooves that were the edges of the world.

Each time, I changed the batteries gently. I would never let the D-I-S-C-M-A-N break.

Never, ever.

Once the batteries were fresh, a green light would come on, the album would restart, and Shelly and Owen James's voices would start to sing again. The album's first song was about a rainstorm and hope. I knew every single word.

There are plenty of things I can never describe about living in the dark, because that's what comes from living in two worlds— the language of one doesn't fit the other. There were times in the closet when all I had were feelings. They were so big I had to make up my own names for them. Regular, other-people words couldn't describe them.

Eventually, a caseworker noticed I had too few school records for the year and called Children's Services. When Mr. Clean's answers didn't add up, the police came to the house. The first new face I saw after more than a year belonged to a uniformed cop, who put his hand over his mouth as tears flooded his eyes. He talked to me in a calm voice until others came. They had to turn out all the lights before I could come out of the closet.

Coming out was like being born again. Some sensations— sight, hearing—felt like the world's brightness and volume had been turned up way too high. My other senses seemed too dull. My hands suddenly had too much to do and my fingertips seemed to go numb, overrun by sorting through the millions of textures everywhere.

I was reintroduced to the world gently. First there were voices, then light, then water, then food. There were people who wanted to protect me, and another person, a "developmental psychologist," who wanted to study what I had lost so she could learn about how kids grow.

I had to learn to walk again because I had sat for so long. I moved like a bird, I heard someone say once—in short, *jerky* movements. Even simple things made me afraid, like the fear that day-to-day being in the world might blind and deafen me. For the first six months, I wore sunglasses everywhere I went. When I went outside and during meals, I wore headphones over my ears, which my doctor at the time encouraged. She said I shouldn't take in too much reality at once. There's more than one reality, I told her, but I don't think she understood. She smiled like she was thinking *poor thing*.

"Welcome back," a therapist said to me the day after I came out. Her hair was pulled back by a cotton headband and there was a shield-shaped pin on her jacket that I knew was from a college. She smiled and swept her palm around like a game show assistant, like I was about to win something. Through the window, I could see a courtyard—soft bushes and a bench covered in bright snow. Everything so real it seemed impossible. I had to tell myself over and over that what I was seeing was actually there, that I could trust my senses, that my eyes weren't tricking me.

This isn't the only world, I wanted to say. It's just a physical place.

Later, we sat at a table, a tray of vegetables between us.

"This is a carrot," she said. "Can you say 'carrot'?"

I'd kind of forgotten how to talk, but I tried to say the word.

"Good," she said, reaching over to pat my back.

I turned so fast that I knocked the tray over, and the carrots and peas and broccoli I was supposed to know the words for went everywhere. I tried not to cry as I helped pick everything up off the floor. I felt bad because I knew she was trying to help me. The therapist talked in a calm voice but looked over her shoulder at the door.

That was what life was like afterward, especially in the first few years. I messed up over and over and over again. I lost some things in the dark. Once, I looked in a mirror and didn't know who I was seeing. I looked like a different person, someone who wasn't *me*—a face and a body that things happened to.

Everyone was very nice for a while. Adults smiled and moved slowly, like I was made of something that could break easily. Before the closet, I went from one home to another, but afterward I lived in a place that was a lot like a hospital and a little like a jail. I lived in two more houses when I became a teenager. In both, I stayed in a bedroom by myself. I went to a small school run by the state for kids who had various disabilities. I hardly talked. No one knew what to make of me. Part of me missed the safety of being in the dark. And the structure. There was no time in the closet, but there was also plenty of time. I did what I wanted.

It is very, very hard to explain.

* * *

I look up when I realize the door to Ms. Parsons's office is open again. I had nodded off, gone somewhere.

Ms. Carr says goodbye to Ms. Parsons but not to me. I don't mind. Her shoes click past me down the hall.

Ms. Parsons looks at her watch. "I'm so sorry, Jessie. Please, come back inside."

I rush past her and sit again in an armchair that is still warm from Ms. Carr. The fabric scratches my arms, but in a good, comfortable way, and Ms. Parsons closes the door, and the office is quiet, and I feel safe again. Outside, it starts raining. The hedges in the courtyard look sleepy and heavy, weighed down by the water. The rain makes the cars pulling in and out of the parking lot seem slower.

"I know that took a while," Ms. Parsons says. She motions toward the paper bag sitting on the end of her desk. "I haven't eaten breakfast yet and I'd planned to have my bagel after our meeting. If you don't mind my eating while we talk, I'm happy to extend our time. You could probably use extra therapy time after having to sit in the hallway by yourself."

She unwraps her bagel and takes a small bite. I can smell the peanut butter—like cream mixed with earth.

"Let's just call this overtime, like extra innings in baseball. An overtime session," Ms. Parsons says, hiding her mouth a little with her hand.

I look at her bagel.

"Jessie, did you eat yet today?" Ms. Parsons sets her bagel on her desk and holds up her index finger while she digs through her purse. Her throat moves as she swallows. "I'll be right back. One minute, promise."

Her door swings open and the squeaks and laughter and conversations of the hallway drift inside. In less than a minute she returns and closes the office door and it's quiet again.

"Well, the most nutritious snacks in the machine were strawberry Pop-Tarts and a granola bar, so you pick." Ms. Parsons smiles again. "Actually, have both. If you want to save one for later, that's fine, too."

I don't bother trying to hide how hungry I am. It's hard to explain, but I love the predictability of Pop-Tarts. I know just what to expect when I tear open the package. I finish both in less than a minute—once the sugar and strawberry flavors hit my tongue, I can't help myself. It takes me even less time to eat the granola bar.

Ms. Parsons quietly chews her bagel. "I've learned something about you today. Now I know how you feel about strawberry Pop-Tarts ."

Kindness can break your heart. I bite my lip because I want to cry so bad.

Ms. Parsons lowers her voice. "Jessie, I want to talk with you about something Ms. Carr said while she was here."

She brushes a poppy seed from the corner of her mouth. Her eyes look concerned and I feel like she is acting, but only a little—the way people have to act sometimes when they bring up bad memories for me.

The sugar has made my mouth water, but suddenly it feels dry.

"She reminded me about what the legal consequences would be if you got close to the James family again. I know that's all behind you now and we're focusing on the future, but since she mentioned it, I wanted to bring it up." Ms. Parsons clears her throat just a little. "I don't want to harp on it, because I know you understand. But that order of protection is permanent, and a condition of your parole. If it is broken, you would likely serve the full extent of your sentence, which is fifteen years in jail. You're very lucky, in fact, to not have to be there now."

I know I am. There are also times when I don't know how to stop. Everyone underestimates me, but that's fine. When it comes to the James family, I'll be very careful not to be caught. I need them in my life. I can't really explain except to say I'm harmless.

"We've talked before about how being alone for so long made you secretive, and that other people don't always understand."

"Yes," I say.

"But you know that if you ever want to tell me something, you're safe here. Okay? I'm on your side, always. Is there anything you're keeping secret now? About the James family?"

My breath leaves me. I can't lie and I can't tell. I keep my face still as stone.

"No," I tell her.

I can't tell Ms. Parsons that I still follow Owen and Shelly James all the time. I can't tell her about any of their things, their memorabilia, that I've bought online. I *know* I shouldn't. I can't explain why I do, except the feeling is a little like the way people describe reasons they volunteer, or attend church—they get something out of it but they have a hard time saying exactly what. Something like meaning, purpose, security, belonging— not one thing specifically. I know I come to those feelings differently than other people do.

I've had a different kind of life.

3

From Ms. Parsons's office I go straight to my job with the catering company.

When I arrive, my boss, Ken, is standing over a table with his hands in his back pockets. He wears Elvis Costello–style glasses and sometimes sniffs in the way one of my old counselors would have called a "tic." Either that, or he is allergic to something year-round. Today, as usual, he wears black Converse sneakers and a black T-shirt. He has spread receipts in different colors and sizes across a table and is punching buttons on a calculator.

"Oh, hey Jessie," he says when he hears the back door close and looks up. Sighing a little, he sniffs. "Glad you're here, there's a fuck-ton to do before the party tonight and I'm stressing a little. You good?"

I nod at him, already turning on the faucet. The warm water runs loudly over my hands into the deep sink. "I'm good," I tell him.

"I pulled the recipes and moved the veggies to the front of the walk-in. Holler if you have any trouble," he mutters, then turns back around, pushing his curly, sandy-blonde hair out of his eyes. "I was worried about finding a new server for parties after Jessica left, but I'm not now. You got this."

He makes a fist, pumps it. I would have guessed Ken was a surfer if we lived anywhere near the coast because of how he looks and his easy-going style. The previous server, Jessica, left the company to go back to school. She smiled at me sadly on the day she left and told me I would do fine filling in for her.

Ken hasn't asked about my life outside of work since he hired me. "It takes all types in the restaurant business," he told me once, rubbing at the tiny dagger tattoo on his hand. "I mind my own business. Some of the people with the worst reputations are the best in a kitchen. Not my concern. We play together, like a team."

Or like a *band*, I thought at the time.

On the refrigerator door is taped a note where he's written the recipe for what he wants prepped. I decide to take the list in order, starting with the bruschetta, and begin scanning the shelves for the ingredients. When I have everything I need, I close the refrigerator door with my hip and lay the ingredients out on the smooth, stainless-steel table.

The kitchen itself is a wonder of stainless-steel surfaces and clean lines. The walk-in refrigerator is a misty cavern. Ken isn't shy about saying that he invested his life's savings in the business, and it shows. He is here so often—always here before I arrive and almost always still working when I leave—that I've wondered sometimes if he actually lives in the storeroom. His drive makes me want to work extra hard—and makes me *wish* extra hard that nothing from my past will disturb the business. He is fair and kind to me and I want him to succeed.

Ken is also by far the best boss I've ever had. When I left foster care, I started by cleaning dog pens. I liked the dogs and they liked me, and I washed their pens with soapy water that smelled like bubblegum and like carpet. Three dozen barked in different voices, caged in a large room while the manager watched me clean and stayed far away, leaning back on his heels like he might take off running. His green shirt had a few holes that I guessed had been made by dog teeth. He was bald on top, but wore his hair in a terrible comb-over.

"After a dog bites, I don't go near it again," he told me once.

He kept his distance from me too, and I kept mine right back.

Once, he called me to his office, closed the door, and said to me, "I know who you are." For a few seconds, I thought my heart had stopped. His chair creaked as he rocked in it. His glasses were very low on his nose and he tilted his head back. After a minute, he rested his forearms on his desk and sighed. "Do you talk at *all*?" he asked.

Concentrate. "Yes, sir."

He laughed like he didn't believe me. "You say anything besides that?"

That was what my previous boss had been like.

Ken knows I'm generally uncomfortable around new people and events, which is why until Jessica quit, I'd only worked as a prep cook.

Ken calls from the other side of the kitchen, "Thanks for everything you do, Jessie. These events start with a ton of prep no one sees." He steps closer and lowers his voice. "I wanted to say, too, that I'm also really glad you're able to help out at the events. Jessica quitting put me in a bind. Until I find someone else, you serving has been a godsend." Ken hesitates before adding, "Obviously, you know, if you wanted to stay on as a server . . ."

I shake my head and smile at him as I pull a knife from the drawer.

Ken smiles back and I go over the instructions again, because I like to plan the order in which I'll prepare everything. I like . . .

the word for being very specific . . . I like *precise* measurements at work just like I do in my apartment. I like the steady, repetitive movements of my hands and the way the knife flashes in the kitchen lights. I like the rhythm and the disappearing and the keeping my head down. I like the feeling of the textures in my hands. I work by myself but also have the safety of knowing Ken is just in the other room.

I don't think he knows about my arrest. I think maybe he is too busy to have run a background check. Anyway, that's my hope.

I slip on my headphones and start on the tomatoes, cutting the pieces into shapes that are *just right*—not chunks or slices so small they would fall apart. The music helps my hands stay on time. Each cut comes down to the beat. I still listen to country, of course, but since the arrest at the concert, I try to listen to all kinds of music. Today is seventies rock, the Eagles. *A Peaceful Easy Feeling*. Ms. Parsons had suggested different music would broaden my horizons, and I tend to agree.

I can pretend. I can dream I've never been in trouble. That it wasn't me who stared at ceiling tiles in jail, listened to screaming fights from the showers, made myself very small under cold covers on my bunk.

But my favorite fantasy is that I was adopted years before. I imagine a mother and a father who pick my clothes off the floor and frown in ways that are really smiles, and that I live in a house that smells like cinnamon and feels like clean sheets. I let myself dream that I have a family, even though it hurts every time the dream ends.

But that has already happened to someone in real life. It happened to Finch James when Owen and Shelly decided to bring her into their lives. A picture of the three of them with their arms wrapped around each other was on the cover of every magazine for a month. Seeing them smile on magazine covers made my eyes sting like they do when I chop onions. Owen's eyes had been glistening in those pictures too. I knew he wanted a child because he told Oprah so in a 2012 interview I found on YouTube.

"I think the time for that will come," he said to her. "When the time is right for Shelly and her career, I know we both want to start a family. It's hard to make the timing right with both of us so focused on work. Probably true for a lot of working families." He motioned out toward the audience. Some of the women nodded.

Focus.

I bring my mind back to the kitchen after I nearly cut my thumb with the knife. I move through the chopping, find a bowl, and begin mixing all the ingredients for the bruschetta topping together.

Ken passes behind me. All I hear is the Eagles as his shadow darkens the concrete floor. He keeps his distance, as if he knows to, taps his watch, and gives me a thumbs up. I check the time, too. We're getting closer to when we'll leave for the party.

I don't like actually working the events as much as preparing food, but this summer I've gotten better at it—learning to stay out of everyone's way and remembering to smile and to take short breaks when I can't breathe because of feeling overwhelmed. I'm still getting used to the idea that when I'm nervous I don't have to run and I don't have to fight—I can just step away for a minute until I feel okay enough to get through whatever it is I'm doing. Wearing a black uniform helps. We wear black hats, too—which I like because the brim narrows the input from the world, helping me to stay dim, especially when we begin cleaning up—picking up dishes and emptying trash. People hardly notice me then.

I finish the mixture for the bruschetta, set the bowl aside, and begin working on dough for dumplings. I like the pressing down, pushing my weight into the rolling pin. The song I am listening to fades out, then the playlist starts over again.

After a while, I look up and notice that the triangle of sunlight coming across the window ledge has lengthened, meaning the hour has gotten late. I check the ingredients list and realize I haven't yet added the baking powder to the mixture, so I pull open the cabinet where it is kept. It's so dark inside that I can barely read the label on top of the box. I can't stop myself from glancing around, and my heart can't help but sink before I slam the cabinet door closed.

My mind drifts to a house where I lived when I was eight or nine. A kitchen with a cabinet.

"Hey Jessie," the oldest boy in the foster home said to me once, squinting at me, measuring me. "I bet you can't fit yourself into that cabinet under the sink."

The cabinet door creaked as he opened it. Inside was dark except for the dull reflection from the U-shaped pipe beneath the sink. A sprinkler went round and round outside the kitchen window over grass scorched the color of toast. Two kids—maybe five and six—were running through the spray in their underwear. Not an adult in sight on summer days—that was foster care. The boy put his hands on his hips, cocked his head, and smiled. Another boy appeared beside him. Both had blue stains on their white T-shirts that looked like Windex, but I had no idea what had made them. It could have been anything.

"I could," I said, like a reflex to a challenge.

"Dare you," the first boy said.

I rested my hand on the sink's metal rim and the boys stepped back. The cabinet door looked like the entrance to a small, dark cave.

"Well?" the boy asked.

I ducked my head and bent my legs, dropped my butt onto the wood and slid my feet inside. Chemical smells made the air thick around me. I pushed aside bottles of I don't know what—plastic that was lime green and rose pink. My knees against my chest, I could hardly breathe.

"See?" I said.

I reached my hand up for a grip to pull myself out, but the cabinet door closed across my knuckles. The sharp edge stung like a wasp. Laughter. I pulled my hand to my chest, gritting my teeth, my mouth filling with spit. I had the scar for years where it cut me.

I heard a scrape as something slid through the handles, locking the door. I banged against the cabinet but there was only more laughter. My heart sped up so fast it felt like it was growing inside my chest, pushing against my lungs, my ribs. The voices outside turned softer, then softer still. I heard the thwack of the kitchen door closing as the boys went outside, and my world became a seam of light and the smell of chemicals.

Later, I could hear them talking through the kitchen wall. Then other voices came from farther away and I knew after a while that everyone had forgotten I was still in the cabinet. I had to breathe in short sips of air for I forget how long. I was there until I fell asleep.

It was the foster mom who eventually let me out. She told us all how tired she was, how she didn't want us playing around. "Someone could get hurt," she said.

This happened three years before I went inside the closet, where I started to make up names for everything—even emotions—just to pass the time. My heart knew *kitchen cabinet* as a mixture of forgotten, sad, angry, embarrassed, and afraid all in one.

But that's over now. I'm living, like Ms. Carr said, "independently."

And I'm working. After I cut out circles in the dough, I begin folding them around pieces of the mixture. I pinch tiny folds into the dough, working my fingers over and over until I can hardly feel. I go to the sink and am flexing my fingers under the warm tap when Ken appears holding a piece of paper in one hand and a pen in the other. He taps the pen against his ear. I tilt my head to let my right earbud fall out.

"Sorry, Jessie," Ken says. "This is for tonight."

My thumb finds the volume button in my pocket and nudges it down. Half the world's noise returns. The world sounds so big when you're not in your head.

Ken uncaps the pen and sets a form on the table beside where I'd just been working. I completed some of my high school classes, but I understand better when I am listening, not reading— especially legal language like what is on the paper. I read as much of the form as I can, but Ken's expression tells me a lot of what I need to know.

"It's basic, really," he says. "It's called a nondisclosure agreement. It just means don't talk about who shows up or anything you overhear at the party. I know you wouldn't do that anyway, but sometimes celebrities who come to these things want to be extra careful. Either that, or their management makes them hand them out. It's just a formality. You know Nashville people are cool about being around musicians, anyway."

I do know that.

Which musicians?

Later, I will look back and wonder if I already knew exactly who—if maybe their names had been right in front of me on that form and my eyes had somehow skimmed over them in the blur of my eagerness and imagination.

I press the pen down and print my name. Someday, I mean to learn cursive so my writing will look less like a child's.

Ken takes the form back and winks a little. "Thanks, Jessie. 'Preciate it."

"No problem," I say, casually, masking the new tightness inside me. *Which musicians?* I wonder again. Something about signing the form makes Ms. Parsons's voice ring in my ear— *the full extent of your sentence, which is fifteen years in jail.*

Ken motions toward the tray of dumplings I had been folding. "Hats off to you. You stay on task better than anyone I've ever seen."

I smile and re-glove my hand. He cocks his head slightly, like he is thinking of something. *The word for staying in a place longer than necessary . . .* Ken *lingers* until I hear someone call his name. Then he bounces a little, as if startled. One of the cooks must have shown up.

"Coming!" he yells over his shoulder. "Holler if you need anything, Jessie. Keep this up." He points again at the dumplings then is out the door, the stack of folded papers sticking up out of his back pocket.

I start cutting croissants, into which I will scoop the chicken salad that Ken made that morning. After that, I will get to work on the mixed salad and the cucumber sandwiches, which have disappeared first at each event I've attended.

As I work, an interview with Owen flashes back to me. I saw it years ago, on the *Ellen Degeneres Show*, before he and Shelly were married. He was sitting across from Ellen on a sofa, legs crossed so his boot rested on his knee. His enormous smile hardly matched his all-black clothes. Ellen wore a white button-down with an enormous collar and made her eyes very wide.

"Owen, I have to say, you look different," she teased. "It seems like something is new. Did you get a new haircut?" She tapped her finger against her chin. "Hmm. You went vegetarian?"

"Nope."

The camera cut to the audience laughing. One woman shook her head.

"You took up yoga? No? Well, maybe you better tell us what's going on in your life, mister."

Owen smiled sheepishly and talked to Ellen like it was only her and him on a back porch here in Tennessee, even though everyone was watching. "Actually, I've met someone special. I've been acquainted with her for a few years professionally but recently we've gotten closer. And then one day I realized I am captivated by her. Just having plans to meet her makes me walk on air."

Ellen made a teasing hand motion.

Owen smiled again. He knew how to tell a story—in a song or on a show. "Sometimes," he said, "I keep my mouth closed just so her name won't fly out. I left her dressing room one afternoon and jumped to see if I could touch the ceiling in the hallway. I missed by nearly two feet, but I was somehow surprised. That's what this lady does to me."

Someone in the audience clapped. One woman lifted her glasses to wipe her eyes.

"Well, *are* you going to say her name?" Ellen asked. She elbowed Owen and made a come-on wave to the audience, who started to clap and cheer.

"Her name is Shelly," Owen said. "And one day I mean for her last name to be James."

The memory sings in my thoughts as I clean my hands, the kitchen quiet except for the hum of machines.

There's a difference between the enthusiasm people portray on television and the quieter way they show feelings in regular life. When I've watched Owen and Shelly in person, I've seen two people who grew up the same way, who don't need constant explanations about rural life (I once overheard Owen say that he loves big cities but they wear him out). Both Owen and Shelly know what it is like to have someone tell them they loved their last album, even if they suspect that person actually hates it, or wants something from them. Neither has to explain to the other the feeling of being watched, or has to teach the other to pretend they don't notice everyone in a room is staring at them.

I wonder if they feel relieved when they're *not* being watched. Or are ever unsure of what to do with themselves when they're alone. I push the question from my mind. Owen and Shelly know how to handle absolutely anything. I just know it.

One of the cooks is whistling, and it takes me out of my head. I smile when I recognize it's Malik. He's moving closer. I wonder if he'll talk with me again. If Malik is so at ease, maybe everything will be okay.

I will look back on everything and wish I'd focused on what I sensed was coming. I'll wish I grabbed Malik's hand, got in my car, and drove away. We could have gone anywhere else. For a day or a week, or maybe just kept going.

If only I'd listened to myself, right then.

If only I'd run.

4

I n the bathroom, I slip out of my prep clothes and change into my uniform. I pull my hair into a ponytail and wash my face with a bar of Dial soap, which makes the world smell orange for a moment, before drying off with brown paper towels. I don't like to wear makeup, but I do want to look and feel clean. I straighten my uniform shirt and lean my elbows on the sink to give myself a quick once-over in the mirror. I look up at the leak-rippled drywall ceiling and try not to think about having to interact with all the people who will surely be at the party. To get through events like this party, I have to focus on maintaining myself—I visualize my facial expression and how to hold my body so I appear at ease. Ms. Parsons told me once to imagine Mario in the game Super Mario Brothers. After he eats a mushroom, Mario becomes invincible for a short time and can run through the game board freely with no fear of being killed. He is safe and purposeful and aglow. In the bathroom, I picture that golden glow around me and tell myself I will be fine. Just fine.

I recognize the voice I hear outside, and then the laughter too. A smile forms on my face. When I come out, I see that the other cook, Andre, has also arrived. He and Malik have propped a cinder block against the back door of the kitchen and are loading Ken's van. Malik has an Afro, and Andre shaves his head. They are both nice to me—Malik especially so—but tease each other constantly, like brothers, and laugh at each other's stories.

The three of us have worked for Ken for around the same amount of time, even though Andre is the newest to town. When we first were introduced, they both looked at me like most people did—distant, unsure—before we got used to each other. Now they keep an extra foot of distance between us and we air-fist bump as a greeting instead of shaking hands.

Malik leans against the door frame, wiping his forehead with the back of his hand. "Ready for tonight? I know you like prep work better than serving."

"I'll be fine," I say as I pick up the stack of linens and walk them to the van.

"It's okay, you know," he says as I head back toward the kitchen. I realize that Ken and Andre are both inside. Malik tries so hard to be kind that I have a hard time meeting his eyes. "Everyone's nervous about something," he continues. "Maybe serving's just not for you. I used to get crazy nerves before open mic nights, but stuff like that gets better the more you do it."

I'm kicking a pebble with the toe of my shoe when Andre appears at the side door. He extends his fist and I extend mine and we bump air. "Hey, what's up, Jessie," he says, his face half-hidden by shadow. He says to Malik, "Get the other end of this table for me?"

Malik nods and follows Andre inside, where they pick up a folding table. I grab a tray and follow them. There is a lot to load up and secure before we head out, and for the first time I realize just how much food I prepared. Obviously, it's going to be a big party.

When the van is full, I climb in the back. Malik and Andre follow, then Ken slides the door closed with that scrape-sliding sound. His keys jangle as he locks the back door. "Everybody ready?" he asks.

"Hot in here," Andre says as he crawls past me and Malik to the front, leaning down to keep from hitting his head. He fans his face with his hands and adjusts the van's air vents so they point toward him. He's not from Nashville and it shows, but he's right—at almost five o'clock the temperature is still near ninety degrees. "Ken, you better get this A/C cranked, my man," he says.

Malik rubs his neck, squinting toward the sun as we start off. I sit on a cooler and can feel the vibration from the street through my fingers. Through the window, I watch Nashville's used record stores and restaurants fly by. Everywhere, a new building, a bar that just opened, a hotel coming soon. The joke is that the city's official bird is a crane. I tighten my legs and grip the cooler handles to steady myself. When Ken turns, ice sloshes inside while smells from the food we made rise up from the folded edges of tin foil covering the trays nearby. We pass from one part of town to the next, the cooks and Ken chatting, me listening to them talk so my thoughts stay quiet. My mind is like a machine that I can hear working sometimes. It helps me to focus on someone else nearby, and to just listen.

We rumble over train tracks before driving onto curved, shady streets and gently sloping hills. The houses on both sides have old trees in wide front yards and diagonal lines cut into grass that seems an enhanced shade of green. The streets are named for trees—Aspen, Dogwood, Live Oak—names that make me think of . . . *the word for when something will always be* . . . The names made me think of *permanence*, of stone, and of strong families—ways of living that anyone would want. Envy nips me like a dog that doesn't know better.

"Almost there," Ken says, glancing at the map on his phone.

"Ken, you sweating, man?" Malik asks.

I look up and notice a clear drop running down Ken's cheek.

He wipes it away. "It's a big account. Good exposure for us, potentially."

Every night after the rest of us go home, Ken cleans the kitchen. A month earlier, I'd watched him put stickers with the company logo on both sides of the van. He wants the business to be a success, and I want that for him too.

I don't want anything about my past to interfere with his hard work, or to mess up my job. I know I need to lay low in order to make that more likely, which is obviously much harder if I'm serving at events and not just prepping food. The thought I always try to push away makes me cold despite the warmth surrounding me: the photo from my arrest seemed like it was posted on every news and gossip site for a few weeks last summer— google my name now and it still comes up.

I hear Ms. Parsons's words in my head—"People forget things, Jessie. Probably no one will know, especially after a while"—and tell myself I won't be recognized. I wonder how long it will be until *after a while*.

I slip on my black uniform cap and tell myself I'll stay dim. I can handle this, I tell myself.

"Now this is what I call a neighborhood," Malik says admiringly. "I think I'll get myself a place here when I win the lottery. In fact, I'll take that one right there." He points at a house set far back from the road, where lanterns flicker beside the front door in the afternoon sun.

"What's with all the lanterns?" Andre says.

Ken brushes away some flour that had settled on the sleeve of his black shirt. "Ah, I forget you're a newcomer. Lanterns mean old money. And those stacked stone fences mean *very* old money."

Malik smiles. "You trying to sound like a native? You've been here, what? Four years?"

"Five," Ken answers. "Nashville's like a mini-LA now. Everybody wants to be here. And the traffic is killing me."

"Five years . . ." Malik says. "You've been here long enough to know everybody's from somewhere else. Besides, any city worth a damn has traffic. We're just in the club now."

Andre asks, "So, lanterns mean old money? What about music business money? That ain't always old money."

Both he and Malik are musicians, working catering gigs so they can spend their free time on music. Maybe they think I'm a musician too. That's what I like to believe. It would make sense— nearly everyone else in jobs like ours plays or writes music. After all, there's a joke in Nashville: *How do you find a songwriter? You go to a restaurant and ask to see a waiter.*

"That's a different neighborhood altogether," Ken says. He'd never said so, but I get the feeling Ken is a musician too.

"Sometimes it ain't old money," Malik chimes in. "But in this town, fame is royalty."

We hit a small bump and the van slows. My hands are sweaty on the cooler handles, but I tell myself to not think. When we come to a stop, the engine turns off and for a second I hear a deafening silence. Ken double-checks the address on his phone, then leans forward and squints as he looks up the long driveway.

"Look at that fucking *house*," Andre says.

The house is a sprawling ranch with white painted brick—no, a color deeper than white, cream. Like a magnolia blossom, slightly wilted. The shutters are chestnut brown and the driveway slopes gently into the backyard like a subtle invitation.

"Please tell me it's a big fucking family," Andre says. "Like a dozen kids or something."

Ken sighs like a teacher. "There's three of them. Lane Peterson is who hired us. Her husband is Brian. Their son, Sean, is graduating." He claps his hands once, like he's snapping us out of a spell. "Okay, guys, let's go ahead and get into our professional mode. It's go time."

"Go time," Malik echoes, and I smile despite my nervousness because Ken says that phrase before any event, which I find funny but also sort of sweet. *Go time.* I take a deep breath and force a smile as I rub my finger and thumb together like Ms. Parsons showed me in order to not get lost in my anxiety.

Andre gets out and opens the van door. A warm wind blows against my cheek as I hear him chuckle. "These people have probably never seen a tough day in their lives," he says. "Money makes 'em soft as little marshmallows."

"The kid may not have it rough, but the adults aren't soft, trust me," Ken answers distractedly as he looks over the order once more on his phone.

Both cooks make noises that sound like disbelief.

Ken sets his phone in his lap, turns around in his seat, and raises his eyebrow at them. "You know what Brian Peterson does for a living? Private equity. He acquires companies, sucks the value out of them, and then sells them off. I read he put 5,000 people out of work last year. The article called him a *sociopath.* Maybe he is and maybe he isn't, but he's done some ruthless deals, make no mistake. It's no accident he has this house."

The cooks' laughter softens as we step onto the street. "Ken did his research," Andre says. I wipe my hands nervously on my pants, not able to stop from wondering how he hadn't looked up anything about me. Above me, I hear the soft shushing sound of leaves brushing against each other as a breeze nudges the oak branches.

Malik hums a beat, absentmindedly. "A psychopath in a suit and tie, huh? Well, now I'm excited. Way to build the suspense, Ken. I thought it was just a fancy party."

Ken opens the back of the van. He looks up at me and winks. "You good, Jessie?"

"All good," I say, although something about the word *psychopath* makes my movements slightly awkward. I look down to find my footing on the sidewalk's edge.

Malik snaps the cart together; then we unload the trays and move toward the back of a long driveway. The food I made is inches away, but my stomach feels full and raw at the same time—a tangle of nervous energy while thought fragments buzz in my head like bees that won't land.

A woman with blue, hawkish eyes comes toward us from the backyard, her hair the color of molasses. She is maybe in her forties but doesn't have a wrinkle. "Hello there! So happy to see you. I'm Lane."

She sounds so cheerful that her voice stops Andre and Malik in their tracks but also somehow calms my nerves. One thing I've learned from delivering food at previous events is that rich people act very, very excited to see one another when they get together. Everyone is sweating except Lane, who looks indecently comfortable in the heat. She rests one hand on her chest and extends her other to Ken. While she and Ken exchange greetings, I run my fingertip along the groove between two magnolia bloom–colored bricks on the side of the house. The paint is slightly tacky from the humidity and I half expect my finger tip to be coated in cream when I pull it away.

Lane points to an enormous wooden structure extending off the back of their house, behind which a white tent fills half the backyard. "We'll keep the food mainly out on the deck area. You know how these things go: the grown-ups congregate in the kitchen, but kids run up to their rooms or hide in the backyard like little hoodlums."

She motions toward the lawn behind the house, where strings of lights hang between trees. It looks like a set from the TV show *Nashville*, but it reminds me too of the outdoor festivals where I saw Owen and Shelly perform last year. I can almost taste cotton candy in my memory and smell the pot burning as their songs rose over joyful, dusty crowds. I may not have a good sense of scale, because my own graduation was so sparsely attended and informal—certainly no party was thrown—but it takes a second for me to remember that what I'm looking at is a high school graduation party. For a moment, my anxiety fades into the background of my mind as I consider the different world that I'm now in.

Malik, Andre, and I take trips back and forth between the tent and the van until all the food is where Lane Peterson wants it. She has left the side door to the house wide open, and each time I pass, I feel a cool wisp of air. On my next trip, I pass through the door into a large open kitchen, where I begin to arrange glasses on the countertop. I set them in five rows of five, each row two inches from the next. I'll replace these as the party progresses so the arrangement stays neat. I'm so precise it drives Andre a little crazy sometimes, but Ken nods approvingly.

The kitchen and living area are basically one enormous space, with a deck that extends off the back where guests have already found shade on the two tomato-colored L-shaped sofas. The deck leads out to the backyard, which seems to fade into hedges beyond the hanging lights. Right where the living room meets the deck area, I notice an iPad-sized control panel attached to the wall, where a dozen icons glow. As I finish in the kitchen, I watch as Lane saunters over and touches the screen. The lights in the kitchen dim slightly, while lights on the deck ease on. When she touches another place on the screen, three fans attached to the pagoda above the deck begin to spin.

Once the food is in place, I set out serving spoons and flatware. I keep my chin down and my eyes on what I am doing as I mind the correct distances between silverware and plates and napkins until everything is just so. As more guests began to arrive, I light the burners, and wide, blue flames lap at the bottoms of the chafing dishes.

People who attend parties like these don't often look at the servers, I notice, which makes it easier to observe *them*. Rich people seem healthier than regular folks, somehow, like walking advertisements for how people should be. It's like they take special vitamins no one else is allowed to buy or even knows about. I look on as perfect families with impeccable hair and flawless, new-looking clothes arrive, one after another. In one perfect family, the father wears a sports coat with a polo shirt underneath, his hand gripping the neck of a bottle of white wine. The mother wears a white-and-blue sundress and cradles a plate of cookies that are iced a half-inch thick.

"This is the land where the Botox flows," I hear Andre say under his breath, nudging Malik, who smiles and seems to pay no attention.

The guests begin to settle in, and I stand back as they pick at the food I've set out. I try to look busy, to make myself dim, so I can to eavesdrop on their conversations.

"Nashville's not just a country-music town. It's a health-care town," I overhear a man in a white polo shirt saying. "It's why we're recession-proof. People don't stop going to their doctor if the economy slows down. Am I right?"

"I wish someone would tell people to stop moving here," the woman beside him answers, in a low voice. "People keep coming and coming, from all over. Half of Chicago must have moved here by now."

"Do you blame them?" the white polo shirt man asks, and the small crowd that's gathered around him all laugh. He wipes condensation from the glass in his hand and sips, winking.

Don't look at anyone directly, I remind myself. *Don't let anyone catch your eye.* That's part of staying dim and going unnoticed. I focus my gaze on the man's chestnut-brown leather shoes and try not to wonder how much they cost, while tiny gusts of wind make leaf-shaped shadows roll over everything.

After a while, I look for Ken. I walk to the backyard, where a tall, muscular boy flips his hair out of his eyes with a quick turn of his chin. This is Sean Peterson, I realize, because he stands like he's at home—leaning back on his heels. He and his friends have hair that brushes their eyelids and all wear polo shirts a size too tight. One has popped his collar up around his neck. I watch as Sean whispers something that makes all the boys around him teasingly shove each other. One pretends to fall to the ground, as if he'd been punched.

"No way," another says. "There's just absolutely no way."

Sean shrugs, his blonde eyebrow rising into a small arch. His mouth forms a reckless smile.

What is it like to talk with other teenagers? To have *real* friends? I can't help the empty feeling in my stomach as I wonder. Growing up, there were times I'd had . . . *the word for people you cooperate with . . . allies*—other kids who watched my back while I watched theirs. Maybe someone I might tell a little lie for, but a real friend? No.

I feel someone move close by. I step out of the way, and when I look, Lane Peterson is beside me, carrying a glass filled with ice, something clear, and tiny sprig of mint. The glass sweats in her hand and the ice inside clinks as she stirs it with her fingertip.

She has the kind of graceful smile that makes people around her smile too. It's like magic. "See?" she says to me. "Sean's already found his position. You'd think he'd want to greet a few guests inside at his own graduation party." She pauses, thoughtfully, like there is an inside joke between us. "Since he won't listen to me, do you suppose his *girlfriend* can convince him to come in and talk to the other guests when she gets here?"

I fumble for words, tongue-tied as usual.

"What's your name?" she asks, smiling as she cocks her head.

I'm staring at her, wide-eyed, when Ken rushes up, wiping his hands feverishly on a kitchen towel. "This is Jessie," he says, "She's a little quiet. Anything I can help with, Mrs. Peterson?"

"Oh, no, Jessie is doing a wonderful job," Lane Peterson tells Ken. "The food looks absolutely superb. But before I forget, one thing I should tell you, that the side door your guys keep coming in and out of blows closed and locks with the slightest breeze. If that happens, we keep the spare key under the planter. Right there." She points past me, nearly brushing against my shoulder, at the side of the kitchen, where the door is propped open for the moment. Beside it is another screen like the one Lane had used to adjust the light and turn on the fans. A shiny metal key juts out from the interior part of the deadbolt, just below the glass. You can never be too careful, I think, remembering stories I overheard in jail about opening doors locked with a deadbolt by simply breaking the window above and turning it.

Lane is so close that I can smell the subtle sweetness of the skin lotion she must use. *Don't touch me,* I think for the second time today, *please.* I can't help but remember my close call with Ms. Carr earlier, and the last thing I need is to have to talk myself

out of a fight-or-flight reflex now. I picture me knocking something over, or worse, then everyone's heads turning.

Lane's eyes twinkle as she moves away, almost like she can
sense I need extra space. I feel my shoulders relax slightly as she
does.

Ken gives me a quick nod and scans the party, seemingly looking for food-service items that need attending to. "Everything's on
point, I think. I'm going to make sure there's enough ice around
drinks in those coolers. Will you make sure those chafers aren't
turned up too high? Last time, Andre almost boiled one over."

More guests continue to file in—some entering formally
through the front door, some coming through the side entrance,
and some coming down the driveway toward the deck and backyard, like we had done.

I go to the buffet area where the rear of the house opens onto
the deck where Lane sits on the outdoor sofa beside the man I
assume is her husband Brian, "the psychopath." He's been in the
same spot since we arrived, leaning back, arms over the back of
the furniture. I'm not the best judge of character, but he doesn't
seem scary to me. Maybe that's the point, I realize. Maybe he's a
wolf in sheep's clothing, as people say. Lane rests her hand on his
arm. When he speaks to her, she tilts her head back and laughs.

Like his son, Brian has sandy blonde hair parted on the side,
just long enough to curl near the end. The collar of his tailored
shirt is wrinkled. He swishes a wineglass around and speaks to
the people around him loudly enough that I can hear him as I
quickly check the chafing dishes. Andre actually *has* turned one
up too high, so I lower the flame. It warms my fingertips and the
back of my hand, which still has a few marks left from where I
wasn't careful enough early on working for Ken. Catering and
cooking can be very rough on hands.

Brian's voice carries to where I'm standing, his words slightly lazy from alcohol. "No, no, it's all Lane's doing." He waves his hand dismissively before scratching at the back of his head.

Lane squints and pinches her fingers together as if showing something small. "Just a *little* helicoptering. But how can you not? Between texting and Snapchatting, and God-knows-what, you really have to keep an eye on everything nowadays. Otherwise, you have no idea what your kid is up to."

A woman seated across from them mock-applauds. Another smiles knowingly.

I move to another chafer and adjust the flame, so close it threatens to singe my skin. I'm thinking about what *helicoptering* means when someone whispers and the heads of a few guests turn. I feel the energy in the room change but force myself to not look up.

Before I see her, before I even hear a voice, I know who has come in the front door.

It's like a dream has begun, and the worst-case scenario I'd hardly let myself imagine when I signed that nondisclosure form comes rushing into the present.

I'm just outside on the deck, but I hear Shelly James singing the word "hell-oooo" and the click-clack of her shoes across the hardwood floor.

5

freeze, too terrified to do anything but hold still. Finally, I set down a glass that I realize I'm holding so tightly it might break, and grip the tabletop to stop the feeling that I'm falling.

Whenever I've seen Shelly in the past, she's looked as if she is *more* than real. Her hair is practically a legend of its own—a wave behind her, blonde ringlets the size of napkin holders. Her skin always looks flawless and seems to actually glow. But a person who couldn't see or hear would still know if she entered the room they were in. She has a presence you feel beyond the regular five senses.

Except the Shelly I'm seeing from the corner of my eye doesn't look like herself. She sets a bottle of wine on the kitchen counter a little too roughly and stumbles as she opens her arms to greet the woman beside her. Her face looks thin and drawn, and her gaze seems somehow distant. Her eyes, even from this far away, look clouded. The pitch and tone of her voice sound right, but I notice a blur between her words, a softness.

Everyone around Shelly seems to move like they are underwater. Brian stands up for the first time and starts toward her. Lane stands too, but does not move except to wring her hands. A woman seated at the far end of the sofa looks like she wants to turn and stare but has managed to keep her eyes locked forward as if through sheer force of will. Nashville has a code of not bothering entertainers, not interrupting them in restaurants. Definitely not asking for autographs.

"Somebody's been having a few late nights lately," I hear a voice murmur somewhere behind me.

"I hear her long nights have actually been going on for some time," another voice answers.

A short chuckle follows.

I want to turn around and glare to show my disapproval. I want to pick up something and throw it at the two gossips behind me. They have no idea what they're talking about, I tell myself as I breathe in and out, deeply, until I feel another shift in energy.

When Owen James enters behind Shelly, I think I will shrink into nothing. My desire to disappear is so intense I feel myself begin to actually fade.

When I followed the tour, I read an article that described Owen as "impish, bright-eyed, precisely scruffy," and "unnaturally thin into his late-thirties." This evening, he wears all black as usual, his pearly shirt buttons shining like they're lit. He looks a little like a cigarette ad in an old men's magazine—except for the fringes of his brown hair, which are frosted at the tips and glossy with hairspray. He is short compared to Shelly, who is nearly six feet tall, but he walks like he owns the world, wearing a deeply lined smile on his very tan face.

My eyes flash back to Shelly, who runs a hand through her hair. Her shoulders poke up from her loose-fitting dress. A guest points, and I realize Owen has left the front door open. I enter the kitchen from the place where I'd been frozen on the deck and rush along the back hallway to close it when I see Finch James appear in the doorway. I stop so quickly my shoes squeak as I slide a few inches across the gleaming hardwood. I turn my face to hide. Finch pauses for half a beat and seems to scan the room before striding past me to the backyard.

Finch: the only child, now grown into a teenager. I haven't seen her, or a picture of her, in months. Tonight, she looks almost my age, maybe partly because of the dark makeup around her eyes. She wears tight jeans and a loose linen shirt that swishes in sync with her hair. The first time I heard Finch's voice was also the first time I got in trouble after the Jameses' tour—the start of being known by their security team. I was crouched beside a dressing-room door under an arena in Orlando. I'd waited until I could catch the handle of a flung-open exterior door, then slipped inside and gone dim, winding my way through the maze of backstage until I heard the voice that stopped me dead in my tracks.

"To *unwind*," Shelly was saying. My back to a wall beside her door, I could see her blonde curls reflected in a sheet of glass on the other side of the hallway. Even in the hall, her perfume smelled like orange blossoms. I held my breath to listen. She was talking to Finch.

"Stop! Mom, just *stop*. No, you're not. You're *not!*" Finch's voice dropped into a gentler tone I could barely hear, "But to where, really? And *why*?"

A chorus of laughter exploded in another room, where people were clearly celebrating. Notes blew from a saxophone. I moved even closer to Shelly's door, but could still hardly make out her voice. Finch's, however, was clear as day. "Dad's with Robert. He'll be here for a while. Let's go to the hotel. Please. I'll order some food. We'll find a movie to watch on TV or something."

Then came a crash—something heavy, like a table overturning and the chaos of rolling cups and broken glass.

"Mom!"

My hand froze in place, shaking over the doorknob. That was me: a helpless observer, unable to participate, unable to intervene—orbiting around, not permitted to land. I made a fist and shoved it into my pocket. There was nothing I could do but listen.

"You're welcome," Finch said.

Shelly asked a question I still couldn't quite hear, to which Finch replied, very coldly, "I'm sure Dad has no idea."

I must have been listening closely because I missed the approach of two men who looked like football players in yellow polo shirts striding toward me. One spoke into a crackling walkie-talkie. It was too late to not be seen, but not too late to run. I took off breathless into the warm Floridian night where the air was so thick it seemed like it should be visible, the guards' footsteps hammering behind me. White light reflected off fountain-generated wavelets in a nearby retention pond. I saw a blur of red taillights as I crossed a road and heard the growl of brakes and the thump of car stereo bass. I tore off running. By the time of the tour's next stop, all security carried flyers with black-and-white prints of my blurred face, wide-eyed, as I dashed away from the blinding light.

Now, my heart is beating so fast it feels unnatural, like I can actually hear it inside me. What's happening feels like a dream that is just about to end—I am both included, and not, and there are too many pieces to process at once.

I have to be careful, I know. The chances someone will recognize me have just increased dramatically. I must be especially dim. I keep my expression blank in order to look relaxed, but what I want is to be invisible. I hear Ms. Parsons's words again in my head. *Fifteen years.* Ms. Parsons told me once with a concerned look that I don't seem to understand risk. Maybe that's true. If I did, even the thought of going back to jail for fifteen years for breaking an order of protection would be enough to make me run out of this party.

But I know why it isn't. Another part of me has come alive. Warm energy surrounds my heart and seems to fill my lungs. Inside, I feel pink. I feel known, in a weird way, like I'm *lucky* the James family has showed up—I have that tiny sense that I'm back with my family, even though, rationally, I know that's not true. Part of my heart *feels* like it is, and for right now that's just enough to keep me where I am.

I know I should hide, but I know too that it will be apparent if I do—there is still so much to be done for the party. I move to the kitchen, where I can see both the patio and the backyard, picking up half-empty cups and dirty plates, listening in on conversations as well as I can, looking at no one directly, as Owen and Shelly come onto the deck.

Through the window I watch as Finch approaches Sean. He drinks deeply from a red cup as she reaches up and brushes his hair from his eyes.

Brian has left the patio and is beside them, his face lit up like a child who has just discovered something. He sets his wineglass down gently in the grass, unlocks his phone with his thumb, and waves Finch and Sean together. He says something to them that I imagine is, "I want a picture of you two."

"Dad," Sean mouths, his voice too low to hear, before biting his bottom lip as his eyes sweep around, as if his father doesn't understand what he's suggesting. Finch straightens up beside him, licks the front of her teeth, and tucks her hair behind her ears. She twists a thin gold chain around her neck. The lights above make stars inside her dark eyes. Brian tests the image on the phone screen, then closes one eye as he finds the best angle.

Someone behind me is watching, like I am, through a window. A voice beside me says to another guest, "*So* sweet. It *does* all go unbelievably fast. One minute they're small, the next, they're grown up and off to school. Look at him especially, so grown up."

"Where . . .?"

I hear the name of a college.

". . . early decision."

". . . as center midfield, what he played in high school. The coach helped Sean network some. Of course, Brian being Brian didn't hurt."

"He gets so embarrassed to be the center of attention. Look."

A flash comes, then another, the teenagers holding their smiles so long the hair on the back of my neck stands up, though I don't know why. When the picture taking ends, Sean and Finch turn away as if slightly lost, disoriented after being released from expectations.

I catch the side of the door frame to steady myself as the edges of the world spin a little. My legs seem to hollow out. My eyes won't leave Finch. I want to trade lives with her. I'm not ashamed to think it.

From the corner of my eye, I catch Lane hugging Owen's shoulder, then hooking her arm through Shelly's, saying, "I'm *so glad* you're here! Come on to the deck, everyone's been waiting to see you." She leads Shelly to a seat on the outdoor sofa while Shelly's eyes sweep from one side of the deck area to the other. When the toe of Shelly's shoe catches between two tiles and she begins to stumble forward, Lane tightens her arm to catch her, keeping a tight smile on her lips the whole time. When she points to a space where she wants Shelly to sit, two people move over to make room.

Shelly mutters something to herself, then throws her head back, laughing at whatever it was. She reaches for a wineglass that belonged to the person who had been in her seat before her, but

Owen stops her, putting his hand over the rim. When Shelly pushes his hand away, her hand catches the side of the glass, which topples over onto the table but miraculously stays intact.

"Shit, shit, shit," I hear her say, as Owen dabs at the wine with some of the cocktail napkins Malik had laid out earlier. My stomach tightens. Part of me wants to look away. What am I seeing? She has looked woozy before, but never like this.

It's like it's not even her.

The gossip I'd overheard earlier reenters my mind with a sharp sting.

Owen glances at Shelly and frowns with his eyes, though his mouth keeps the smile I've seen on a dozen magazine covers. His teeth gleam. He stretches his neck to one side, like it's stiff.

Shelly's hair catches the light as she pulls it off her neck with one hand while fanning her face with the other. Even in whatever strange state she's in, she is breathtakingly beautiful—a person who seems created to be looked at, watched, admired. She dabs at the sheen of sweat on her nose. In the middle of her neck is the tiny butterfly tattoo she got the year before—I remember it from a magazine I saw in the grocery-store checkout. It is a simple blue outline with a few tiny orange stripes. The article had called the tattoo a "marker of Shelly's mid-life crisis," but it looks very pretty to me. Sometimes at home, I've tried to draw it on myself with a pen.

For a moment, everything seems to calm down. Owen settles beside Brian. I watch his lips move as he begins to talk. From where I'm standing, I can only understand about half of what he says, but I fill in the pieces I can't hear with bits I've read in magazine articles, heard in interviews, and listened to in overcrowded arenas. Any fan knows Owen grew up riding his bike around "Nashville's leafy streets," listening outside its honky-tonks, playing guitar, and "daydreaming beside the Cumberland River," where the wind carried his mistakes away.

"Where is everybody?" Shelly asks, suddenly.

Heads turn.

The women sitting across from Shelly look at her strangely.

"Everybody?" one of them asks. Even more guests have arrived, and now at least fifty people are milling about on the deck and in the backyard.

It seems as if Shelly meant to ask *something*, but the wrong question came out of her mouth. She sweeps her hand toward where Sean is leaning against the trunk of an enormous oak, and Finch leans against him.

I see Owen swallow. He drapes his arm around Shelly's back. He winks at the others with an uneasy smile as his hand becomes more of a grip around the point of her shoulder, as if he's holding her in place.

My heart skips a beat. I think about the exchange between Shelly and Finch I overheard in Orlando. I've read rumors online about "substances." I didn't want to believe them, but I know what I'm seeing. The strained expressions of the people sitting near Shelly tell me that I'm not seeing this wrong—she's acting strangely.

Her fans see her as a self-made rebel. They admire her as a woman who speaks her mind. And she *does* speak her mind, it's true. She's the *real thing*. The year before her first record broke, seven of country's top ten artists were male. Sixty percent of country's audience was female, and the stereotype was that women bought records from good-looking men who sang them love songs. Shelly turned that around completely. She took on interviewers, sometimes calling out reporters who asked inappropriate questions. Once, at an airport, she snatched a camera from a too-close paparazzo and tossed it down a flight of stairs.

People actually applauded when she turned and faced the man, her hands on her hips.

But that rebel energy feels different tonight. Her movements seem sloppy and her eyes appear unfocused as she shifts restlessly in her seat.

Lane Peterson stands up slowly and comes toward me. I busy my hands so she won't know I've been watching so closely.

"Jessie," she says. I can't believe she's remembered my name. "I think Ms. James might like some sparkling water and I forgot to put any out. Could you check the refrigerator in the garage? I think there are some cold bottles in there."

I hurry through the kitchen to the garage and close the door behind me. For a second, all the sounds hush. The garage smells like grass clippings and gasoline and rubber boots. As my eyes adjust to the dark, my fingertips connect with the light switch, and a blue-white light the color of skim milk fills the space. Light reflects in crescents off the hoods of three vehicles. I don't know much about the makes of cars, but they all look heavy, sleek, and expensive. What Ken said about how much money Brian has seems more and more clearly true.

I take the handrail and start down the stairs, feeling like I might fall, but also like I should hurry. I spot the refrigerator Lane Peterson meant against the back wall and weave between two of the three cars. The paint of each of the cars looks like liquid in the faint light—two huge SUVs and a small white convertible that I lean to squeeze behind. My fingertips trace the letters above the taillights. P-O-R-S-C-H-E.

I open the refrigerator, and the escaping light is blindingly white. Inside, cans and bottles are arranged with the tidiness of a well-kept grocery store. I don't know which type of sparkling water to grab, so I take two different types, close the refrigerator door with my hip, and head back up the steps. The cold bottles chill my chest through my uniform shirt. As I pause at the door, a whoop of laughter reminds me of the world on the other side— the James family and fifty people I don't know, any of whom might recognize me from the concert.

Lane Peterson meets me in the kitchen.

"Thank you so much," she says, taking both bottles. She sets one on the counter and takes the other back to Shelly James, who looks as if she doesn't understand what's happening, as if the thing Lane Peterson means to hand her makes no sense at all. Like she's being offered a houseplant, or a scarf. Shelly eventually accepts the water, gives it an odd look, then sets it on the coffee table.

Then, a chill passes through me. Another person has joined the party in the short time I've been out of the room: the Jameses' manager, Robert Holloway. Even from behind, I would recognize him anywhere—his lanky height, the stoop of his shoulders, his full head of longish red hair. The evening just got much more dangerous for me. I glance at my watch and pray that wearing a uniform and avoiding Robert will be enough to keep his eyes from settling on me. I need to go outside.

Of anyone, Robert would be the most likely to identify me immediately. He spoke to the police—both on the tour and later, and at the station following my arrest. He was present at my sentencing hearing, smirking with folded arms from across the courtroom. All it would take tonight would be for him to look up at just the right time. To catch my eye. To call out my name. That would be the end of my new life.

I catch another glimpse of him before I circle back to the chafers. He wears a button-down shirt despite the heat, so well-pressed it looks made of metal. He leans toward Owen with an elbow propped on the sofa. His legs crossed, his cowboy boot jiggles over his knee.

But Owen faces away from him. When Robert speaks, Owen seems to pay no attention. He keeps his arm tight around Shelly's shoulder. I see him glance at his watch, then squint toward the backyard. Someone asks Owen a question and he clears his throat.

"The album? It's almost finished, actually. The recording is done, I'm just mastering it now. Fortunately, I have the convenience of working from home."

"They called James Brown the hardest working man in show business, but it's actually Owen James," I hear Robert pipe up.

Owen's face stays still, showing no recognition of Robert's comment. Instead, he says, "And luckily, Shelly's right there, too. Also very convenient for the process. I can't tell you the number of times I've asked her to come upstairs and re-record a vocal."

Shelly nods and smiles.

My heart thuds. I can't believe I'm close enough to hear this. Close enough to hear *Owen's voice.*

As I walk away, I notice something aggressive about the tension in Owen's hand on Shelly's shoulder, his veins twisting like tiny rivers. He leans for the bottle of water Lane brought her, unscrews the cap, and sets it back in her hands. Shelly rubs the side of the water bottle over her forehead. A drop of condensation runs to her chin and hangs there for a long second, like an icicle.

Outside, I nearly run into Malik, who quickly steps aside to avoid a collision. "Everything good in there?" he asks, a look on his face that tells me how busy he's been. I nod and smile as I pass and mutter something about checking the ice, which is just my excuse to move away from the Jameses and Robert. My head is trying to process what I've seen—not just Shelly's behavior, but Owen's too.

This evening, he seems so much more serious than the Owen I've watched before. For a second, I'm reminded of an event more than a year earlier, before I'd even started working for Ken. I'd hidden at the back of a banquet hall as waiters in black jackets buzzed over burgundy carpet while onion-shaped crystal chandeliers rained glittery light. I'd followed Owen inside, just wanting a harmless glimpse. It was a fund-raiser and there was a raffle. I leaned into a curtain while Owen chewed his fingernail before crouching beside a boy at the last table. I was close enough to see the boy show a red ticket to Owen, who nodded and tousled his hair. When Owen went to the stage and reached into a black box, he squinted at the ticket in his hand and called out a number. The boy from the back of the room jumped up and rushed forward to take a signed guitar. My heart fluttered like a bird's wing because I'd just watched magic.

Where is *that* Owen tonight, I wonder?

My head spins. I retreat to the van, pretending to take a break.

I flash to the summer I was arrested—the darkest time in my life. Darker than abuse. Darker than my closet year. In there, I was safe. Out in the world, I got lost.

Memories flood me.

* * *

When I left foster care, I moved to a room in a house where a lot of people lived, but I didn't like other people being near my things. I didn't like the no-control feeling. I kept a bed there, but it felt strange being inside with everyone coming and going.

Sometimes, I slept outside in the car I'd bought—sometimes parked in the house's driveway, other times behind a grocery store where it was very quiet.

I didn't tell the other people who lived in the house, or the tall lady who'd helped me find a job, or my manager at the kennel, because I knew they would say my staying outside was unsafe. Different things feel unsafe to different people. I kept a knife under my seat.

I saved the money I made at the kennel and barely spent time at the rooming house. I wanted out. No, just out. I'm not embarrassed to say that I wanted to be a part of what felt like a family. I knew that Owen and Shelly James would start a tour early that summer, and I knew I would quit my job to follow them. It may . . . *the word for very, very sad* . . . It may sound *pathetic*, but they were more my home than a physical place. Owen and Shelly's music was like a home inside me.

But I did have a few problems. Freedom, for one. How do you explain freedom as a problem? *Free-doom* was how I thought of it. There were no walls restraining or protecting me, just the dizzying sense of balancing on top of something tall, on one foot, waving my arms to keep from falling. Freedom was terrifying.

Then there was money. Despite having saved, I was running out I tried to think about that as little as I could. The state had given me an allowance when I graduated from foster care to "get started." The lady in the long dress had explained that it was more than the usual amount because of what happened to me when I was eleven. I'm not smart, but I know subtraction, and I was moving through what I had very quickly.

Luckily, I didn't need very much. My phone, gas for my car, food, and concert tickets—I figured out how to buy single tickets resold through an app on my phone. Sometimes I could manage to buy one from a scalper just before the show started. Three times, I snuck inside.

That summer was the hottest on record, and everyone kept saying it. For two months, my body never stopped sweating. During the daytime, I would wander through suburban shopping centers, eating free popcorn. No one bothered me if I watched TV in Walmart. There were always news channels on, stories about concert safety, about people firing into crowds. They seemed to flash constantly on the screens. The images made my stomach tighten. In the spring, a man in Kansas had rushed at Jason Aldean on stage. His security had swarmed to take the guy to the ground, but they found a buck knife in his pocket that he said he'd forgot he had on him. Maybe he *had* forgotten, but you never know what people might try. Sometimes people want to make other people feel pain. I never understood why.

After a while, all the cities began to look the same, especially the outskirts. I knew people complained about sameness—I heard them—but for me, sameness was comfortable. It helped me know where to find food, where the safest places were to park and sleep. I wasn't going to ask someone. This was before Ms. Parsons. Before trust existed inside me. I had to figure out everything on my own because I was on my own, and the whole world felt new. I felt like maybe I was losing my mind, but I didn't care. I had nothing to go back to. I told myself I was like the groups of kids who followed festivals around, except I did it alone. I didn't speak to anyone. I didn't want to explain myself because I knew no one would understand me. I carried my knife like I always had.

So, following the tour didn't feel very different from how I had been living. I washed myself in the sinks of fast-food restaurant bathrooms, lost track of daylight in dusty suburban public libraries. I napped behind shopping centers in my car, or under highway overpasses, traffic rumbling overhead like steady but distant jets. When I got to the venues, I would look at faces on posters for long stretches—country stars from every decade. I knew them all of course. Some looked stern. Some smiled like they knew something I didn't. In Owen's and Shelly's posters, they looked right into the camera. Shelly's eyes said they would be sad if I'd stayed home. Owen looked like he was thinking. He seemed to want to tell me something.

I kept my phone charged in my car and would scan the "ticket" inside each time I went into a venue. The scanning beep sounded the same in every city—a short, high chirp of a tiny robot bird. My heart leaped each time it welcomed me home.

I saw the whole tour, starting in Boston. Fifteen cities. Then, the last show, back in Nashville. Home. Most of the security team worked for the venue where the concert was held. Only a few followed the tour. I knew their faces. I was sure they knew mine. Auditoriums smelled like popcorn, even outside. Also, like sour-sweet dried-up beer on concrete, and like hair products. The crowds are seas of yellowed trucker caps and black-and-white T-shirts and denim and smells that are salty but also like perfume at times, and sway when music begins—sometimes, in unison, like one enormous organism. Most of the modern venues look like narrow shopping malls. They have columns so high you can't see the top and banners of whatever sports team plays there waving under giant vents. And they all have metal detectors.

I always tried to look bored when I went through security. I'd keep my mouth open a little, my knife taped to my leg, as I stepped through the metal detector. I went through eleven times and only got stopped three. Each time I found a way to play dumb. Only once did I flat out have to run, but still my heart raced every time, so loudly sometimes it felt like the guards could hear the liquid swooshing in my ears or see the thumping under my shirt.

The night of the last concert, I went through beside a family— an older couple and a kid who was maybe their granddaughter. The grandfather looked at me once, like I smelled. Behind him, someone spilled a Coke across the floor. Bits of half-melted ice and syrup-water spread everywhere. Everyone turned and looked at it for a minute, like the way people freeze when someone drops a plate in a restaurant.

"Goddamnit," a guard said.

I shoved my way to the middle of the family and emptied my pockets into the plastic bin that was passed around. Two of the security guards were busy with the spilled Coke when the metal detector whined. The one who was paying attention fiddled with a toy car that belonged to the little girl, glanced at the line forming behind us, then waved us forward. I collected my keys from the bin and went to the ladies' room, where I found an empty stall and locked the door. I could hear water rushing from the line of sinks. Someone was humming a song I didn't recognize, the sound going around and around the room like a pinball machine.

I pulled off the knife I'd taped to my leg, wincing, and slipped it into the back of my jeans. I let my shirt fall over the handle. When I left the bathroom, I went dim—staying near the wall, behind groups of people, but not too close behind. I found a seat in the last row where I could see most of the stage and most of the stands.

I watched for an hour. The warm-up music was the same at every arena. The sound check was a rolling thunderclap inside the auditorium. I'd memorized the order of the songs and sang along inside my head as I watched. The stage crew looked like the shadows of ghosts—they wore black shirts and black pants that seemed to blend in against the floor. They checked the blocking, the tuning of instruments, the order in which everything was to happen. I didn't know their real names, but I'd made up names in my head: Grey Ponytail, Tall Skinny, and Grandpa.

Robert Holloway stood at the side of the stage too, his back to me as he barked orders at the other three, pointing. Without the house-lights turned down, I felt vulnerable even at that distance. I knew

Robert from old press releases. He'd been Owen's manager since 1994. By then, I was pretty sure he knew me from security flyers I'd caught a glimpse of my own face on one after sneaking in through a loading dock halfway through the tour, and it took my breath away. I figured those started after I was chased out by security in Orlando. I'd read blogs that described Robert as stern and unforgiving, which fit the way he talked to the crew. Even if security would more likely recognize me first, something about Robert's presence filled my gut with fear. I exhaled when he faced the other direction.

My head felt empty the way it does when I don't eat. When was the last time? I couldn't remember. A granola bar or some Pop-Tarts in my car that morning?

There was a flash at the far end of the stage. I reached behind for the knife, stopped. Just someone testing a lighting kit. But my heart was still pounding. Some part of me knew that a bad thing might happen. My . . . *the word for knowing instinctively* . . . intuition. When you look back on situations, the way you should have acted is much clearer than it is when life is happening. Maybe I wanted to get caught, I wondered later. I knew I had pushed everything too far. I knew security would catch up with me eventually.

The knife blade scraped against my skin as I leaned back. I let out my breath. Around me, seats were filling up. The warm-up music got louder. I could feel little vibrations in my chest and in the chair beneath my legs. Fatigue from travel and hypervigilance must have caught up with me, because I didn't notice the guard as he approached. He almost touched my shoulder before I flinched.

"Miss, I need you to come with me," he said. I didn't respond and hurried out the other side of the row, then down the aisle. I knew what this meant—I'd been identified by security. It hurt knowing I would miss the last show, but it was time to get out. I looked over my shoulder and saw him speaking into a radio.

I had to run, but security guards blocked the exits behind me. The only way away from them was down—closer to the stage. Maybe I could lose them once the lights went out. I bounded down a flight of stairs, jumped a barrier, and ran along the back of another group moving onto the arena floor. I kept looking over my shoulder, watching for the security guard who was watching for me.

Shapes moved fast toward the stage, a rush. People touched my shoulders and back. It was accidental, I knew, but it still made my skin burn. I had to get out, but it was like I was painting myself into a corner and couldn't stop.

Then all the lights went out. People started screaming. Phone screens lit up like eyes of animals all around me. There was a burst of light from the stage so bright I saw green-and-red floaters and the river-like outlines of blood vessels inside my eyes.

I tried to remember the word for when a person goes crazy.

Shelly appeared on stage, waving, the crowd surging toward her. I pushed ahead, knocking someone out of my way who fell down and looked at me and I had no words to say sorry. My skin felt like it was on fire from all the touching.

Then someone shoved me hard from behind. I turned to see a guy in his mid-twenties, scowling at me because I'd stepped in front of him. He gripped my shoulder.

I pulled my knife. I wasn't thinking. Finding it was *reflex*. I had been so, so tired for so long. I had no thoughts. I tried to scream, but my voice would never let me scream. I felt the rubber grip of my knife slipping as I held it toward him and watched the scowl drop from his face.

I was shaking my head, *no, no, no. I'm sorry. I'm just scared.*

Had I cut him?

It was dark, but I could see him holding his upper arm.

Around me, people were screaming. People started running, gripping each others' shirts, pulling others away from me. Was someone behind me? Someone I didn't see?

But the someone *was* me. I'd done something terrible. I couldn't breathe. A hand gripped my neck. Another hand gripped my arm, jerking my hand. I caught a glimpse of a face—not a uniformed security guard but an actual police officer.

I would learn later that this was Detective Marion, working overtime as added security detail for the Nashville show. He would appear at my hearing to testify, where he would tell the story matter-of-factly and conclude by saying, "I hope she gets every bit of the help she needs." I knew that under his suit, his left forearm probably still had a bandage from where my knife had cut him as he took it from me.

Flashes popped—one from a photograph that appears on websites around the world any time my name is googled, but also in results for "crazed fan" and "stalker."

I heard my knife clatter across the ground. I felt my jaw crack against the cold cement floor. Pain shot through the front of my face as I felt one of my teeth break apart—pain so sharp it felt white. I felt a weight on my back that made it hard to breathe as my arms were twisted and my wrists were cuffed.

Then I stopped feeling my body and my mind fell into a deep hole.

There was no trial—my attorney encouraged me to plead guilty to reckless endangerment, trespassing, and simple assault. The state dropped an aggravated assault charge. I had a sentencing hearing where a judge heard from Detective Marion, and my case-worker from the state, and Robert Holloway, who testified that Shelly, Owen, and the crew were aware I'd followed the Jameses' tour across the country. My lawyer told me this was to establish that I hadn't acted impulsively on the night I was arrested. He said the state wanted to make it look like I'd been planning an attack at a concert for weeks, and Robert agreed that it seemed I had. He reviewed safety measures the crew had taken to identify me and described the flyers picturing my face that the crew had all seen. Shelly and Owen had seen my picture too, he said. They were aware that I had trespassed into a dressing-room area and agreed I posed a threat. Each venue's security, of course, was responsible for keeping me from entering the building in the first place.

When it was time for the man I'd stabbed to testify, my eyes dropped to the floor and stayed there. A force stronger than gravity pushed them down, keeping me from looking at him while he spoke. He said he was angry, and confused. He didn't know if he could ever feel safe at a concert again because of what I did. His voice shook a little as he talked about his ambulance ride to Vanderbilt, the stitches he got, the cut on his upper arm.

I hated myself.

Then I was taken to jail—where I spent a year.

I lost track of the James family after that, along with the rest of the world. I had to think about me—which was a good thing, in that way, I guess. Every now and then, there was some information about Owen and Shelly I couldn't escape. They were famous after all. Their pictures popped up online, on magazine covers, everywhere.

Everyone knew the Jameses' faces.

And apparently, the Jameses knew mine.

* * *

After my break, I head back to the Petersons' house, where I pick up a tray and pass through the kitchen to the outside area. Ken and Andre are tending to the food. I know I have to keep my distance from the Jameses and Robert, which shouldn't be hard to do for a while—there is plenty of work to tend to elsewhere.

By now, I half expect to see Detective Marion too. Since the concert where I was arrested, he's worked as a special consultant and security guard for Owen and Shelly. But, no, I tell myself, he wouldn't come *here*, with them, would he?

The backyard has filled with guests— mostly teenagers. There is a peculiar stillness to the dusk, a gentle bracing. There is little breeze now to make the strings of lights sway, just the sorrowful calls of suburban birds, and music through outdoor speakers so soft it seems subliminal. I hear a word in the air—*boyfriend*—followed by hoots of laughter.

Do they mean Sean?

I wonder what it is like to have a boyfriend. A boy who wants to see you, who waits for you. Who texts you, remembers your birthday, speaks to your family. A boy who occasionally leads you into darkness because he wants to put his hands on you.

A boy you want to follow into the dark.

I see how Finch faces Sean. The way she tilts her head when he talks. That is what Finch wants him to be—her boyfriend.

But watching him, I can't tell if he is. His body is angled away. She laughs when he talks, but he looks over her shoulder.

I do all the things I had planned to do, keeping as far away from the deck as possible, and to my relief, my tactic seems to work. The more time goes by, the more people begin to filter out. I just might make it out of this party, I think hopefully, even as my heart is still beating like a jackrabbit's.

For more than half an hour I manage to keep away from the part of the house where the living room meets the deck, until Ken asks me directly to check the status of the glassware in the kitchen. I nod, having no excuse that won't raise suspicion, and tell myself I'll be okay. I'll stay dim, I'll slip inside the side door Lane propped open. Checking and rearranging the glasses will take less than a minute tops, if I'm quick. A timer starts inside my head as I walk through the door. My chest feels like I'm holding my breath.

But the second I step into the hallway, I'm frozen by the sound of Owen's voice. ". . . don't need to drink any more tonight. What's with you? I'm starting to get . . ."

My eyes search the shadows around me for something to focus on and find a family portrait: Lane, Brian, and Sean Peterson all wearing white button-down shirts and khaki shorts on a beach somewhere, the sky behind them pink and blue from the perfectly angled sunlight.

"No, I *am* worried," Owen is saying. "You're a mess. Talk to me. It's *me*."

It's like there's some sort of force drawing me back toward Owen and Shelly despite my best efforts to keep my distance. I lean into the shadow of a pantry and listen. I can't *not* listen.

Shelly replies in a tangle of sobs. "I'm ruining tonight, I know. Take me home, will you? . . . Didn't want to be *here* in the first place."

"But these are our *friends*. Shell? Will you please tell me what's going on with you?" Shelly says something I can't hear, to which Owen half laughs. "Okay, fair, maybe *he's* not our *friend*, but everyone else is. And this is about Finch tonight. Let me get you some more water. There's just a week or two before Sean leaves, and . . ."

"I'm asking you, *please*." Shelly's urgency is breathtaking. I'm not hearing two people perform, I realize, suddenly—I'm listening in on an intimate conversation between a married couple.

Earlier—last year, even last week—I might have found the idea thrilling. But now Shelly's tearfulness and Owen's tender humor cause my stomach to sink, guiltily. I don't feel included like I have in the past. Suddenly, I feel like an intruder.

I think of the words Robert used during my sentencing. He said everyone agreed that I posed a threat. I want to run back outside, but I'm afraid any movement will make a sound.

In the stillness, I hear Owen sigh. "You've started taking them again. Don't deny it."

Shelly answers by staying quiet.

Them, I wonder? Taking *them*?

I suspect he means whatever is putting the slur in her voice and making it so that she can't walk in a straight line.

"I know you," he whispers. "What I don't know is how to help. Let's *talk* . . . when we get home. Okay?"

Another pause.

"Shelly?" he asks, before concluding, "I'll go tell Finch it's time. Just stay here. We can all walk out together, okay?"

I hear Shelly's muffled agreement, then the scuffing of Owen's boots on the hardwood, headed into the interior of the house.

I'm still partly holding my breath, I realize, drawing in tiny puffs to keep from passing out, my chest burning. Shelly is just a few feet away from me, I know, on the other side of the wall from where I stand. I need to move—to leave as quickly as I came—but silently, because I know any move I make can be heard from where she is.

I see the shape of someone passing up the driveway toward the street and recognize my chance, hoping my footsteps will be masked by the noise they're making. But as I spin into the hallway to go back out the door, Shelly does too.

And just like that, we are facing each other. I can't move.

Her eyes are glassy as she takes me in, and then widen as she raises her hand to her mouth.

My heart hammers, my pulse whooshing in my ears. The dark driveway behind me, I know half my face is lit by the iPad panel beside the door.

"You're . . ." Shelly begins, her voice at once trembling and slurred.

On the iPad, the icons are arranged in tidy rows, like glasses set out for a party. They're a mixture of symbols and letters that would take hours to understand how to operate, I'm sure. But from the corner of my eye, I see two icons I clearly understand:

ALL LIGHTS ON.
ALL LIGHTS OFF.

I push the bottom one as Shelly begins to scream.
Then everything goes black.

6

A chorus of screams follows Shelly's as I feel my way to the driveway and close the hallway door behind me. I nearly trip over the planter where Lane said the spare key was kept and hurry toward the front of the house, where I can hear voices from inside, some laughing at the unexpected thrill. Then comes Lane's voice, somehow both commanding and sweet, calling out, "Everything is okay. Someone probably just bumped the light panel."

A moment later, the lights all come back—this time, all on at once, including floodlights bleaching the lush front lawn I cut across on my way to the van. How could I have been so stupid? Why did I take such a risk? Maybe Ms. Parsons was right after all—I don't understand risk—I think, balling my hands into fists. I feel like knocking them against my own head. Not just because of the stupid risk I just took, but because the conversation I've just overheard made me feel like I trespassed. Shelly's crying and Owen's pleading with her to get help made something click inside me. It made them both *real* somehow.

Now I feel like a fool—one whose realization came a moment too late and now will be headed to jail, most likely. I climb in the van's passenger seat and close the door, panting like I've just run for my life.

I don't know what good hiding will do, but as I watch people begin to filter out of the house, I bend forward in my seat, doubling over like there is an actual pain in my stomach. It seems like the momentary darkness I created inside the house somehow signals an end to the party, or at last quickened the pace of everyone who was already on their way out the door. I watch as people wave their goodbyes under the floodlights—Lane, I realize, must have pressed the iPad icon ALL LIGHTS ON,—because from where I sit, everyone is clear as day.

Maybe ten minutes pass, and then I see them: Owen, Shelly, and Finch James—as they walk along the brick-paved path from the front door. Owen is looking straight ahead with the steady expression he has on stage, but Shelly stumbles, her arm linked through his. Even from this distance, I can tell she's been crying, and she gestures with her hands like she's trying to explain something to Owen, who winks at her and calmly shakes his head. Finch trails slowly behind them both, typing something into her phone. They make their way to Shelly's white Mercedes SUV parked along the edge of the lawn. Owen helps Shelly into the passenger seat before he and Finch climb in and they drive away.

There is obviously a lot happening in their lives, but I know at least a part of Shelly's crying relates to me having scared her—a thought I feel awful about.

I'm thinking about what else I could have done, how else I could have gotten away, when the van's rear doors fly open and the interior dome light pops on above me. I turn, nearly jumping out of my skin. It's just Malik, a tray in his hands. "Whoa, hey. I didn't mean to startle you. I'm just putting away some of this stuff. How long have you been out here?"

I run my hands through my hair and force myself to draw in a deep breath. "Just a minute," I lie.

Malik's smile is caring but unknowing. I wish I could tell him the truth. "You probably got nervous and came out here when the lights went out, right? I get it. Want to come back inside? Ken was wondering if I'd seen you."

"Sure," I say, and follow him back toward the house. I know it isn't *safe* to go back inside—especially since I haven't seen Robert Holloway leave—but I can't think of a good excuse to stay sitting in the van, alone.

I follow Malik around back and begin straightening up. I turn off the chafers and circle the outdoor sofas, picking up the cups and plates left behind. The plates I pick up clink together in my hands, their edges both sticky and slick. The night seems to have gotten even warmer somehow, and I feel my cotton shirt clinging to my skin as I move around. The evening breeze is only a slight relief when it touches my neck. I scan for Robert, but there is no sign of him, and I hope he left out the front door after the Jameses did.

We work steadily for another hour, me taking as many trips to the van as possible and lingering there to stay out of the way. I hesitate to let my guard down, but everything seems to be going as normally as possible for the moment—no police have arrived to arrest me for breaking the order of protection, and no one from the Peterson family has accused me of being where I don't belong. A small part of me wonders if I just might actually leave quietly and sleep in my own bed tonight.

When the van is finally loaded, Ken, Andre, Malik, and I climb back in and start the drive back to the company kitchen. The neighborhood is much darker now—the long lawns sloping and shadowy. My breathing has slowed down, and while I still feel terrible about having startled Shelly, my insides relax a little. I start hoping the story of this night has ended, and that I'll look back on my close call with a little more wisdom and perspective.

I've learned I can't "idealize" the Jameses, to borrow a word I've heard Ms. Parsons use. I even wonder if I might start to get rid of some of the memorabilia I collected. Maybe I could donate it, or sell it and donate the money—that might make a nice end to my involvement with that time in my life.

The radio crackles as Ken drives. I'm not paying attention to what music is playing, but I look up immediately when Ken switches it off as we turn into the kitchen's parking lot. When we come to a stop, he cuts the engine and the slight vibration I feel through the floor and the cooler I'm sitting on goes still. When Andre opens the door, Ken says, "Guys, hang on a second." Andre closes it again, halfway, the dome light above him shining its pink-orange light down on all of us.

"I want to say a few things," Ken begins, in the tone he uses when giving us one of his pre-event pep talks. "The party tonight didn't always go smoothly, but I thought we handled everything really, really well. All our preparation showed. I thought we maintained our cool and kept our heads in the game even when the lights went out . . ." Malik and Andre both chuckle. "Even a momentary blackout didn't throw us off. So, great job everybody."

Andre holds onto the door handle like he's waiting for Ken to finish so he can get to unloading everything and head home. His eyes look tired, suddenly. Malik's too.

Ken pushes his heavy, black glasses up the bridge of his nose and clears his throat, then looks at each of us. "I also have big news. This is important. I need everyone on the schedule for next Saturday night. About halfway through the party, Owen James came up to me and asked me if we can work an event at their house in Belle Meade, starting at seven PM."

Ken's voice cracks from the thrill. He makes a fist and pumps it, eyes closed, like he's won something.

But my head spins, dizzily, my stomach dropping into freef-all. "I can't," I blurt out.

I've said it too loudly, I realize immediately, stopping myself from covering my mouth with my hand.

All three turn and look at me.

"Unfortunately, it's not really a question, Jessie. This is a must-do. This would be the biggest event that's happened to this company. We can't afford to miss it, even if it's late notice." The tiny tattoo on his hand flexes as he grips the steering wheel. His eyes seem to radiate intensity through the shadows.

"I just can't," I mumble.

"We can talk about it later." He answers in a deep, more serious tone of voice. "There's really no choice on this, I'm sorry to say. It's an all-hands-on deck moment."

Malik looks back and forth between Ken and me, his expression tight. Then his lips pull into the kind of frown that says "no big deal" as he raises his palms. "This is a good thing, Jessie. We'll handle it. It's okay."

But this is *not* okay, and I know I can't say why. I need to find a way out of going as quickly as I can. Even if Ken said there's no choice, there is. As much as I would hate to, I know I will quit before going to a party at Owen and Shelly's house. My temples are damp, and the back of my neck burning hot, like I've been standing too close to a fire. There's simply no way I can go.

I'm almost too upset to listen as Ken explains the way Owen's offer came about. "The event is for the release of their new album. Apparently, they already *had* a caterer, but I got the idea that Ms. James can be tough to work with."

I zone out as he tells more of the story. I watch as Andre wipes his forehead with a cocktail napkin, then folds it in half and wipes again, letting out a sigh.

Once Ken's finished, we unload the van. I keep quiet, hurrying on each trip to the kitchen and back. I grit my teeth when Malik starts to whistle a tune that normally makes me smile.

On my last trip, I nearly walk straight into Ken, who holds up his hand. I look at my shoes. The pavement is dewy, like it's sweating. "Jessie," he says. "Listen, this will be fine. Don't I always look out for you? You did so well tonight. You can do this."

He's thinking this is about me being shy, I suppose. I start thinking of an excuse, but I'm always available, and Ken knows it. If I make up a lie, it will have to be believable, and I'll have to keep it up forever.

One lie can lead to a thousand more.

For a second, I wonder if Ken knows about my following the tour, my arrest. He didn't seem to earlier when he handed me the nondisclosure form. But just like now, his eyes were calm and satisfied, and my head tells me he couldn't have—if he knew, he would have shown it before now.

But I wonder sometimes, am I reading him right?

My head spins as I drive home.

I lock myself in my apartment and try not to think.

*   *   *

Later that night I stare at my ceiling instead of sleeping. How could I? I sit up in bed and force myself to take deep breaths. I've already been more than stupid. I know this. Going to the Petersons turned out to be a very bad idea. Going to another party *at Owen and Shelly's house* would be completely insane.

Shadows of branches shift across my ceiling as I try to put together the Shelly I've seen on stage and the person I saw tonight. I wonder: is that *really* how she's been all along? I picture the way Owen acted in front of everyone, and how that changed when he and Shelly were alone. He sounded embarrassed when he talked over her, steering the conversation.

I think about Finch James. She was like me in the way that she didn't have her real parents. But I went to state care, and she went to live with the most successful country artists in the world. I wonder if she was surprised when she found out where she would go—twelve years old, being told she was going to live with stars.

And then she was famous too. Just like that.

I guess I do sleep some eventually, because I dream about a story I read once about a man who made wings from wax. He wants to fly to the sun, but when he gets too close, the sun's heat melts his wings and he falls to earth like a stone. I dream that I am him, falling, my heart pounding inside my chest, my arms failing as they try to flap. As the ground rushes toward me, I wake up, screaming.

* * *

On Wednesday, I stand in the catering kitchen sorting through recipes for events for the next few weeks while Ken paces back and forth between his office and the back door, rubbing the back of his neck.

I consider a dozen possibilities about what I will tell Ken to avoid working the Jameses' party. I need my job—and Ken is so good to me. I know "calling out" is something people talk about doing to skip work. If Jessica hadn't quit a month earlier, prep would still be all I do. Ken knows I feel awkward around crowds of people, I just don't want him to notice I'm *especially* uncomfortable around *this* event.

Thank God I still haven't heard anything about Shelly having recognized me at the Petersons' party. At least in that case, if I am found out I can deny knowing they would be there—not even Ken knew for sure. But if I'm seen at Owen and Shelly's, there will be no explaining it. There is no mistaking who lives in their house, and my wearing a uniform would even make my presence look even sneakier.

Ken has gotten a haircut and his shirt looks as though he pressed it. Each time I hear the thump of his shoes as he passes, I expect him to say something.

Finally, he asks me, "You're coming with us this afternoon, right?"

"Where?" I ask, though part of me already knows. Ken has called Andre and Malik in too. Andre opens the side door as if on cue.

"Owen and Shelly James's, of course. Ms. James is going to show us everything we need to know for Saturday's party."

I grind my teeth as I twist the cord to my headphones. "You're doing it for sure? Catering their party?"

"Absolutely." He whistles, then draws his eyebrows together like he's confused by my asking. He sniffs the way he does when he's nervous. "Were you thinking I wouldn't take it because of the short notice?"

I nod, and my stomach clenches up.

"I'll absolutely scramble to do this one. Listen, you don't *have* to go today. I just thought maybe you'd want to see their house and all. Get familiar. Plus, you know, it's the home of a famous couple. Fun to see . . ."

If you only knew, I think.

"There's too much to do here," I say. "I saw the prep list and I figured I would get started on it this afternoon." I close my hand around my earbud, from which a tinny song rises.

Ken shrugs as if to say *good point*, just as Malik steps forward.

"You're not going? How can you *not* want to see that crib?" he asks. His question sounds innocent enough. Malik touches the screen of his phone, sets it on the table, and turns it to show me a picture: the Jameses' gray and beige mansion—the size of a castle, but newer, designed to look modern.

I look at the photo and nod, trying not to show my interest. Even though I've seen the same photo hundreds of times, it is so regal-looking that each time I do, I always feel like music should start playing.

They both lean toward the photo.

"Backs up to Warner Park," Ken notes, pointing at the tree line around the rear and side of the house. Warner Park is the nicest, biggest park in town—almost two thousand acres. It's where rich and beautiful people go to be in nature.

"Nice," I say, quietly.

Andre walks in behind Ken, nods at me. "Sup, Jessie? Sup, guys?"

Ken seems to consider Andre's clothes, then glances at his watch. "We've gotta get going. You guys ready?"

Andre smiles. "We're not even supposed to be there for forty minutes. Somebody's excited, I think."

Ken shrugs.

Andre asks, "Jessie, you ain't coming? You're going to want to see this, I promise."

Because: who wouldn't want a tour of Owen and Shelly James's mansion? Who wouldn't want to meet Shelly James?

Me.

I shake my head and turn my attention back to the recipe cards, writing down a note about some ingredients that Ken needs to pick up. I know they can sense I'm not comfortable going, and I pray that Ken thinks of it as no different than my unease with any other event.

"You guys smell like weed." Ken frowns like he doesn't approve even though Andre and Malik know he doesn't care.

"Jessie got us high," Andre says, winking.

My head snaps around.

"Stop," Malik says. "Don't let him bother you, Jessie."

"Aww, Jessie knows I'm playing."

"I'm fine," I say, but my heart is beating like a rabbit's. I haven't slept more than a few hours a night since I learned about Owen's offer. I'm in no state to take a joke.

"Just don't fall into the pool, or like, talk. At all, guys," Ken says to them both. He and I go over my instructions for what I can prep while they're gone, then he practically skips out the back door.

"Later, Jessie," Malik calls. He waves to me, then gently pulls the door closed behind him. A few seconds later I hear the rumble of the van starting.

It makes sense that Owen and Shelly are throwing the party as a way of generating some buzz for their new record. I lean against the counter, listening to the refrigerator hum, then pace around, trying to stay out of my head. I picture the others making their way over to the Jameses' house and wonder if Ken will take the same route to the house that I have before. I imagine the van driving through a neighborhood even nicer than the Petersons'—where the houses really are mansions with neat-cornered hedges a dozen feet tall and storybook chimney tops, and stone walkways, and third stories.

I can picture just where Ken will turn down their side street, and where he will stop and look up their steep driveway. He will check his phone for a security code, punch numbers into a keypad, and a gate will slowly swing open. I've wondered before about that combination while watching delivery trucks pass in and out of their driveway—but of course I would never have thought to try to actually *go in*.

I shake my head to clear the images away, slip on an apron, and decide to start on the mirepoix. I figure it won't hurt to contribute to the event, even if there's no way I'll actually work on it, and practically whatever Ken and Shelly decide on, this type of prep can happen days in advance—Ken uses mirepoix as a base for nearly every party he caters. As usual, I get lost in the rhythmic cutting—the onions gently give way beneath the knife. I turn them and chop, turn them and chop, making little piles on the edge of my cutting board. I put more of my weight into the celery, having to press down faster, harder, for the cut that I want. I pile the pieces in separate stacks, slipping one tiny piece into my mouth. I skin two dozen carrots, then chop them up too.

I nearly achieve a state of calm.

A few hours pass before I hear the tired cry of the van's brakes. My pulse speeds up again, but I pretend to shuffle the recipe cards. The back door opens and Malik and Andre burst in, laughing.

"What's happening, Jes-say?"

"You missed out," Malik shrugs like he's truly sorry I didn't come along.

I set the knife down and wipe my hands on the apron. "What was it like?" I ask, hoping they can't see my pulse throbbing in my neck.

"What was it *like*? I'll tell you what it was like," Andre cracks up. "It's like that lady's never thrown a party before, for starters." He looks out the door, where Ken is pacing up and down, his phone to his ear.

"There was a lot of waiting around outside, trying to stay out of the hot sun," Malik says, through a calm smile.

Andre makes a motorboat noise with his lips that means *I don't know.* "The only reason we were there is because Shelly

James fired the last, like, three caterers. She may be crazy for real, but Ken wants the gig, so we stayed on our best behavior."

The word "crazy" hits me, but I don't let my face show it. I want too badly to hear what they have to say.

Andre says, "Honestly, the whole trip over there was a waste of our time. Soon as we get there, an old dude assistant came rushing out to meet us."

"The manager," Malik clarifies.

Robert Holloway, I think, picturing his red hair and goatee.

"He looks the three of us over and asks if everyone in the company had come along. Ken explained you were here working. The manager told us only Ken could go inside, at least at first. Ken said he would try to introduce us before we left."

"Not Ken's fault," Malik adds.

"Still," Andre says, clearly annoyed. "The manager dude takes a call as we stand there, so we sit on the hill in the backyard to wait in the shade, and Jessie, it's like *Lifestyles of the Rich and Famous*. Twenty feet of perfect grass before the woods start. Leaves floating down around us. Heaven." He puts his hands together and wiggles his fingers like a falling leaf. "Honestly, it was so nice, I nearly forgot we weren't allowed inside."

I know just the place he's describing. I nearly got there myself once, but was never able to get so close to the house. I can almost smell the early summer woods, the sharpness of pine.

Andre says, "The house's back walls were glass. *Anyone* could see right inside—but since it only faces the park, I guess maybe that's okay. Just animals and trees."

If I had been there, me, looking into their house . . .

"Except we can see inside. Right? And guess what we see?"

Malik hides his mouth with his hand as he looks out the window. He's blushing, I notice.

"We see Shelly. Upstairs. Doesn't know Ken is there yet, I guess. Walks past a huge sofa, into a bedroom, and holds out an old flip phone *as she unbuttons her shirt halfway down her chest.*"

"Stop," Malik says.

"Truth. She was taking a selfie!"

I swallow, hard. I feel like walking away, but I'm afraid it would look odd.

"Jessie doesn't want to hear this, man," Malik mumbles.

"Then she goes downstairs and shows Ken around, all in a hurry, waving a wineglass around while she walks, pointing like," he makes a high voice like a woman's, but with a sort-of British accent. "I'd like the main buffet over here, with a little table in this corner for silverware beside it." (Andre throws his hands in the air and starts slow dancing.) "But Ken don't care. He thinks he might *get some* from Shelly James. She had on these huge sunglasses." (He makes his fingers into circles and raises them to his face to show the size.) "And she walked around in these little white shorts while Kenny pretended to write down what she was saying."

I look at the back door, wondering if Ken is in earshot.

"Ken's in love. But that's okay, I guess. *Everybody's* in love with Shelly James. I think *I'm* in love with Shelly James. Half of Nashville thinks they have a shot. I guess Owen ain't taking care of her anymore."

"Nah, Shelly's married," Malik says, and Andre lets out a laugh that seems to rattle the windows.

I hate to admit it to myself, but he's right. *The word for behaving like you're attracted to someone . . .* Shelly James is *flirtatious.* Sometimes when she talks with men, she reaches out her red fingernails and touches their forearms or their cheeks. She gives quick glances while walking off stage, and during interviews, and with certain fans, and with her security guards. And I've noticed the looks men give her back—longer, like they're breathing her in.

I always wanted Shelly not to look at men like that, and also wanted Owen not to know that she had. I wanted to have misunderstood all of that, but always knew I didn't.

"No Owen James though. I guess he was at work."

"In the studio."

Andre shrugs. "Maybe she's a flirt because Owen works too much."

I think of interviews when Owen has said that he sometimes turns out the studio lights and sleeps there.

"Man loves to work," Malik agrees.

"He didn't get that house by doing nothin'. So, check this out," Andre says. "Right as Ken is taking the tour, the girl, the teenager, appears in the kitchen, saying something to the manager, Robert."

Finch.

"*Then* she *storms* out the back door, right toward us. 'You two are with the catering company?' she asks, her cheeks all red, her hands in fists on her hips. And we're like . . . uh, yeah? And she raises her voice and says, 'I sure as hell hope you weren't taking any pictures with your phones' and points up."

"We weren't," Malik assures me. "And we told her we weren't."

"But she climbs up on the hill, right beside us, and squints up at the house to see what kind of view we have of the upstairs. Malik asks her if everything is okay."

Malik rubs the back of his neck. "She was pretty worked up. I guess she thought we were watching the upstairs. I don't know if she knew what we saw or what, but I guess she saw our reactions."

"It *was* kind of crazy," Andre says. "You know, seeing Shelly James taking a half-naked selfie."

"But we weren't looking for it," Malik reassures me.

"Yeah, it's not like we *knew* what we were gonna see," Andre agrees. "Or went up on that hill meaning to look in the back of the house, which turned out to be *all glass*, like some kind of stalkers."

Malik laughs softly.

Ha ha, I think. I flash to my dream from the night before of falling to the earth. My stomach feels like wasp stings again.

"Then she says, 'There's nothing going on worth laughing at, got it?' And she storms off. And what can we say but 'Yeah, we got it.'" Malik gives a little salute as they both share an uneasy laugh.

"She looks just like her mom. Or her mom looks just like her." I hadn't thought of it that way, but it's true. Last winter, when Finch cut her hair shorter, Shelly went out and got the exact same haircut.

"Other than all that, the place itself was cool," Andre says, shaking his head.

My eyes must go blank as I'm picturing it, still half listening to Andre describing how similar Shelly and Finch can look. A shadow crosses my eyes as Andre waves his hand, his eyebrows raised. "Earth to Jessie. You in there? Ken said we could take off. You comin'?"

I shake my head and point at the stack of recipes I'd been going through.

"Suit yourself," Andre says. "You know that party don't start till Saturday."

They're heading toward the door when Ken comes in from outside, index finger up like he was saying *wait*. "The guy who runs their security for parties wants to meet everyone. He's on his way now."

I stop right where I am and let out a little sound like a gasp. I can't help it.

Detective Marion.

Ken turns, his smile kind but unknowing. "What?" he asks.

My heart is thundering in my ribs. I have to find a way out of the kitchen, but it feels like it's closing in on me. My head can't work through the blurry cloud of Andre and Malik's story— Shelly's selfie, Finch confronting them, Robert asking if *everyone was there.* Does he know about me?

Ken looks at his watch. "Guys, this will take no time at all. A few minutes, then we can all go."

Behind him, Malik lets his head fall back against the wall. He laughs a little and rubs the spot where it hit. "Man, Ken, I got places to be." He starts playing air drums, mimicking percussion sounds as his hands work up and down.

"Ten minutes, relax. The guy just needs our information so he can run background checks."

"Background checks? To work a party?" Malik asks.

"High profile," Ken answers.

"Shouldn't they have done that *before* we went over there?" Andre asks. "What kind of guard is this?"

In my heart, I know exactly what kind—the kind who has already proven his bravery during a crisis. An *actual* cop, who works the Jameses' parties and special functions during off hours, who's not afraid to tackle and cuff a suspect carrying a knife. Inside my mouth, my tongue finds the rough edge of my chipped tooth. Of course, Detective Marion works security for the Jameses. Not many people would have risked their own life to stop a crazed fan. And I *know* Marion does special jobs like this. I've seen his photo online. If anyone would recognize me, it would be him. My hand finds the place on my lower back where his knee pinned me against the concrete floor that night.

I hear a car door slam in the alley. Everyone's head turns.

"Well, shit, that *was* quick," Andre says.

I open my mouth to speak, but nothing comes out.

Ken cocks his head to the side like a curious dog. "Jessie?"

"I have to go to the bathroom," I say, starting to back out of the room.

Too late. I'm trapped. The kitchen has two doors—the side entrance I know Detective Marion is about to walk through, and what Ken calls the front door, which was actually at the rear of the building. Marion will be between me and both. From where I stand, I can see the frosted glass of the bathroom window, and for just a second I think about escaping through it. Just running. I don't want to think about what would happen next if I did. It feels like the end of a board game that I'm losing: there are fewer and fewer open moves. The choices get worse and worse. Still, I *have* to find a way out.

Marion will know me instantly. He will add everything up. He will think I'm planning to go to the Jameses' house and know I'd seen Owen and Shelly at the Petersons' party. I'd been less than twenty feet away. When he looks at me, the face he will see will be the one picture taken by someone's cell phone—the one of me on the ground, a trickle of blood flowing from between my lips where my face had been slammed down. The one that comes up on Internet searches. Marion will look at me and then . . . what?

Report me? Have me fired? Call Ms. Carr?

Draw his gun?

He could, I know, take me away right then.

Ms. Parsons's voice comes back to me: *Fifteen years.*

Ken smooths his hair as he starts toward the door.

In my mind, I see the metal rail above my bed in jail, and smell the bleach-mud scent that is on everything inside. I flash back to my feelings from then too—the suspicion all around you, like air, like something sharp close to your throat, even when you're asleep.

I hear a knock. Malik and Andre straighten themselves, tugging at the bottoms of their shirts. Andre checks his breath in his cupped hand. Malik raises his eyebrows. My eyes sweep over the freezer—large enough to hide in. A bead of sweat runs from my hairline to my lips. My fear tastes like salt.

The side door opens and Ken extends his hand. Andre and Malik step forward. The temperature rises from the heat outside flooding in.

I drop my chin and take a step toward Detective Marion, just as he walks in.

Except it isn't Detective Marion.

The man in front of me is tall and blonde. Aviator sunglasses rest on his forehead, and he wears light-blue jeans and a polo shirt the color of the basil I'd just added to Ken's list.

Ken's voice gets high and nervous-sounding again, like when he first spoke to Lane Peterson. "I'm Ken, from All Out Catering. Ms. James said that you'd want to meet before the event."

The not-Detective-Marion-man whistles as he looks around the kitchen. I can tell Ken is introducing Andre and Malik, but the whoosh of my pulse in my ears keeps me from fully hearing him. Relief fills me, but a small part of me has already begun to wonder about Marion. *Maybe a work issue prevented him from being here?*

The blonde man holds a tablet with a shell-like black case and makes a sort of approving frown as Ken shows him around the kitchen. I blink away my fear as my hands unclench and hear him introduce himself, saying, "I've just started working for the James family but will be managing security for events at the house going forward. I apologize if the background checks seem excessive, but there've been issues in the past . . . You've met with Ms. James, I understand?"

"We just left there. Everything's pretty much set for Saturday. She wants the event to start around seven, so we're planning to arrive around six."

The man touches the pad. "How many in your crew?"

"Myself and three assistants, so four of us altogether. We actually all met Owen and Shelly at the Petersons' event last week."

The man looks up from his pad. "Oh, it was you guys working that party?"

"Sure was," Ken says, like it happens all the time.

"Small world. So, for today, I'll need to see . . ." The man's phone chirps. He raises his index finger and slips his sunglasses off his forehead as he answers it, then turns away when he realizes the four of us are watching.

My heart jumps a little. I can hear enough to know it's Shelly James on the phone—I would know her voice anywhere. I can't make out her words, but her tone is excited. Maybe even upset. I watch the blonde guard twirl his sunglasses by the stem. Malik and Andre glance at each other while we wait, and I realize how thankful I am that I'm not on the ground at the moment, being handcuffed.

But another part of me wonders where Marion is. I keep thinking about this new guard explaining he's new on the job.

Why would the Jameses need a new head of security?

Still, I know what the guard will need to see—everyone's ID. And if he runs mine, it won't be long before everything crashes.

I eye the door again as the guard walks in a tight circle, his eyes up to the ceiling.

His mouth tightens before he says, "Be right there, Ms. James." He drops his phone into his pocket and looks at his watch. "Anyone in the crew that I should be worried about? Any felonies I should be notified of?" he asks, his voice different, suddenly. He looks at Ken with mild irritation, like this meeting is an imposition, like it was Ken's idea.

Ken smiles. "No sir, absolutely not."

"Okay, well, just check in with me Saturday once you guys..." He looks over at me for a second. "This all looks fine."

Fine?

A second later, the door slams closed behind him and I hear his car start in the alley.

I let my breath out.

"That was it?" Malik asks.

"Apparently," Ken says, standing on his toes to see out the back window. "Not a big deal, I guess. Jessie, you still here? The security guy already took off."

It takes me a second to remember my excuse about needing to use the bathroom. "I'm here," I call as I step out.

The cooks both leave. On his way out the door, Ken tells me he'll see me Saturday, and I don't know how to find the words to tell him he won't. I'll have to message him later.

I'm not usually the last one to leave, but I'm lost in my head. I pull the back door closed behind me, lock it, and drop my keys into my pocket.

I'll go home, I think, and figure out something to tell Ken to get out of doing the event. Even if it means lying to him or losing my job.

I've just turned toward my car when I hear it.

"Hey."

Just that one word. It breaks the silence of the alley and snaps me away from my thoughts, back into the world. I feel my hands clench into fists as I stop in my tracks. I recognize this voice, I realize. I turn to face who spoke to me.

Robert Holloway steps from the shadows. His red hair is a little longer than he wore it on the tour, his beard more neatly trimmed. He wears a navy baseball cap now, which he's pulled low on his forehead. His palms are turned up as if to say he means no harm, but my heart instantly starts pounding. I look over my shoulder for a way to run, but realize I'm backed against the closed end of the alley. I step back and he steps forward. I see the bumper of his truck and realize from its angle that he has parked to intentionally block in my car.

I try to shut down the fight-or-flight reaction, but it surges. My teeth grind together. I can almost feel my pupils dilate. I was a fool for telling myself he hadn't seen me at the party, just like I was a fool for not running the second I saw the Jameses and for letting my curiosity draw me in, again. I try to read what Holloway wants from the little I can see in his eyes as he takes another step toward me.

"Jessie, I need your help."

7

Robert Holloway opens the passenger door of his truck and motions for me to get inside. I'm not sure I have a choice. I glance at the back of my car, inches from his front bumper. I *could* run, but how far would I get? And where would I run to? He found me at work; he could find me again. Easily. I realize with a shudder that if he knows where I work, he most likely knows where I live.

He's been watching me.

The visor of his cap shields his face but his voice sounds gentle, almost kind.

"Please."

I get in and sink into the passenger seat while he hurries to the driver's-side door. Inside, the truck smells like leather, expensive cologne, cigar smoke. Bits of paper that look like receipts line the rubber floor mats, which my feet barely reach. The cab hardly rocks as he climbs in and closes his door. Slightly out of breath, he presses a button and the engine rumbles to life. The cabin floods with a blast of air-conditioning, which he lowers with the press of another button.

His eyes have a kind twinkle I've never seen in them before. "I'm sorry if I startled you. I didn't mean to sneak up on you like that. My apologies. I waited until the others left, Jessie, because I wanted to speak to you alone. I wasn't sure it was you at first when I saw you at the party. I caught you out of the corner of my eye and wondered if I was seeing things. It's been a long time."

A year, I think. Longer for me than for you, I bet. Still, he sounds sincere.

"But then Shelly said she thought she saw you too. I know she was having kind of a rough night. Owen thought she might have been mistaken but . . ." He pauses. "You look *good*. Really good, actually. Healthy. I know you've had your struggles in the past, like we all have . . ."

A sudden, violent urge to smash his face surges through me. Struggles he can't possibly imagine. But what he's saying settles over me: Shelly not only saw me, she'd *told* people she had, including Robert—the very person I'd specifically hoped would not find out.

". . . but now you've got a job where you're part of a team. The food is incredible too. What can I say? I'm impressed. You should be proud of how far you've come in such a short amount of time."

I force myself to interrupt. "You said you needed my help?"

A smile slowly creeps over Robert's lips. "I did. Actually, it was Owen who asked me to find you."

"Owen?" I try not to show how taken aback I am, but my heart jumps inside my chest. I clench my teeth, not wanting to give away any of my feelings to Robert Holloway.

"I . . . need this to stay just between us. Can we agree to that?"

Even if I knew how to answer, I'm not sure I would be able to force the words out. My head is swimming as I look at the face of the man who'd smirked and waved bye-bye as I was driven away in the back of a police car the year before. Robert, who witnessed the most horrifying moment of my life. What message could he possibly have from Owen? I'm too stunned to do anything but agree.

"Sure," I say.

"You're surprised to see me, I'm sure. I didn't expect to be here myself, quite honestly. I hadn't thought about you in a long time, but when I asked to check the nondisclosure agreements for the party, there was your name."

Of course, I think. It wasn't like signing my full name was very subtle.

I glance behind us, over the truck bed, and see Robert catching me look.

He unpeels a breath mint from a roll and pops it in his mouth. A second later, I smell wintergreen as I hear it clicking against his teeth. "I know you must be nervous to see me."

To say the least.

"If you're worried about getting in trouble because of working that party, don't be. Believe me, I'm nervous to see you too. I just want to say, when your arrest happened at the end of the tour, I was just doing my job—protecting Owen and Shelly at all costs. My basic rule was to take care of them first and ask questions later. You got burned, unfairly, and I'm sorry."

I nod once, tentatively.

"I'm here because they want to meet you."

I shift in my seat. I'm sure I haven't heard correctly. "They what?"

Robert's smile broadens into a grin. His eyes hold steady. "They've been talking about finding you for some time. Truth be told, you going to jail didn't look great in terms of public perception. After what happened, they learned about how you grew up. They have huge hearts, Jessie, and, honestly, once they learned about your past, they felt sick. Owen believes in second chances.

And you know how he respects hard work. He loved finding out that you'd been working, and just between you and me, it's why he offered your boss the gig for the album party. He and Shelly want a chance to meet you, and maybe have a photo taken together. They want to do right by you. It would be a nice turn of events, don't you think?" He pauses. "Besides, I have to admit, PR-wise, with the album coming out the timing would be perfect."

My head tries to conjure the images of Shelly telling Owen that she saw me, and then him going to find and hire Ken.

Does this mean Ken knows?

My stomach turns from the rush of too many thoughts and feelings at once, and from the disorientation of half-trust. But what comes on most strongly, what threatens to swallow me whole, is disbelief. It's all I can do to stay grounded like Ms. Parsons showed me as I manage to ask, "A picture?"

Robert chuckles, soothingly. "Only if the timing is right. Everybody understands the situation. But think of it—the story coming full circle. Essentially, you'd be working for Shelly and Owen. Knowing you're coming would mean the world to them."

The muscles in my legs relax, slightly. The leather seat is so soft it seems to pull me into it. Hope is dangerous, but it begins to rise in my chest. I can't help it. I've wanted so badly for my intentions to be known. God, to be *forgiven*. How many times have I wished I had a time machine to go back and undo everything about the concert, to be more careful, less of a monster?

I feel a flutter in my stomach as my tongue finds the edge of my tooth, still cracked from that night. "What about security? A guard was just here, checking on us."

"Not an issue." He waves his hand, laughing like he's relieved. "I wanted to wait till you agreed before speaking with security, but it won't be a problem. You're *invited*."

I think back to the blonde guard I'd seen a few minutes earlier, a part of me still trying to make sense of his visit. "Will Detective Marion be there?" I ask. "At the party?"

Robert's eyebrow twitches. He stammers some before his calm tone reemerges. "Marion is no longer employed by the family." His hand rises a few inches, and for a second, I think he means to pat my knee. "I get why seeing him would be upsetting. But, no, he's focusing on his main job being a Metro detective as of about three weeks ago. Nothing to worry about there."

Detective Marion's departure makes perfect sense, but I find it strange somehow. Maybe because I'd pictured him with the Jameses for so long. Something about Robert's hesitation tells me there is more to the story.

Robert leans back a little, the look on his face suggesting that something has been decided. I can tell he means for our meeting to end. "So, Saturday. You'll come for sure?"

"I guess."

"Say yes, please." He holds still in expectation.

"Okay," I say.

He makes a fist that becomes a thumbs-up as he shifts back and forth in his seat. "There'll be a lot of guests, I'm sure, so look for me when you arrive. I'll let Owen and Shelly know you're there, then we can visit and maybe do a photo." His chin drops. "They can count on you?"

"Yes," I say. "Yes, they can."

He tugs a little at his ear as he glances behind the truck. "Very good," he says. "This is very good."

We say our goodbyes and I climb back out of the truck. He calls out, "See you Saturday," before I close the door.

I watch him pull away, my head filled with that just-waking sense when it's not clear whether what just happened was real or a dream. But this *was* real. I watch his blinker flash as he turns onto the street, the smell of mints and cologne fresh in my mind.

When I get in my car, my eyes jump all over the dashboard, searching for the odometer. My hand shakes as I log the reading in my gas notebook. I drive slowly and distractedly home, wondering what I've agreed to and how in the world I'll say anything about it to Ken. Maybe, I decide, it'll be better if he doesn't know until the time.

How could he possibly be upset if Owen and Shelly give me their blessing? Won't that make him look good too? After all, Robert said it was why Owen had offered Ken "the gig."

The chance to set everything right feels like a gift that is somehow also scary as hell.

That night, I vacuum my living room twice. I walk circles around my kitchen table. I could never lie well—my stomach aches and I start blabbering. To keep that from happening and my words from getting jumbled and confused, I'd meant to text Ken the following morning. I'd meant to say: *Ken, I can't work the party. I'm so sorry.*

Now, everything has changed.

I lie in bed, the shadows on the wall monstrous exaggerations of the trees outside. In the distance a siren wails like a warning. Just as I lie down, my phone lights up. I turn the face toward me. I sit up some when I see it's a message from Malik. Ken had insisted we each exchange numbers in case one of us had to call out, but he's never texted me before.

Hey Jessie, just checking in on you. You seemed quieter than usual today. Or something. Let me know if you want to talk.

Part of me is touched by him reaching out, but another is frustrated—I don't want to talk, I want to think. Even if I knew I could trust him enough to explain what was going on, where would I begin telling the story? The terrible hugeness of it.

I type back:

You're nice to ask, Malik. I'm fine.

Then I turn my phone face-down on the nightstand. It is dark for a second before the screen lights up again—a sliver of light reflected off the tabletop, so faint, I almost miss it. I turn it back over. He's replied:

Have coffee with me sometime?

I delete the message thread and turn the phone off.

Not now. At least, not yet.

Talking would probably lead to Malik's knowing about where I've been—kept in the closet, following a tour like a maniac, lying in a prison bed—parts of life I hardly want to think about myself, let alone explain to anyone aside from Ms. Parsons. He thinks he wants to know about me, but he wouldn't like what he would find out. Besides, the unexpected meeting with Robert left my head feeling full. Maybe, just maybe, if Saturday night goes like Robert said it will, there will be space to start talking with someone.

But not now.

* * *

Over the next two days, I work normally. What is about to happen feels so unreal, I hardly allow myself to think about it. Instead, I keep my head down, and my earbuds in, and stay focused on the prep work Ken hired me to do in the first place. I follow the recipes to the letter, interested as I go about the food Shelly has chosen. Asian slaw for pork barbeque sliders. A mustard sauce for a bacon bar. I wonder, will they invite me to eat any of this stuff?

On the afternoon of the party, my apartment is silent and still. I clean again and rest on my bed. From upstairs, a guitar riff starts.

Then a girl begins singing. My window unit kicks on and rattles like my heart. I feel the cold air on my cheek, but my eyes are fixed on the black sleeve of my uniform shirt, poking out from my closet. Soon, it will be time to get ready to go. I get up and pace, practicing what I may say, how I may greet Owen and Shelly. I try to imagine what their facial expressions will be like when they see me. I force my face into the happiest, most grateful-looking smile I can.

I want to meet with Ms. Parsons, to tell her about the plan, but my next appointment with her isn't until the next Tuesday. I have hardly slept any of the last three nights since meeting with Robert, and now my eyelids are impossibly heavy. I lie back down to rest for just a minute.

But when I wake up, I realize the sun is going down. Panic floods through me, and when I check my phone I see four missed calls from Ken. I check the time and text him to say that I will meet him at the party. I get ready faster than I ever have, practically hyperventilating as I rush through my shower. I can't remember the last time I've eaten, so I grab a package of orange peanut butter crackers and shove them in my pocket for later, then run out my door without even vacuuming up my footprints.

I have no idea how much gas I'm burning as I speed toward the James house. I smudged the pencil on the notepad and now I just have to guess. I step on the accelerator, hoping I won't run out of fuel. How could I have let this happen? I cut down a Belle Meade side street where trees grow in a canopy from both sides, blocking the last daylight. Fireflies' highlighter-yellow flashes light up the front steps of Warner Park while my headlights create a path along the darkening road.

As I turn onto the Jameses' street, I am greeted by a line of red taillights. *Shit.* Some boys wearing emerald-green shirts and khaki shorts run along the shoulder before jumping into SUVs and pulling away. At the top of the hill, the mansion is lit up like a concert is going on inside. The windows are giant white rectangles through which light rains onto the grass, catching some of the trees in the massive, sloping yard. I watch people-shaped shadows ascend the long driveway and hear a joyous tangle of voices in the front yard as my car idles. I check the time again. Because I rushed so much, I'm barely late, but there is no way I can wait in this line of cars.

Ken's van is parked in the driveway, the rear double doors hanging open. He's waiting, I know, counting on me, but the line of traffic makes entering and parking behind the van impossible.

I crane my neck to look over the steering wheel, then lean forward as I cut along the side of the road to avoid the other cars and drive straight ahead through the grassy shoulder, the full moon a dull reflection on my hood. I rumble forward until I can slip back onto the paved roadway. I drive a few hundred yards to an empty gravel lot at the back entrance to Warner Park, get out, and start walking back toward the mansion.

I remind myself that this is my chance. I'm lucky, I tell myself, my steps light as my shoes crunch on the loose stones beneath them. I try to ignore the voice that's saying, *You should not be going up there. Don't be a fool.*

As I near the road, a pair of headlights appear. They weave a little, like cars do when their drivers are texting—distractedly drifting across lanes before they suddenly look up and correct back to center. I step to the side, but the car is coming so fast, and is so close to the edge, it nearly clips me. I manage to catch my balance and keep from falling into the weeds. When I look again, I realize I know the car very well.

I'm staring at Shelly James's white Mercedes SUV as it slides into a space beside my car. Her taillights redden the night as she slows.

I panic and duck behind the trunk of a tall tree, my thin cotton pants protecting my legs from the branches of brambles. Leaves crackle gently beneath my shoes as I move among the shadows.

What is happening? Why is Shelly leaving her own party just as it starts?

I know I need to get to the party, but I watch.

I can't help it.

Did she see me? No, I guess, probably not. If she had, she wouldn't have nearly run me over. But what if she recognizes my car? Even if she does, will it even matter? Something tells me no. Something tells me she is keeping a secret of her own. She seems to have hushed the night, silencing the insects in the weeds and woods behind me. Her house is close enough that I can hear distant cries of laughter, carried on the wind, from where I hide. Laughter that sounds somehow dangerous, now.

And I feel crazy, really crazy, like the world won't let me stop watching Owen and Shelly James no matter how hard I try not to. *Just as I'm about to make everything right. It's what I always do*, I think frustratedly, *watch and dream*. I know what it would look like if someone saw me there—like I'm the thing I hate being called the most, a *stalker*. I'd look like I was *stalking* Shelly James, and I guess I am—but what else *can* I do? *What it means to accept something you don't like* . . . I feel a sense of *resignation*, like duty too, even as fear grips me.

Circles of overlapping light fall on the ground as her SUV door opens. Separate shadows appear inside them, as if there are two Shellys. I lean against a tree trunk and watch very carefully as she hunches over, staggering and bouncing, trying to get a pair of shoes on. When she straightens up, she runs her hands over her hair, then slams her door closed. Then she moves toward the base of a hill, where a trail begins.

My breathing is shallow and fast as the soft sound of crickets returns to the night. Above me, branches creak as they sway. I watch Shelly's shape climbing the trail—dark inside dark, more a movement than a shape. I imagine her expression as she walks—it's like she's in a trance, being drawn forward.

Her SUV lights pop off automatically, night-blinding me. I know the blackness will last only a few seconds—there is still the moonlight. The dark calms me, but in it, in that brief instant, I lose Shelly. She has gone into the woods.

Maybe it wasn't her.

But no, I'm sure it was. I would know her anywhere.

I shake my head, like someone trying to knock away room-spins from too much medication. Questions swarm in my mind, but I feel like a timer is running inside me. I picture Ken's worried expression, his tic, his glasses sliding down the bridge of his nose.

I curse under my breath because there is not enough time to make sense of what I saw.

I find the house lights again and follow them slowly, trying not to think about what just happened, not to feel like I am neglecting some deeper duty to keep her safe. I tell myself to follow the plan Robert laid out and explain everything to him the moment I see him. I put one foot in front of the other along the roadside, listening to the crickets and the gravel and the call of an owl from somewhere nearby. Lights from the guests' vehicles fill the roadway and the wooded area where they're being parked. Mostly all SUVs, like Shelly's. The valet boys wildly run to and fro, their floppy hair bouncing over their collars. I keep my eyes straight ahead, willing them not to pay me any attention as I enter the gate.

Halfway up the driveway, Ken's van is in the same place, both back doors still open. I fall in behind a couple wearing formal-looking clothes making their way up toward the house. The hem of the lady's dress nearly brushes the ground. I'm close enough to hear the swish of the fabric as she walks. Her husband links his arm through hers, steadying himself with a cane that makes a clinking sound each time it touches the cement.

Behind me, I hear one valet say to the other, "Owen James's friends are definitely *old* Nashville."

It seems like a nasty thing to say, even though I see what he means. I keep a quiet distance from the couple, despite my desire to rush past them.

I think of how Shelly hadn't just been *leaving* the party but *speeding* in the other direction. I glance behind me into the swallowing dark and wonder, somehow, if who I saw wasn't her. I picture the overlapping circles of light that showed her shadow in two directions. Did I really see what I think I did?

Please be safe, I think, whoever you are.

Ken emerges from the van carrying a tray, smiling as he sees me. His forehead is shiny with sweat. "Oh, Jessie, you're a lifesaver. Perfect timing." Once he's closer, he leans down, whispering, "Not like you to be late. Everything okay?"

I make my face blank to hide the terror inside me, the confusion over what I've just seen, and what I hope may happen soon. I actually look past Ken's shoulder, wondering, somehow, if I might find Robert standing there, ready to welcome me.

"I'm good," I say to Ken, actually a little out of breath from the walk up the steep drive.

I'm sort of starstruck just by the house as I follow Ken to the back, around the pool where light from the second-story windows reflects on the tiny ripples below. Around us is a low rumble of conversation. Laughter rings out, loudly now, before disappearing into the dark line of trees along the backyard. I see the hill where

Andre and Malik sat a few days earlier. I can't count how many times I've spied on the front with drive-by glances, but the rear of the house is exactly as the cooks described it: nearly all glass. The backyard is a manicured slope lined by pine forest.

Ken leads me to a table with a black tablecloth and glasses turned upside down on it. He has obviously done a lot of work setting up—everything seems to be in its place. Through the glass, inside, I can see trays of the food I've been preparing all week. I feel a tinge of guilt for having shown up late. "I'm really sorry I didn't get here on time," I say.

But Ken is buzzed with energy and hardly seems to have considered it. "No worries, especially not now. The guys rode over with me, we managed."

"They're inside?" I picture them passing Robert and wonder briefly if he has asked about me.

"Yeah. But out here is where I need you. Cool?"

Definitely cool with me, I think, preferring to have some space to breathe. I look around and notice the amount of alcohol set out—more than at any other party I've ever been to. Two cases of wine are stacked beside two coolers full of beer on ice. Bottles of every type of liquor line the station. In one, gold flecks float in what looks like a thick, clear syrup.

I lean close to Ken so no one else can hear me ask, "How many people are coming?"

He straightens a stack of paper napkins that are already perfectly straight. "Ms. James asked us to cater for seventy, but I brought enough for ten more, just in case." He notices the way my eye is focused on the alcohol and explains with a low laugh, "I didn't know either about all of that booze. She had it all brought in and set up. Here, hand me those?" He points to a stack of napkins, which I hand to him as he explains how guests may ask for simple cocktails but will mostly likely help themselves to beer and wine. I catch every third word or so of Ken's instructions, but I understand enough—I am to occasionally pour drinks, but mostly collect the empty glasses and plates that are left about.

I scan the patio for Robert, but there is no sign of him. I wish he would appear, even for a second, to signal me, to reassure me that there will be no misunderstanding. I'm more than a watcher tonight—I'm both supposed to be here and not, which is horrible and thrilling. *Stay focused, stay focused. Just do your job.*

"Jessie?" I feel a tug at my sleeve. My head snaps around. Ken's eyes are worried, but his mouth is smiling. "You sure you're okay?"

"Sorry, I'm here. Just taking everything in."

He glances back to the lit glass wall of the main house, where Owen's friends move around the enormous kitchen. Even from that distance they seem so much older than Shelly.

Why did she leave? I hope she's come back. Maybe she already has.

"Okay, you got this," Ken says. "Just keep filling up the water and champagne glasses. Wine is on ice behind the table. I just opened a fresh bottle. I'll be right inside if you need anything." He practically skips back to the house. I see his black shirt through the window, the outline of his glasses.

Soon, more party guests arrive. I take deep breaths. I smile as I pour. Twice, I walk the perimeter of the pool to collect glasses on a tray. The woods at the edge of the property draw my eyes. I stare at the subtle shapes in the dark, part of me wanting to run off between the trees, to vanish.

But not tonight, I think. Tonight will be different. *But when?*

I try to estimate the time because there is still no sign of Robert. When I fill my second tray, I realize I need to take it inside and exchange the dirty glasses for clean. I can see Ken's back through the glass wall. Beside him is the edge of the crate where the clean glasses are.

I hate to leave my station, but it should only take a minute to get in and out. I'll take the tray inside, set it beside Ken, and come out with a fresh tray that should get me through the rest of the party.

I try my best not to be overwhelmed, to use some of the *coping skills* Ms. Parsons taught me, and not fall into my old ways like *vanishing into myself* or finding somewhere small to hide. I breathe in to a count of four, hold it inside for two, then let my breath out to a count of four—just the way I practiced in her office. But my heart will not calm down. It wants to run wild because I'm *walking into Owen and Shelly James's house.* That fact rings through me as I load up the tray and go quickly through the back door.

The kitchen looks like it should be in a restaurant or on a cooking show—it's larger than All Out Catering's space. Every light seems to be turned on, which makes the space very bright, like a movie set. The refrigerator, range, and dishwasher are all stainless steel, gleaming. Unlike my apartment, the James house doesn't smell like a mossy window unit—it smells like flowers and baking, like orange and lemon mixed with sunshine. It smells *perfect*, like a fancy retail store, like I've always imagined a house is supposed to smell.

A place where nothing goes wrong.

I nearly stumble into one of the dozen wooden stools lining the kitchen bar, but manage to set the tray down on a marble countertop. I wipe my sweaty hands against my pants. At least until I see Robert, I feel the need to keep my eyes down to keep the risk of being recognized as low as possible, but I can't stop myself from looking around some. The crystal chandelier in the dining room fills my eyes with light. It seems to turn as I pass, each gem flashing like a camera.

Ken waves me over as he answers a question from one of the guests, his fingers searching his shirt pocket for a business card. Beside him, I try to stand still as I look around.

"Doing okay?" he asks me when they walk away.

"Okay."

Andre passes carrying hors d'oeuvres. His eyes look blank but he wears a thin smile.

"Can you pass through the front room again?" I can hear the nerves in Ken's voice. They are nothing like mine.

"You got it, Ken," Andre says, exiting.

I start back outside with a tray of clean glasses, but Ken says, "Hang on one sec." I listen while a guest asks him how spicy something is and he answers.

Then Owen James's voice comes from the other side of the room, and the hair on the back of my neck stands up.

Should I say something? Where is Robert?

Owen is saying, ". . . I *do* like to cook but it took some fiddling around to figure out how to actually turn any of it *on*." He motions toward the double range as he enters.

I freeze, my eyes focused on the moon's reflection in the window—a white circle trapped in the glass like a tiny ghost. It's shaking a little from the air conditioner or the footsteps across the floor. I'm like that. Trapped and shaking. I try to make myself small in Ken's jagged shadow, but anyone can see me, I know.

The couple I followed up the driveway earlier stands beside Owen. The man taps his cane as he asks, "Where is ol' Shelly, anyway?"

A group of people laugh encouragingly, like they mean for someone to search the house for Shelly, like a family would look for a hiding house pet.

One lady whoops, "Yeah!"

". . . was here just a minute ago."

". . . bet she's just . . ."

"Upstairs, probably," Owen says tiredly, like he wants no part of the game.

I step halfway into the pantry to stay dim, hating that I know the answer. Knowing reminds me of my own curiosity. *Why did she go into the park?*

More laughter. Across the room, something spills.

"Shell?" a voice calls.

I hear phrases, whispers as they look for her.

". . . worse than before."

"Having an off night . . ."

"I heard that . . ."

Then someone clears her throat so loudly the guest nearest to me jumps a little. Her accent is sweet as syrup. "Y'all, Owen is about to play a track from the new record in the studio if anyone wants to come hear it."

A few of the guests exchange glances, then empty into the hallway. I hear the stairs creak with footfalls.

Ken snaps me back from my trance. "Jessie? I was asking about wine. You brought in a lot of glasses."

"There's plenty left," I tell him, which is the understatement of the year, before heading back through the double doors into the warm evening. I rub the back of my neck and bite my lips. *Something is wrong,* I think, as muted guitar chords begin from deep inside the house. Shouldn't Robert have approached me by now if he was looking for me? There is a word for the fear I'm starting to feel. *Naïve.*

But for a few seconds, time stops and I'm not where I am, or even who I am. My feet feel the music's slight vibration as my hands shake like that reflection of the moon. I'm away from the risk I'm taking and I forget about the order of protection I'm so obviously breaking. Hearing *Owen's new track* lifts my heart, and I strain to listen.

This is why I love music.

It's the eye of the storm, like it always has been.

It isn't until the song stops that the questions flood back. *Did Owen mean to distract everyone from the fact that Shelly is gone?*

I glance across the patio, where more people are arriving, and pray silently to see Shelly's headlights.

I grind my teeth together. I force my face into a smile when a guest asks to check the time on my phone.

When I look back at the kitchen windows, I see Ken, standing with his back to me. I can tell he's talking with someone by the way his head moves, and I tell myself it's a guest—that maybe he's about to hand out another of his cards. But then he turns and looks over his shoulder, right at me.

The way he looks at me is different from a moment before. His eyes show a confused intensity.

Then I see Robert Holloway standing to Ken's left, eyebrows raised, mouth moving. Robert moves beside Ken and they stand shoulder to shoulder.

I take a step toward them, then I stop cold. I can tell something is very, very wrong from the way they're both looking at me.

Robert scowls and Ken shakes his head. I hear myself gasp when Ken moves to the door. Behind him, Robert raises a phone to his ear.

8

Robert Holloway disappears into the house. The way he looked at me was the same as last summer, when he stood on the beer-soaked loading dock, watching as the police dragged me to a car. His arms were folded, and he cast a triple-sized shadow on the concrete wall behind him. He mouthed a word at me I didn't catch except to understand it was unkind.

Now Ken walks toward me slowly, his eyes dark with disappointment and fear. He glances at the guests on his left and right—a man chuckling as his wife leans down to touch the water in the pool, as if testing whether or not it is real.

He comes close and speaks to me slowly, the way Mr. Folger used to talk to wild dogs. "Jessie, the Jameses' manager just told me something about you." Ken gestures over his shoulder with his thumb.

My breath comes in short bursts, as if I've been punched in the chest. I shake my head slowly back and forth. I want so much to find the words, to explain. I try to start at the beginning, "Robert wanted me here. I'm supposed to meet Owen and Shelly." But as words come out of my mouth, they sound all wrong—ridiculous, like I'm making up excuses that can't possibly be true. My face starts to feel numb.

Why did Robert do this? Have I been stupid, or is this a terrible misunderstanding?

Our whole story is in Ken's eyes—him hiring me, teaching me, taking me to events. For a second, the memories come back so vividly I grip the knife's rubber handle as I cut vegetables. My job, and maybe the life I've built, are about to end.

He grimaces before saying, "Jessie, he's calling the police right now."

I start to have a thought—just a tiny flicker of an idea: Robert has tricked me into coming here. Why, I don't know yet. Did he change his mind about me? Or learn something new about me? Does this have something to do with Detective Marion? I feel that wall-caving-in feeling of being set up.

For a second, I can't think of the word "sorry." I want to say it to Ken. I try to swallow but my mouth is dry. I look over at the pool, the driveway, wanting to run.

Ken can tell. "Jessie, let's just stay here, okay? Let's just keep calm."

Keep calm?

When I see Robert heading to the back door, I start toward the gate.

"Jessie, wait." Ken's whisper is a hiss. I hear his shoes slipping on the pool tiles, then I don't. I know already he won't follow me. I hear the heave of my breathing over the fading bass and drums of the party, the back of my throat registering the cotton-thick night air. Through the dark, a stray laugh trails after me, but I understand it has nothing to do with me at all. Whoever called out belongs to a club I never will.

The angle of the driveway carries me forward like a push against my back. I picture Ken trying to explain his decision to hire me to the security guard who'd come to his kitchen on

Wednesday. I picture the cooks being interviewed—their recalling to investigators how long they've known me, how we met, how I've always been so quiet, so unassuming.

It's always the quiet ones. That's what everyone will say. I have just proven everyone right, without the slightest sense that I was doing it. I feel like I walked into a trap that I don't understand. The one time I want to put everything about the Jameses behind me, I end up stalking them in spite of myself. In my head, I already hear Ms. Carr asking me, "If Robert Holloway invited you, why didn't you stay and sort everything out with the police?" Because I know how this situation looks. And because I don't enjoy being thrown on the ground.

"So, until I think of some better explanation, something that will fix this," I want to say to Ms. Carr in my mind, "I'm making this up as I go along, walking as fast as I can."

I go through the open gate, pass the valets all huddled around a single cell-phone screen, one of them saying, "Well, now it's a full count."

Will someone come after me? Yell for me to halt? Or will Robert want to keep everything looking perfect? That's what I want to believe. I don't want to go to jail.

I wonder: What if I left? *Really* left. Got into my car and drove out of Nashville and started up somewhere new. I had enough practice moving as a kid—I know how to do it.

But then my stomach clinches. *With what money?* The state would stop my stipend if I disappeared, I'm sure, and I barely scrape by on my salary as it is. Every month I have to be careful not to overdraw my account. Ken can't pay much, and I've made some bad decisions with money. I survive because I live sparingly. I don't even know how many tanks of gas I can buy if I spend every dollar I have, or where I could go that I wouldn't be found.

Points of gravel press against my shoes as I walk along the side of the road—which is now darker, quieter. The way back to my car seems like forever.

I dig into my pocket for the orange crackers. I'm nowhere near hungry but I want the salt in my mouth, something to focus on besides my shame and fear. I open the package and press so hard on one of the crackers that it breaks apart in my hand. The peanut butter dries on the roof of my mouth instantly, the sensation an odd comfort. I try to swallow what I can.

Clouds have begun to gather above and less of the moon shines down. I smell rain in the air now, and between tree trunks I see a splinter of lightning reaching down between two clouds. A quick flash but no sound.

As I come to the edge of the park's parking lot, I see Shelly's SUV is still here, still blocking the view of my car. Night has fallen completely during the time I was at the party, but there is no sign of Shelly—no light shining through her tinted windows, where she might be reading or on a call. No, she is still in the woods, I realize, looking at the shadowy stalks of pine. *What is she doing in there?* Part of me doesn't want to know, not anymore. But part of me can't stop myself from thinking about it.

I tap the base of my hand against my skull and tell myself to stop wondering about Shelly. As I get closer, I hope she'll stay in the woods, at least until I'm gone. I don't want this night to look any worse than it already does.

Like I somehow followed Shelly to this place. Like I followed her into the dark, right after I'd been caught, again.

A raindrop hits my neck, warm and sudden—the heavy, full sort that comes at the beginning of a real storm. I rest my hands on the roof of my car for a second, the metal still warm under my palms. Another few drops hit the gravel as I open my car door, keys dangling from my hand.

From the trail I hear the sound of crackling leaves.

I stop. I look at the trees, like charcoal lines on gray paper. My skin turns cold as the rain continues to fall all around me. The cricket sounds end, and the trees seem to become still.

And then there's a voice, calling out.

I look toward the trail. The sharp edges of my keys cut against my leg as I shove them into my pocket, my feet carrying me into the dark. Was the voice calling out to me? I hear it again, over my own breathing.

Up ahead, a branch snaps. I make out the word "stop."

When I look up, there's just enough light for me to see the shape of a man looking down from the top of the hill. I can tell it's a man—tall, broad-shouldered, wearing a baseball cap. Light shines across his face for half a second as he raises a phone to his cheek. His is the voice I heard.

The rain picks up. I feel my shirt sticking to my skin.

Then he starts toward me. He is maybe a hundred and fifty feet away—so hard to tell distances in the dark. I forget about the trouble I'm already in and turn back to my car. I don't know what's going on, but everything inside me tells me to leave. I have a little head start.

Through the sound of my own breathing I hear the pounding of his footsteps as he follows. I yank my keys from my pocket, drop into my car, and start the engine. The windshield is a mess of streaks as I pull onto the road. My shirt and hair are nearly soaked, my chest heaving as the glass immediately fogs up from my breath. I can hardly think beyond the basic tasks of aiming my car toward the road and hauling ass away.

The move from gravel to pavement allows me slight relief. I pass the James house without slowing, where the thump of music still carries into the night. Do I tell? I find my phone, turn it over on the seat beside me, then wonder, Will it start to ring? What will I tell the officers who come to arrest me?

Don't think. Just drive.

Shadows from branches flow like waves on the streetlight-yellow road. I grip the steering wheel and press down on the gas pedal. I wipe my hand on my pants, hurriedly, brushing away the crumbs and oil from the cracker I'd crushed. I take my eyes off the road for just a second.

That's when I nearly hit Finch James.

My brakes squeal as I slide to a stop. Through the fog on my windshield I see her staring back like a frightened deer. How close did I come to hitting her? Fifteen feet? Ten? The road's curve hid her from sight until I was almost upon her.

I get out of the car. The open-door ding insistent as I look behind. The man who chased me could catch up any second. Through a clearing, the Jameses' house is visible on the hill across from the park. The distance makes it look like a model, the moon-sized windows glowing with blue-white light, then darkness around the curved road. Still out of breath, I half expect to see headlights coming toward us and hear the sound of an engine gunning through the rain.

I close the door halfway as Finch James and I face each other in the pouring rain. Her skateboarding shoes have clumps of light-brown mud that the rain spreads onto the dark asphalt. I think of the story Andre and Malik told about her confronting them, and I expect her to be angry.

Instead, her voice is a small cry. "Can you help?"

Finch is wearing a black tank top and jeans, her hair is wet and dripping onto her bare shoulders. Her pale chest heaves. She clasps her hands to it, shivering, her eyes wide like she's trying to make sense of what I'm doing in the world.

"Please?" she asks, just as the sky opens up even further—the thunderstorm becoming a downpour.

I squint through the rain at the still-quiet road and nod, pointing to the passenger door. Emergencies stop time. I forget about the week before, even ten minutes before. My head buzzes with confusion about what's happened—too many things at once that I can't understand—but I know this for sure: I have to get her off the road. I can't be a *watcher* anymore. I have to get us both away from whoever just ran after me from the trail.

Finch gets in the car, then I drop into the driver's seat and we go—both soaked to the bone, speeding into the pounding rain. It comes down so blindingly hard that for a few seconds my windshield wipers do nothing to clear it and I have to try to focus on the twenty feet directly in front of us, praying we don't crash into some tree along the roadside.

For a long moment, Finch doesn't speak. Are there right words for this situation? Then she runs her hands through her hair before pressing her palms against her cheeks. Her eyes peek at me over her fingertips. "Thank you." I clear my throat as my mind forms a thought, but then she says, "Oh my God. Oh my fucking *God*."

"What . . . happened?" I struggle to ask. I wipe my eyes with the heel of my palm. Rainwater runs down my arms, forming heavy drops at my elbows. Everything is drenched.

When I look at her, I realize her jeans are muddy and torn. She has a tangle of red scratches on each bare shoulder. Her hands stay pressed to her face, a protective barrier. But her eyes grow even wider. "I think someone just killed my mom."

My foot slips to the floorboard. I nearly slam on the brake. I stare at her for a long beat, then have to swerve to keep the car on the road. I have to remember to press the gas pedal again. *Drive.*

"You saw it?" I ask.

Finch nods, frantically. "My parents had a fight. She was leaving and I called after her, but she drove off. She goes to the park sometimes to walk and think . . . I went to look for her there. I could hardly see, but when I found her . . ."

Her voice cracks, a heave of pain breaking through.

Killed?

The word re-echoes over and over in my mind, my hands so tight on the steering wheel they start to go numb. I saw her mom leave too, I realize, just as I got to the party. I remember the careless weaving of her SUV, and how I had to step off the road to avoid being hit. I'd watched her put on her shoes and start into the woods. It looks like I saw Shelly too—*right before someone killed her.*

It seems impossible for the rain to come down any harder, but it does, so crazily that the windshield is washed white for a few seconds.

"Someone was with her," Finch says. "A man, standing over her. I think she had gone to meet him."

She looks at me like she's recalling a nightmare she can hardly believe, like she wants reassurance it didn't happen.

"He turned when he heard me coming. She was lying on the ground. She wasn't moving. I screamed. I could tell from the way her neck . . ."

No, I think. *No, no, no.* Denial is a wave, washing over everything. *I just saw her.* "Why . . . what made it seem like she'd gone to meet him?"

Her voice drops. She turns away, looking out the window. For a second, I see her blank eyes reflected there. "My parents were fighting . . ." She hesitates like she means to say more, then says, "I think he murdered her."

"Who?"

Finch shakes her head. "I don't know. A *man*. It was so dark."

The man who'd chased me. In my mind, I see the flash of his phone lighting up the side of his face—the blue-white light on the profile of his jaw—the power in his stride as he charged down the hill, the shadowy velocity.

We just barely got away, I realize.

"Oh my God," she says again, her mind seeming to retreat into disbelief.

"Finch, we have to go to the police."

She stares straight ahead.

"Finch."

She nods very slowly, her chin an up-and-down metronome.

The police, whom I practically ran from fifteen minutes earlier. Robert called them—were they on the way? Will they know what to make of any of this? Or even be able to see in this rain?

"The closest station is Belle Meade," I say. "Right?"

"I . . . guess?"

She sounds unsure. Why wouldn't she be? Suddenly she seems so young, and I remember she's a person I've somehow looked up to—and been jealous of—despite her being younger than me.

A man, standing over her. I think she had gone to meet him.

My heart pounds as I drive, pushing away as determinedly as I can the persistent fact that keeps overtaking my mind: Shelly James is dead. It feels like the world is ending—like an earthquake that goes on and on and on.

I feel her eyes on me, and I turn my head.

"You . . . you're Jessie Duval," she says.

"Finch, you have to tell the police," I say. "Just what you told me. Try to remember as much as you can."

She doesn't speak.

"Finch."

"Okay, I will."

Already, I know I'll be talking to the police too. I'll be explaining how I was invited to the party, that I was chased myself, and that I only meant to help Finch.

But they won't believe me.

I can't think about that now though. I have to get her safely to the police station.

We come to an intersection lit pale with streetlights. The rain slows as I pass through a four-way stop. Up ahead, I can see a yellow-orange glow that I know is the station. Three cruisers are parked out front. From the parking lot I see a dark uniform through the glass door. I can't go inside, but Finch will be safe here. She seems too dazed to even ask why I don't get out.

She leans on the open door for a second and our eyes meet. She says a word that sounds like "thanks," because what is there to say? I watch as she starts across the parking lot, headed toward the front door.

I turn the wheel and pull onto the street, the rain pouring steadily as I drive straight home.

I imagine Ms. Carr asking why I didn't go inside with Finch.

Here's the answer I would give her: I was scared. I wanted Finch to be safe, but I wasn't ready to walk into a police station.

Everything—starting with my meeting with Robert in his truck—is a jumble in my mind. I need to try to understand everything that's happened.

In my apartment, I lean over the toilet and throw up over and over. Each jolt makes my hair fall forward and I have to retuck it behind my ears. The sickness comes from deep inside me. It pushes outward until only air is left, like my body is trying to remove what I've seen—like it is trying to expel *Shelly is dead*, and the man on top of the hill, and driving Finch to the police. But I can't forget. I try to recall the shape of the man I'd seen in the woods—to burn his form into my memory.

Could Finch have been wrong? No, my heart knows she was telling me what she saw. Her hands were shaking. Her voice wavered through her tears. Her world was over. The world I've lived in, too, for years, has ended. The songs I hummed when I was in the dark, the woman I've dreamed of as my mother—the world where Shelly James is alive and singing and waving and lighting up a crowd with her smile, *that* world is gone now too. My stomach tightens again and again, until I'm sore. I wrap my arms around myself and tip over, resting my forehead against the warm linoleum floor.

While I lie there I have a strange desire. A part of me wants to go back into the dark, into the closet. Counselors told me I had made up a world, but the world itself is made up. It should be better than it is. I wonder if my staying in the closet would have kept everyone imaginary, and safe.

The closet was more than a dark place. It was everything. I knew there was a world outside, but after a while it seemed unimportant. Twelve months and nine days was how long I spent there. But what were months? How long was a day? Measures of time didn't matter. I had a birthday, a Christmas, an Easter Sunday, a Fourth of July—dates that may have been important to some people. Instead, I told myself stories. I put the people I thought about into situations in my mind like characters in a movie. They had all sorts of feelings and did all kinds of things, some good and some bad. Sometimes, I interacted with them. Counselors called them *narratives.* I know they thought I'd gone crazy, but it was really the opposite. Stories kept me from drifting into space, and falling, falling, falling. I knew that if I ever really let go, I'd never find my way back.

Now, I press my palms against the warm floor and close my eyes. For a second, I try to go back to the world I'd once made—where everyone was safe. In that world, no man stared down from a hillside. No one chased me. No one murdered Shelly James.

But I know that world isn't real—it's just a place I made up years ago to keep myself sane. And I know what I have to do, no matter how much I don't want to.

I pick myself up off the floor and find my phone. My finger is trembling so terribly I can hardly dial the number. When a voice answers, I explain who I am.

Reality rushes toward me. Sometimes I feel like it may drown me. I may be sending myself to jail, but what choice do I have? The fact is this: a woman has been murdered and I need to help find her killer. I *saw* him. He *chased* me.

"I need to file a police report," I say.

9

The banging on my front door is so heavy and loud it rattles the plastic picture frames in the hallway. The music being played upstairs gets softer, then I hear a question asked in a muffled voice. I picture my flimsy front door and the back of a fist.

The police. I've been waiting for them.

Through my bedroom window the clouds look low and dirty in the day's first light, still full from last night's rain. I made myself lie down but never fell asleep. How could I? My stomach feels hollow. My head spins like a state-fair ride gone haywire.

I've been rehearsing what I'll say, going over the pieces of what had happened since I made the call. I just have to tell the truth, I tell myself, but part of me knows the police won't judge me fairly, even if I'm the one who called them—a fear confirmed by how loudly they're knocking.

The banging comes again just as I get up from my bed—even more intensely this time. I wonder for a second if this is how police are trained to knock on doors, even during the early morning hours. I hate to think that my neighbors might complain, or my landlord might wonder why officers are visiting my apartment and decide to take a closer look at who they've rented to.

But those are just trivial worries now.

Through the peephole, I see two men in the yellow hallway light. One is Detective Marion. He's wearing a black polo shirt and jeans and has the edgy, unshaven look of someone who hasn't slept. Aside from that, he looks the same as he did during my sentencing hearing at the courthouse. The other officer wears a police uniform. I don't recognize him. He must have seen me darken the peephole because he barks, "Metro PD."

When the handcuffs on his belt catch the overhead light I grit my teeth.

I try to tell myself they'll just want to talk about the night before, that I'm going to help, and that what they're here for is information. Helping them is the *right thing to do*. I'm on *their team*. But now that they're here, my muscles coil like springs, my body ready to fight.

The second cop raises his fist as if to knock again, inches from my face, when Detective Marion reaches and gently takes hold of his arm. "Ms. Duval?" he asks.

Come on, Jessie, I think. *Face this.*

The lock screeches as I slide it. I crack open the door, my toes digging into the worn carpet like I mean to stop myself from being blown over.

Detective Marion speaks first. "Good morning, Ms. Duval. We're here because of your phone call. Are you okay to talk with us this morning?"

Under pressure, it's even harder for me to find words. I wonder if Detective Marion remembers this about me, or if he expects me to answer normally. I try to answer, but it comes out like a stutter.

He nods, patiently, like he's prepared to take it slow. The other officer's eyes glow like iron on fire. "This is Detective Williams," Marion says, gesturing toward the man beside him. "When you called earlier, you said you wanted to file a report?

We understand you were at the James residence last night. May we come in?"

I look at their black, thick-soled shoes. I look over my shoulder. I hesitate. I can't help it. I keep my apartment just so. Since I moved in, no one but me has been inside.

"Everything okay, Ms. Duval?"

I let out a slow breath. "It's okay."

I back up and they push past me, both looking around, scanning my things, their shoes thumping across my kitchen floor. I breathe through my nose in tiny, quick puffs. I never drink alcohol, but at that moment I wish I had something to help calm me down—something stronger than Ms. Parsons's grounding techniques. I wince at the chaos of their shoes and steps and movements in my space.

Detective Williams is tall with black hair. His movements are quick, like an animal's. He makes me nervous as he glances at the vacuum lines in the carpet and whistles. "This place sure is tidy. You always keep everything this neat?"

"Yes," I say.

Maybe he's trying to add a little humor and ease the tension, but the smirk he wears makes my heart clench. He looks at me like people do when they don't know what to make of me. When he reaches for a shelf where I keep my rows of souvenirs, I shuffle my feet, and his hand stops. He squints like I've just spoken a word he never learned.

He and Marion exchange a look, and I know what it says—they're talking with someone who is a suspect in what happened last night, despite the fact that I placed the call and said I wanted to file a report. My history makes me someone with a *motive*.

I anticipated this. After all, I broke an order of protection by trespassing just before Shelly was killed. What else is there to know?

I guess I'm about to find out.

Detective Marion pats the back of a kitchen chair. "Will you have a seat, Jessie?" he asks.

I smell coffee on his breath and notice his hand is shaking a little. I realize part of me is expecting Marion and Williams to throw me on the ground, press their knees against my back, and shove my face into the carpet—I know what happens when you get arrested—but I sit down and they sit too, facing me. On the table, they set the white coffee cups they have both been holding.

My apartment feels much smaller with them inside. I feel like I might float above us, like my spirit might leave my body and look down on the three of us—at me. I want to run, or for them to leave, but this is what's happening, I tell myself. This is life now.

It's strange. I've been afraid of Detective Marion, but between the two officers, he's the one I *feel* I can trust.

During my hearing, he told the judge his version of my arrest. His story was different from mine, but it wasn't a lie. When the judge asked if Marion thought I would be a danger to anyone going forward, he said, "I'm not to say. I think that's up to her psychologist or social worker to determine." He looked at me once from across the courtroom with a tired, regretful glance that made me want to never get arrested again.

I remember I felt . . . *The word for feeling really bad or ashamed about something.* . . . I felt *guilty*, because I could see he truly felt people were in danger when he arrested me.

Now my eyes are wide and wild from no sleep, so I fix my gaze on the vacuum lines in my carpet—all straight until they curve at the end of each stroke. I try not to look at my dresser, and especially not the bottom drawer. I keep some things there that I know will give the wrong idea.

Things I want to keep private.

Detective Williams leans back in my kitchen chair until it creaks, snapping me away from my little daydream. Puffs of steam rise from their coffee lids like smoke from gun barrels. The day's first sunshine is a faint, diagonal streak, a triangle spreading toward us.

Detective Williams says, "There's a permanent order of protection held against you as a condition of your parole. You're aware of that?"

Then, I understand: Williams thinks my mental deficits are more than they are. He assumes that the trouble I have speaking means trouble thinking.

He goes on, "Being in violation of the order by pretending to work for the caterer, you have a very good reason to cooperate with us this morning. You understand that, too, right?"

I look at Detective Marion, who rubs the bridge of his nose. He speaks softly to him. "She's got it, man. Jessie, just . . . yes, of course you know about the order of protection. He's trying to say that if you violated that protection order to *work*, we get it. You called us. We want as much information as you can give about the details of last night. Where you were and what you saw. Just be as honest as possible, okay?"

I nod.

I begin to explain when my vision grows blurry and I realize I must be crying. I wipe my eyes quickly with my sleeve. "I wasn't *pretending* to work. I was . . . doing my job, but I was invited," I say. "I was supposed to be there."

I start to explain about Robert when Williams shakes his head and interrupts. "Invited? If you didn't *understand* you were in violation, just say so. Right now, we have a report that someone matching your description was leaving the crime scene. That's enough to arrest you already."

"Let's give her a second," Marion says as he goes to the counter, finds a paper towel, and hands it to me. "You're doing fine, Jessie. I know this must be hard."

Williams levels his eyes, watching me, judging how upset I get while we talk. Watching and noting, watching and noting. Gathering evidence against me.

This was a mistake, I think, part of me wishing I'd never called.

"I didn't want to work the party at first," I say. "I wanted to get out of it when I realized whose party it was. But then Robert Holloway found me at work after everyone else had left. He told me Owen and Shelly wanted to meet me, and that we could make things right . . ."

I keep talking, telling them how I came to be where I was the night before. I'm describing the boys running cars for valet and explaining why I left my car at Warner Park when I notice a confused expression on Williams's face. "Okay, yeah," he says quickly, like he doesn't believe me.

I go through everything to the point when I saw the man on top of the hill and drove away.

Marion says, "So let me say this back to you. The sequence of events went like this: You went to work the party but you were running late, so you left your car at the park and walked to the house. That was when you saw Ms. James go into the park. That park has five separate entrances. There are three main trails, plus a horse trail, plus the paved loop—they all intersect at various points. You saw her go up that trail, where you both were parked."

"Yes."

"The Jameses' manager, Robert Holloway, spotted you at their party around seven. Then you left and walked back to your car. That was when you saw the man on the hill, looking down at you."

Williams says, "Forensics will want to pull dirt samples off your tires and compare them to dirt samples from each of the lots in the park."

A rush of raindrops brushes the sliding glass door, forcing my attention toward it.

Both cops see me look, but Detective Williams is the one who asks, "How about that rain? Cleans things up nice, right?"

I think of Ms. Carr's warning and I do the math. *Nineteen plus fifteen.* I would be thirty-four when I was released from jail.

Marion asks, "When you left the park, you went where?"

"I drove up Chickering Road. That's where I saw Finch James."

Williams looks at Detective Marion but Marion does not look back. He folds his hands then asks me, "You *saw* Finch James?"

"Walking on the side of the road." *I almost hit her with my car*, I think, realizing I'd better not say so, exactly. It might sound like I'd meant to.

"You . . . spoke to her?"

"Yes. I pulled over, got out. I kept looking back toward the parking lot to see if the man on top of the hill had followed, but there was only empty road." I remember the road behind us disappearing into darkness, the low, tired growl of my car's engine. In the air, I could already feel the rain that was about to fall over everything. "She was scared. She said she'd been chased."

"Chased?"

"She said she'd gone to look for her mother. Didn't Finch tell you that? She said her parents had had a fight. And that when she found her mom, a man was standing over her, and that man chased her and she ran through the woods. I think it was the man that I saw on top of the hill."

Neither detective says anything.

"She looked like she'd come through the woods. There were streaks of dirt and mud up the sides of her jeans, bits of leaves in her hair." My voice cracks. Tears are hot in my eyes from wanting them to believe me.

Finally, Williams says, "And then what?"

"Then she got in my car with me and I drove her to the Belle Meade Police Station."

"Is that right?"

My heart pounds.

"Ms. Duval, this was around what time?"

I have to think. Time is bent by what happened. It has become strange. I feel like it is still happening, like I'm still there, like there is no such thing as time now. Why are they talking to me like this when Finch filed the police report? Is this a trick?

"You were asked to leave the party around seven, correct? So, walk to your car, then drive up Chickering puts us at what? 7:15 or so?"

Williams keeps looking at Marion. "Finch James had been at her friend's house since earlier that afternoon," he says.

But that can't be. I saw her. I picked her up, dripping wet, terrified, and drove her.

I did not imagine it.

I'm shaking my head, as the hot press of tears returns from confusion, frustration—feelings I don't have time to feel because Williams asks, "Do you remember where you were last week?"

"The Petersons' party?"

His speech slows again, like he's trying to bring a small child up to speed. "And you knew Owen and Shelly would be *there* too, right?"

I shake my head. "I knew there might be celebrities, but I had no idea it would be them."

131

Detective Williams pops his knuckles. "You mean, just by complete coincidence, the very people you'd been following around the country happened to show up at the party you were working? I think you knew there was a chance." He looks at me like he expects I'll change my story.

Did I know? Am I only telling myself I didn't, making up a story the way I did during all that time in the dark? The thought makes me shiver; I don't want it to be true. I want my memories and thoughts to be completely real, like everyone else's. I remember the uneasiness I had while signing Ken's form, and when the front door of the Petersons' house opened, I sensed *something*. Didn't I? Didn't part of me recognize Owen and Shelly were there even before I saw them?

I'm still thinking about Williams's question. I don't answer right away. When you don't talk, people think all sorts of things. They take their fears and put them on you.

Type *Shelly James stalker* into an Internet search engine. There's my picture.

Type *Shelly James biggest fan* into the same engine. Same picture comes up.

When I worked at the kennel, a girl who worked with me said, "Oh, I like the James Family." And I said, "Not as much as I do." Then she said she was sure she was a bigger fan, and I told her how the word *fan* didn't apply to me, and when I started to talk about their set lists, she got quiet and made a funny face and said, "All right, whatever, I guess you win," very snarkily, before she said, "Did you ever think maybe you like them a little too much?"

That was a month before I left to follow their tour. By then, I already knew I shouldn't talk about Owen and Shelly. No one would understand.

"Jessie?" Detective Marion asks me. "Just so we're clear, did you know Owen and Shelly would be at the Petersons' party?"

I look at them both before I shake my head.

Williams lowers his chin. "Was it you who brought Shelly James the opioids?"

I feel my eyes go wide. It's like he's asked the question in a language I hardly know.

"No," is all I can say.

Williams closes an eye and points at my bedroom like he is taking aim. "How do you feel about us having a look through your room?"

"Fine," I say, though I try not to look at the dresser's bottom drawer.

Detective Marion nods, but Williams leans toward me so far that the side of the table creases his shirt. He's testing me, maybe, asking something off base to see how I will react.

But my mind is racing. I remember the slur in Shelly's words the night of Sean's graduation party and replay the conversation I overhead between her and Owen. I picture her smile on the last two magazine covers I saw her on. I flash to the warmth, the *love* in her voice as she thanked everyone during the CMA awards. And then to the way she nearly tripped walking off the stage.

To hear the police say it is a nightmare that keeps finding new levels, a dream that continues unfolding like origami. But they're right to ask. And I wonder about the connection, too, between those pills Owen wanted her to stop taking and where she was going the night before, right before she was killed.

I tell the police a little about what I'd heard her and Owen discussing at the Petersons' party, and about how she'd seemed less than sober as she made her way through the party.

Marion asks, "Did you hear Owen mention where any substances came from?"

"No."

"Or which substance specifically he was referring to?"

"No."

Williams interrupts. "For being as close as you were, you weren't actually listening very carefully, were you?"

The question hits me like a slap across the face.

"Hey," Marion says to him. I see his jaw tighten and his lips press together. His chair screeches as he pushes back from the table. Both their coffee cups shake so hard I think for a second they might fall over. "Talk to you a second?"

He puts his hand on Williams's shoulder. Williams looks at me like I've just gotten him in trouble before following Marion through my sliding glass doors out onto my porch. The door makes a heavy shuffling sound as Marion pulls it closed. Most people don't know about how strong my hearing is, or forget. I block out all the other morning sounds and focus on just the sounds of their voices. I miss a word every so often, but I can tell what they're saying. I understand a lot about what they're saying just from the tone of their voices, and from the way each of them stands.

The way Williams folds his arms and leans against the railing reminds me of a boy who lived in the foster home where I was for a while. Once, he slapped the back of my head so hard my scalp stung above my ear and asked me, "The fuck do you always wear those headphones? The fuck are you listening to?" I was walking, away, anywhere. I held my CD player against my chest, the plastic warm in my hands. For a year after I left the closet, I couldn't fall asleep unless my hand was touching the CD player.

"Hey," the boy kept on. He shoved my back—he talked like mean laughter. "You fucking deaf?"

I walked faster. When I thought about trouble, I pictured having to move to another house again, I pictured more packing, more introducing. My stomach felt like *spoiled food.* His foot slammed into the back of my leg. I fell forward, my pants ripping open at the knee, dust and bright-red blood at the edges. He shoved my shoulders into the gravel. Somehow, I kept my hands around the CD player like a shield that kept it from breaking apart. The rocks reddened the tops of my hands. He reached for the Discman.

"Gimme that."

I took hold of his wrist and sank my teeth into his arm until I could taste his blood. He started screaming, yanking his arm away, and I ran into the shadows to hide. Soon, I could hear shoes brushing through grass, voices calling out to each other while I stayed very dim and listened to the wind making a shushing sound like the trees were talking. *The word for something that is difficult to explain* . . . The wind sounded like a *mystery*. I stayed hidden until the light touching the forest's edge became dark.

Now, neither officer takes his eyes fully off of me as they begin to talk. I wonder if maybe they want me to listen.

Marion asks, "What's the matter with you?"

"The matter with *me*? You could be a little more dialed in. You work for the family, right?"

Marion drops his gaze very slightly. "What are you getting at?"

"I mean, don't you care? We're talking to a murderer."

My hands seem to go numb when I hear that word, and the edges of my vision blur slightly.

"We're talking to a troubled person," Marion answers calmly.

"You're not thinking right."

"This girl called us. I think she's trying to help. Look, it makes sense she'd want to watch them or even follow Shelly or whatever, but why would she want Shelly dead? Think about it," Marion says.

Williams crouches down, pinches something off the concrete and examines it. "Rejection," I think he mumbles. He sounds impatient.

"She's had plenty of that already. Eight months in jail and a restraining order? What would've been different this time?"

Williams drops whatever he was holding and stands. "Maybe she hit her breaking point when Robert Holloway turned her in. Maybe she knew that was really going too far."

No. I feel my head shaking back and forth as I rub my hands over my legs.

"Even if someone's in a *state*—a manic state, paranoid, whatever—even if they're deluded, there's a *logic* to what they do, right? If you buy the premise, their behavior usually makes sense. If you think the CIA really *is* watching you through your television, it'd make sense to be scared."

"So?"

"I'm just saying, if she wanted to be included so badly, which is what she said when she got arrested, why on earth would she want to kill any of them?" I hear an emotion in Detective Marion's voice that I can't name no matter how hard I try to think of the word.

"You're forgetting that she'd planned to stab them already."

My stomach tightens. Of course, I realize, he's just saying what everyone already thinks: I was dangerous before, why wouldn't I be dangerous now? But Marion seems to be defending me. That, I don't understand.

"I . . ."

"What?" Williams makes a sound halfway between a laugh and a snort.

"I was never convinced she *meant* to attack anyone," Marion says.

"Sure as hell looked like that to me. But it's *your* left arm that has the scar."

Then for a moment they turn and I can't hear what they are saying no matter how hard I listen. All I can think is: Finch was at a friend's house? *What? I took her to the police station. I know what I did.*

Everything swirls in my mind. Maybe they know I can hear and are trying to trick me, I can't help but think.

I know what I saw: A person had chased me off the trail. A man—I remember his baseball cap and his phone. I *know* I saw him. Finch did too. It is like her memory backed mine up.

But something Williams said to Marion sticks in my mind: "You work for the family."

That's not true, I realize. Marion *worked* for the family until a few weeks ago. I learned that when the security guard showed up for a background check and I went to hide in the bathroom. I'd expected Marion then.

And not that I would believe a word Robert Holloway said, but he'd confirmed it: "Marion is no longer employed by the family. He's focusing on his main job being a Metro detective as of about three weeks ago."

A shiver goes up my spine as I watch Marion's and Williams's lips move, but I can't hear what they're saying. And I start to wonder: Was Marion fired? If so, why? Could the reason have made him so upset with Shelly James that he would want to kill her?

I study the shape of Marion's head, the angle of his neck to his shoulders, his close-clipped hair, trying to match them with the man on top of the hill. The dark had made seeing details hard. Still, I know it was a man I saw from the way the shadow moved and the heaviness of his footfalls. I can't see any direct similarities between Marion and the man I saw, but then a new thought makes me stop looking for any. If Marion were the man who had chased me, why would he be defending me now? Why would he have told Williams he thought I was trying to help them?

Those two facts wouldn't fit together.

I hear a chiming sound and Detective Williams takes his cell phone from his pocket. A few seconds later, his lips mouth the word "fuck." "Hey, I have to take this," he says to Detective Marion.

Marion nods once quickly, then comes back inside, sits down, and folds his hands on the table. Williams closes the door behind him. It makes a noise like a bag being sealed, trapping air inside.

I don't know how I can look at Detective Marion, but I don't want to look away either.

"He'll be right back," Marion says. He scratches the side of his head and looks around awkwardly, like he isn't sure how to look at me either. Or what exactly to say. His head falls slightly to the side. His voice sounds a little like Ms. Parsons's as he asks, "How are you doing with all this?"

I can't tell if this is a detective trick or not. "Okay," I answer.

Like a reflex, my hand slides to touch the spot where I've carried my knife in the past—that place on my thigh seems bare now.

He shifts restlessly in the chair, glances in Williams's direction, and asks me, "Did you get any sleep last night?"

The pace of my breathing has picked up. I shift in my chair as I search for words. "No," I answer. "I didn't sleep at all, I think. You asked me a lot of questions this morning, but has anyone asked you . . . where you were last night?"

"No one yet," he says. His skin seems to flush a little. He works his jaw back and forth before answering. "I've been up since yesterday morning. I was packing up to spend the night camping when I my phone rang. I work . . . I used to work security for the James family. You knew that?"

I nod.

He narrows his eyes a little. I expect frustration, defensiveness, but I realize from the way he puts his elbows on the table and leans forward that he's curious. Truly curious.

"Jessie, what makes you ask that question?"

I swallow, my mind racing through the possibilities. I think of how he reached out to me after my arrest last year. My gut tells me I can trust him.

From the corner of my eye, I catch Williams looking in, at Marion. I wonder what my neighbors think about a uniformed cop marching around on my porch. I can only hear the edges of Williams's voice from outside; he's dropped it to a whisper.

"Jessie," Marion asks quietly. "Did you hear something about me?"

I want to tell him what I'm thinking. I draw a breath when the glass door slides open again. Williams's shoulders are pulled back. He has a strange look on his face.

Something has changed. I feel the difference in the air, and it scares me.

Marion's head swivels and his professional-sounding voice returns. "What's up?" he asks. He doesn't seem to sense the same danger in the room that I do.

Williams frowns at me before shifting his eyes back to Marion. "We need to go," he tells him. "Right now."

*   *   *

Detective Marion tells me not to leave town, and it isn't long before the front door is shut behind them. Finally alone again, I remember something. Something I saw a year before and forgot. *No*, something I made myself forget because I didn't want it to be true. I told myself I couldn't have seen what I did, that what had happened was a joke, or that it wasn't actually Owen and Shelly.

The show was in St. Louis—one of the biggest crowds of the tour—and they were late getting on stage. The tech guys were running back and forth across the stage, signaling to the sound booth. There was a rumble of restless energy in the crowd, a small sigh when another warm-up song began playing through the PA. Then, finally, a thumbs-up, lights dimming. I could see the side of the stage from where I sat—high and on the side, which usually let me see everything.

Owen and Shelly were there—her two steps ahead, him carrying his guitar by the neck. But before she went forward, her head turned. Owen grabbed her arm, roughly enough that her curled hair shook. She said something; her mouth seemed to spit out the words.

And then his mouth formed the word "bitch."

Shelly smiled and shook her head. She walked on stage, waved, and the crowd went wild. Owen waited for just a beat and then followed her.

10

The regular sounds of daytime return: the chugging of old air-conditioning units, singing from upstairs. Across the courtyard, someone plucks a bass in an odd, complicated rhythm. I try to process what just happened, but the energy for that has drained out of me. I set my head down on my kitchen table. It feels empty from worrying. I must fall asleep because I begin to dream.

I'm inside Ms. Parsons's office when I see two police cars through the window behind her. She shakes her head, guilty over being the bait in a trap. "They arrived right before you got here," she says, "I'm sorry."

Then the hallway door opens. Police circle around me, their dark uniforms seeming to block out all the light. One wears a small microphone on his left shoulder that squawks like the old radio in my first foster home. Daylight looks like a precious thing I may not see again. My legs begin to shake as footsteps echo in the hall. When Detective Marion steps through the door, my stomach sinks. Marion presses his lips together, looking at me just as he did when I was sentenced to jail: confused by who I am—and sorry, and careful.

He clears his throat. "I need you to turn around and put your hands behind your back."

I do just as he says. I lean against the cold tile in the hallway and hear the zip of handcuffs. I hoped I would never hear it again, but it is too late. Ms. Parsons raises her hand, waving good-bye as Detective Marion shuts the door. Her expression says she knows she'll never see me again, and I want to tell her it's okay, and that I appreciate everything she's done for me, and that giving me the strawberry Pop-Tarts and granola bar was so kind it made my heart hurt. But I can only walk straight through the double doors at the end of the hallway into the cruel light of day. I hear Detective Marion's footsteps behind me, his breathing, the rattle of his keys. I feel eyes watching us from the courtyard as he walks me to the police car . . .

Beside me, my phone is ringing, bringing me back. I'm in my kitchen again, pushing onto my elbows, rubbing my eyes. I follow the sound to my bedroom and answer, looking out my window as Ms. Parsons's voice enters my ear.

"Jessie?"

"Hi," I say.

The space outside my window looks normal—waving branches and sun and squirrels—but the worry in Ms. Parsons's voice makes my heart ache a little.

"Oh, thank God. Jessie, are you okay? Where are you now?"

I feel my eyes start to water. "Just here . . . at home." I don't know what to say about *how* I am, or how to begin to talk about the night before or the police visit just now, but her concern—the sincerity of it—touches me and I thank her for asking.

She lets out a small breath. "Can you come in?" she asks. "How about near the end of the day? Four-thirty."

"It's Sunday," I say.

"I'll come in," she answers.

The green numbers on my bedside clock read one forty-nine. I tell her I'll be there, then shower, put on fresh clothes, and wait.

I want her to know I didn't hurt Shelly James. I trust Ms. Parsons to listen to me—even while a tiny part of me worries if she can anymore. I wonder: *Will there be too much doubt in her now*? Replaying how the police reacted to my telling them what I knew only makes me more confused. Especially Williams's hurry just before they left. Who had called him when he was standing outside? My throat feels tight, nervousness making it hard to swallow or draw a full breath.

I drive to her office and park at the far end of the lot. I log my gas, put down my window because of the heat, and stare at the sun's reflection in the rainwater pools on the black asphalt. At a quarter past four, I go inside.

Ms. Parsons is sitting on the bench outside her office—the place where I listened to her and Ms. Carr talking. She wears what some people call a "hippie skirt" and holds her hands in her lap. When she sees me come into the hallway, she stands up and opens her arms like she means to hug me, then drops them to her sides. Her eyes shine as she guides me inside her office and pulls the door closed.

We sit in our usual chairs among her stacks of books and I inhale deeply to take in their sweet, dusty smell. Through the window behind her, I see only bushes and trees, not the police cars from my dream. Ms. Parsons's eyes tell me that if she has doubts about what happened the night before, they haven't made her turn her back on me.

"It's been all over the news," she says, just as calmly as that. "You weren't mentioned by name, but I saw the logo of the company you work for. I assume you were there." She raises her eyebrows in a way that asks for confirmation, and I nod, solemnly.

"I can't believe you did that, considering the risk involved. But before I start lecturing you, are you *okay*?"

I clear my throat, force words from my mouth. "I had to go. Robert Holloway—But I didn't know—I wouldn't—I didn't hurt Shelly. I . . ."

Ms. Parsons leans forward, her eyebrows drawn together. "Jessie, I'm here for *you*. I know you wouldn't do anything like that. No judgment, okay? You know that."

I remember a week earlier, when I expected to have a different conversation during my appointment. I imagined telling Ms. Parsons how the first party changed my sense of Owen and Shelly, and that being recognized was the shock I needed to put that part of my life to rest once and for all. A week ago I'd felt, briefly, like I'd just grown up—a realization that seems naïve and self-centered now that Shelly is dead. I wanted to let go of last week. Now, it wouldn't let go of me.

I look into Ms. Parsons's eyes and start again, slowly. Gripping the front of the chair cushion, I tell her everything, from the start of the Petersons' party through the police visit to my apartment. I can't believe how much I talk, like I've somehow forgotten the problem of my voice and how bad I am with words. Pieces of sentences keep coming out, fragments, but Ms. Parsons nods like she mostly understands. Once, her eyes bug out a little with disbelief even though she doesn't mean for them to. I tell her about seeing Robert whisper in Ken's ear, and about the look in Ken's eyes when he talked to me outside after putting everything together. *After he understood who I was.* I try to forget the squeak of his shoes on the pool tile, him following me those few steps, then letting me go.

Ms. Parsons lets out a small sigh. "The job part will be okay, I'm sure. Even if you don't stay with the same catering company, there's a lot of work in Nashville. Sometimes jobs come and go you know." She waves her hand like she's shooing a fly. "I promise, that will be alright."

I try not to show my heartbreak. I try not to feel it, either.

Ms. Parsons takes a lot of care not to treat me like I'm damaged, but sometimes she gets a worried look on her face, and this is one of those times. She leans forward, resting both hands flat on the arms of her chair. "I know you wouldn't hurt Shelly James. But I also understand *why* the police wanted to talk to you. And you get why too, right?"

"I get it." And I do understand about *why me*. "I'd have interviewed me, too," I say.

"How did the questioning go?" she asks, a wrinkle of worry between her eyes.

"Detective Marion wanted . . ."

Her face tenses. Not a wince, less than that. "Detective Marion was there this morning, during the questioning?"

I nod, curious now. She obviously knows something I don't.

"Was there anyone else there? Another officer?"

I tell her about Detective Williams, and Ms. Parsons leans back slightly, glancing at the door, like someone might come in. "Has anyone contacted you since then about Detective Marion?"

My words begin slipping back inside me, as though gravity were pulling them down. I shake my head.

"Detective Marion has been taken off the case, Jessie. He's being questioned for possibly having a role in Shelly's death."

My stomach drops into freefall.

This was why they left, I think. *This was what Williams heard about on the call he took on my porch.*

Ms. Parsons looks the way people do when they realize they've caused hurt feelings. "I thought someone would have let you know, or that you'd have seen the news yourself. He hasn't been formally charged yet, I think. But his being taken in means the police have a good reason to talk to him."

In my head, the world becomes a buzz. I replay what Robert Holloway said about Marion no longer working for the family and try to fit it together with him reporting me for being at the party. I think back to the way Marion treated me earlier, and how Williams glared at him when he said they had to leave.

When Detective Marion questioned me, he'd seemed sincere. He asked questions he didn't know the answers to, like he really was trying to figure out if I had been in the woods the night before. Like he hadn't been there himself.

But maybe he's just a skilled liar. *Police lie*, I remember one of my early foster roommates telling me. *They trick you with half-truths.* I have the bewildering feeling of being lost in a crowd. There has to be a way it all makes sense, but I can't see how yet.

Ms. Parsons tilts her head sideways and asks if I am okay, then if I am thinking about Detective Marion being questioned, and I say I am.

She pushes a tissue box toward me. "I'm sure your thoughts are crowded right now with everything going on. But the police talking with Detective Marion is good news in a way. It means they're moving the investigation forward."

She means to be helpful, I know, by saying it's good the police are not focused on me. And it is. I feel tears starting to well up behind my eyelids and a sense of lightness from the relief. What she'd said a moment earlier about me finding other work flashes back and I see a way that maybe, for me, what happened can be left behind. Calling the police, telling them what I'd seen, *was* the right thing to do, I think, even if they had a reason to suspect me. Still, I don't like picturing Marion being led into his own department for questioning. Despite my relief, I can't put together him defending me to Williams with him becoming a suspect. It feels *wrong*, even though I doubted him a little bit too. If he was guilty, wouldn't he have encouraged Williams's suspicion of me to keep the focus off himself?

When it's time for the session to end, Ms. Parsons says in a slow, calm voice: "Jessie, I'm here for you. I'll be here all day tomorrow. If you need anything at all, tell the front desk it's you and they'll interrupt me. I *want* them to interrupt me, okay? This is important. You're going to get through this. Everything is going to get back on track."

Back on track.

When we stand, I try to make my face look normal, to not show how lost I feel. I wave good-bye, close the door, and make it no farther than the bench in the hall before pulling up the local news on my phone.

(NASHVILLE)
At the top of the news story
The body of country music star and national celebrity Shelly James was found by Nashville police in Percy Warner Park on Saturday evening. The remains were discovered near a park trail while a party was being held at James's residence less than a mile away. The Metro Police Department is investigating the death as a homicide. An autopsy has not yet been performed, but a police spokesperson indicated that her head sustained multiple blunt traumas . . .

It doesn't seem possible, and yet here it is—right on the screen.

In my head, I hear Finch's voice saying, "He chased me," and anger flies from my stomach to a place behind my eyes, burning red like butterflies on fire. Could Marion have done this?

I can't imagine Shelly James not being alive. She could stand in front of fifty thousand people and make them feel whatever she wanted them to—emotions they didn't know they had. She filled auditoriums with fans who felt she was talking directly to them, people who sang her songs back to her, every word.

For a summer, I was one of them.

I scroll down. Just below the first article is another, an update:

NASHVILLE

A Metro Police Detective is being questioned about the murder of Shelly James. Sunday afternoon, Detective Jason Marion was questioned at the Downtown Precinct about his possible role in Shelly James's murder Saturday night. Investigators say Marion has been employed part-time as a security officer for the James family for the last year. Marion is being questioned about the extent of his relationship with Shelly James and his whereabouts over the weekend, though police say no formal charges have been filed at this time. The investigation remains open.

There is a photo of Detective Marion climbing the police station steps, two other policemen right behind him. My eyes jump around the page, picking up only a word here and there. I draw in a deep breath, let it out, and force myself to read slowly enough to understand. I read the story over and over, taking in a little more each time. I try to piece together the facts with what I saw that night and what I know.

I never saw Detective Marion at the party, which means he could have been anywhere else—including in Percy Warner Park waiting for Shelly and Finch. But he doesn't look like the man I saw standing on top of the hill. And why would Detective Marion kill the woman he spent a year protecting?

I push open the door and step outside, where the light is still strong. While I was in Ms. Parsons's office, the traffic picked up on Charlotte Pike—horns are honking, an engine revs. I don't know how much gas I have, since I didn't log any of last night. I'm not sure I want to go home, but I don't know where else to go.

As I get close to my car, I notice another car parked next to it. It's backed in, facing the street. I don't know cars very well, but it's old—an American car, avocado-colored, rusted around the bumper. I wouldn't have noticed it at all if it hadn't been right beside mine.

And then Detective Marion opens the passenger door, blocking me. It opens with a creak as he looks past me, up toward the building.

"Jessie, get in please."

Earlier this morning he'd looked tired and on edge. Now, his eyes radiate intensity even as the dark circles beneath them have deepened. He wears a faded denim shirt and dark brown cowboy boots that seem to make him lean forward slightly, like he's ready to jump at something. My head spins with the fact that only a minute before his picture was on my phone. He was in my apartment this morning, and then later in my dream.

I hear the *putt-putt* engine of the car. He's left it running. I remember the way he held me to the ground during the arrest, and my dream from earlier. I feel a quiver in my stomach as my legs turn heavy and I wonder, *Am I in danger?* I look behind me, wondering how far I could get if I were to take off running. Far enough to get away from him? Back to the Center's door, to bang on it? I know he would catch me before I made it halfway up the steps. I briefly imagine being dragged backward, the pavement scraping my palms. He could catch me if he wanted to—there would be no point in trying to get away.

If I *could* scream, would anyone even hear me?

Marion looks around, his eyes showing worry, impatience. "Please," he says again, then points. When I look inside the car, I seem to fall forward—maybe with a gentle nudge at my back. The door closes behind me. I search for a handle, but instead pull a crank that drops the window some while Marion comes around to the front of the car. He gets in, slams his door, and we start moving. Suddenly, my insides feel like I'm flying, dropping— *almost disappearing into nothing*. I know the sensation from the dark. The fading sensation is something like blacking out, something like going outside my own body. Ms. Parsons told me it is a coping mechanism, protecting me from the full force of reality.

My heart pounds as the mental health center shrinks in the rearview mirror and we merge into traffic and speed away, because now I have no idea what is about to happen. I press my hands against my knees to stop my dizziness. I look at Marion, trying to match the shape of his head and shoulders with my memory from last night. I thought it didn't fit, but was I wrong? *Was* he the man on top of the hill? In my gut, I don't feel that he means to hurt me or that he killed Shelly, but I can't help the fear that at any moment I will feel his hand on my shoulder, or a sharp point of a knife in my ribs, or the rough push of gunmetal against the base of my skull.

He's taking you somewhere to kill you.

The only witness.

I know that's not fair, but I also can't help but remember Ms. Parsons's cautious tone as she told me he is a suspect. And after what I saw the night before, and after being tricked by Robert for whatever reason, I've run out of trust.

"I'm sorry," Marion says. "I didn't mean to catch you off guard. You're safe, I promise. I know this is scary and not what you're used to. I just don't have a lot of time to work with."

"Don't touch me again," I say.

He looks back and forth between me and the road. He grips the wheel. "You're right, I know better. I'm sorry. I won't, you have my word."

"Where . . . are we going?" I manage to ask.

Marion tugs at his ear. "Just up the road here, to a safe spot. I just need to talk, to ask you a few questions." He glances over both his shoulders. "I don't mean to be mysterious, Jessie, but I also want to avoid a lot of attention. I'm not here right now. You know what I mean?" A vein twists down his temple like a river.

I'm not here.

The words slip out of my mouth. "You mean because you ran from the police."

He winces, like he hates how it sounds. He rubs his eyes with his knuckles, then his muscles seem to relax, just slightly.

"I'm not running from anyone. Not exactly. I'm not going to be arrested. There's no problem verifying where I was last night. But I have been kicked off the case, and as of right now I'm suspended indefinitely."

Around us, the low branches of trees move as wind whistles through the half-open window. When Marion glances over at me again, I see something shift in his expression.

"Jessie, are you going to be sick?"

"I don't know," I say. I realize I'm clutching my stomach.

"Hang on, okay?" The car slows. We buck over a small curb and stop under the shade of a pine tree in a parking lot for some sort of business with no real storefront. No other cars are around. I pull the door handle and lean over the pavement, my stomach roiling as I try to catch my breath. I smell the sweet-bitter asphalt as the warm air rises over me despite the old, chugging air conditioner. Marion rests his hand on the back of my seat as he looks behind us.

"I know you're nervous but I won't let anything happen to you." He holds up his palms as if showing they are empty. "I know all of this must be a lot to take in. But please, just hang in there with me a little while?"

I draw a breath and the world's spinning begins to slow down. The edges of everything lose their blur. I nod and tell him "okay," and the car door, made before I was born, creaks loudly when I pull it closed.

"I'm going to start driving again, alright?" he asks, and I nod again.

We start down a series of side streets. To slow my breathing, I make my chest so still my heart begins to burn. I let my breath escape, slowly. The car smells like newspaper and oil and it squeaks on even the smallest bumps. I realize that it probably doesn't belong to him but I don't ask. At a red light, he turns right and we rumble over train tracks before cutting down a service road. I remember my eagerness for the comfort of Ms. Parsons's couch an hour earlier. Now I'm headed to who-knows-where, my head is buzzing with confusion, my heart is hot with fear.

Eventually, I find a way to say, "What do you want to ask me about?"

"I need to hear more about what you saw last year during the tour. I guess you could call it an informal questioning. I need your help. And I happen to know you need mine. Officially, I'm off the case, but I can't *not* work on it. Even though they questioned me, I know they still consider you a suspect, which I also know is off base. They think they're following sensible lines of motives, but they're not seeing the full picture."

Is this a trick? He seems too nervous, too sincere to be deceptive. On top of that, he sounds exhausted.

We drive a little farther, and I stop recognizing the neighborhood. The houses turn older; the tree branches seem long and rain-heavy and untended. The road slopes down a steep hill as we pass a church with bright white paint and beet-red windows.

We slow as we approach another intersection, then speed up again to cross when Marion sees it's clear.

When we reach the end of the street, he clicks a garage opener clipped to the sun visor and the garage door on the last house on the right swings open. Before we are fully parked, he clicks the button again, and a few seconds later the engine is off. A yellow seam where the garage door meets the driveway is the only light. The dark shapes of tools hang on the wall, dull from grease and age. The thought flashes in my mind that if Marion wants to kill me, now is the perfect time. He opens his door and a dome light pops on above. He starts toward a stairwell on the far side of the garage, but when he sees I haven't moved, he pauses.

I could reach the garage opener, I think, where it hangs limply from the visor. I could open the door and run, but I think back to the way Williams had looked at me earlier and decide I at least need to listen to what Marion has to say. I have to know what he knows.

His shoes squeak from the rainwater he's tracked in as he returns to the car. I look at him over the curved edge of the window.

"I know detectives don't give out information," I say. "They keep part of what they know to themselves. Right?"

"That's right." His eyes are patient even as his feet shuffle on the garage floor.

"I understand why that is. But if you want me to follow you inside this house, I need to know *everything* you know about what happened to Shelly."

He bites the inside of his cheek then sets his jaw. "That's fair."

"And you have to tell me where we are."

His eyebrows rise and fall like he forgot something obvious.

"This is my uncle's place. He and my aunt go up north every summer, so it's empty. I'm staying here, until . . . something changes with the case. Until the news and everyone else stops looking for me. Do you feel okay enough to go inside?"

My head is spinning from wanting to be out of the closed-in space.

I was a watcher, a follower, a fan. When I tried to leave that life behind, I got pulled back into it. If I tell him to take me home, I'll just be sitting there waiting to hear from the police again. I could do that, or I could find out what Marion knows, and try to help. I know already what my choice is. I follow him up a flight of painted wood steps, and we enter a kitchen lit only by daylight coming through the windows. The air smells dusty and still and is very warm. I wipe my forehead where it has begun to sweat and notice there is no display on the microwave, no ticking from the clock at the center of the stove.

"Sorry about the temperature in here. Everything is turned off. It's better, less noticeable from the street," Marion says, pulling a chair away from the kitchen table. He motions for me to sit down, then sits on the chair across from it.

He sets his hands flat on the table as if laying out what he means to say.

"Where should I even start? I'm still in shock to be honest, still processing what happened. Since my phone rang with the news late last night, everything has been a blur. But if I think like a cop, I understand Shelly's murder is the biggest crime Metro PD has faced in a decade. People in Nashville are angry, and scared. Metro has to arrest somebody, bottom line. The longer they wait, the worse it looks, and the more time that passes, the more evidence goes away. Rain has already turned the park into a mess. You saw someone last night. And you *watched* the *entire* last tour. I wish like hell you weren't in this situation, but you're suspect number one. And until the other detectives verified my location last night, I was a suspect too. And I know neither one of us is guilty."

I give him a look. *How does he know it wasn't me?*

He reads my mind, shrugs a little.

"Was I imagining it, or were you a little suspicious of me when we questioned you this morning? You asked where I'd been the night before."

A week earlier, I would have kept quiet because of the protection order. "Yes," I admit. "I know you weren't working . . . security for them. As of three weeks . . ."

"Because the new security interviewed the caterers," he says, realizing.

I nod.

"You were the first person who came to mind when I heard the news about Shelly, I'll admit. But it was so obvious you were telling the truth during the interview. You hadn't even wanted to be at the party last night, I could hear it in your voice."

"I didn't. I tried to get out of going."

"I believe you did. So, we have to back up. Tell me again what Robert Holloway said to you. He told you Shelly and Owen wanted you at their house for a PR stunt?"

As a reason, it sounds crazy when Marion says it back to me, probably too crazy for me to have made up. I start at the beginning, when Robert found me in the alley, and tell Marion everything that was said.

Marion slowly shakes his head. "I don't get it. I'm confused, I'll admit, but I don't see any motive there. The trouble is, there aren't many people in Shelly's life who would want to do her harm. Whoever killed her was angry at her for sure, or at least extremely determined. Forensics told us she was struck at least nine times. In some cases, victims have a list of enemies a mile long, but Shelly is beloved."

Is. I notice he can't use the past tense. A gust of wind blows a branch against the window, the leaves brushing the glass like they're asking to come in.

He rubs his eyes. "Let's talk about what you saw on tour. Maybe you shouldn't have been there, but the truth is that you were. It might be weird to talk about, especially with me, but there are things that probably only you saw and might remember. Owen and Shelly had a lot of people working for them. You watched those people, show after show. Basically the whole summer, right?"

I nod, hesitant. I glance at the tiny scar my knife made on his left forearm.

"Go back to the first show. Boston. I assume you drove up there?"

Putting the memories out of my mind was like cleaning my head. Opening them back up is like finding souvenirs I once thought were special but look strange to me now.

Marion leans forward.

I tell him how I left Nashville and drove straight through the night, the speedometer at sixty-five to save gas, staying in the right lane of the interstate all the way up the East Coast. It felt like I was driving to Mars—with no idea what Boston would look like, or where I would go once I got there. I tell him about how once I found the arena, I paid to park with a crumpled ten-dollar bill and wandered sidewalks until it was near time for the show to start, my arms wrapped around my chest because the wind from the harbor felt cold even in June. I ate a candy bar because I felt weak, went into the arena as soon as it opened, and listened to the last of the sound check echo over the empty seats. This was before security knew me—I noticed a few looks, but the guards seemed to think I was homeless. I guess I *was* homeless. Except the music was my home. It was more my home than any physical place. In the dark, that music was woven into me.

"Tell me about the crew and the other musicians. Was there anyone who stood out? Maybe who you saw after the show?"

"In Boston I left right after," I say. "I thought maybe my car would get towed. Then I'd have no way to get to Pittsburgh. That was the second stop. I drove at night again, laughed to myself at the thought that I was a kind . . . of driving vampire. I stopped for gas, bought two Red Bulls, kept going."

Marion rubs his eyes like I'm losing him, but I'm not sure which details are important and which aren't.

"I want to show you a few pictures," he says, turning his phone screen toward me. "Tell me if you ever saw these people alone with Shelly or sensed that anything could be off between them, okay? Thomas Dixon," he says as the first image comes up. "The sound engineer."

I shake my head as I look at the man who worked the boards during sound checks.

Marion nods, scrolls through his phone, then shows me another. "Angela Lamb," he says.

She managed lighting and effects. I shake my head again.

"Right," he sighs, seeming like he doesn't believe it could have been any of them, like he's going through the motions by asking, reviewing suspects he already considered and ruled out.

"Tana Nolan," he says. She managed all the merch tables. I picture her long purple-red hair, her all-black clothes.

"I didn't buy any merch at the venues. It's too expensive."

"Where do you get it then?" The side of Marion's lip draws up a little. I'm sure he's remembering the pictures they showed at my hearing of my collection—proof, they said, that I was dangerously obsessed with the Jameses.

I shrug, trying to avoid giving away how much I used to spend. "On eBay. There's all kinds of stuff on there. I bought a few of Owen's handwritten set lists. I bought a scarf Shelly wore on their first tour. There are other clothes, ticket stubs, and things like that, but VIP passes too. I could never afford those, though."

Marion frowns. "VIP passes? The all-access kind, on eBay?

"Yeah."

"Like phony ones? There were only four of those passes issued for each show, sold only through Shelly and Owen's website."

"They didn't look phony to me, and they always sold. For a lot, too."

His eyebrows knit together as he asks, skeptically, "How much?"

"Five thousand."

He blinks a few times, fast, then slowly leans back in his chair. "And how many, would you estimate?"

I have to think. "Five? Six?"

"Total?"

"For each show."

Marion buries his cheek in his palm as he looks out the window. "Where do people even get that stuff?" he asks, not expecting an answer.

"I think Robert Holloway sold me most of it," I say.

Marion's hand drops onto the table with a thud. He cocks his head at an angle. "What did you say?"

And so I tell him every detail I can recall. I talk slowly, not able to hide what remains of my shame. "He didn't know he was selling anything to me. But it was easy to hide who I was, and he didn't seem too careful about it anyway. He used a few different accounts, but I knew them all. You could tell the photos were taken in basically the same place each time. Some of them looked like they were above a tiny sink, like in a tour bus. His reflection was in the mirror once, but it was basically the same photo over and over, even though the account kept changing."

Marion's voice drops into a very deep tone. I can see he believes a part of my story that didn't make sense to him until now. Very slowly, he asks, "Tell me again about what Robert asked you to do when he approached you outside your work."

As I talk, his eyes begin to burn.

11

Marion turns away from me, his back rising with each breath. His neck has reddened just below his clipped hair, and I imagine his mind working as he twists his boot on the floor the way people do when they're putting out a cigarette.

I've triggered something in him but I'm not sure what. He's put something together about Robert, but when I ask about it, he doesn't answer except to curse under his breath. In my mind, I recall the outrage in Robert's eyes as he spoke to Ken. Outrage and something close to joy, like it made him happy to catch me.

Marion picks at the frayed hem of his denim shirt, the back of which is dark with sweat. Finally he stands up, shoves his hands in his back pockets, and says, "Ready Jessie? I'll take you back now."

Outside, a bird perched on a branch watches us like we are actors in a play and he wants to see what will happen next. Marion hooks his finger through his key ring.

I stand up. "You're going to find Robert?"

"I have your number. I'll be in touch soon," he says. His mumble sounds preoccupied. Already, his eyes are on the door we came in by.

"I want to come," I say.

He doesn't look at me. "No, you don't."

"Why?"

"Because I said so."

Words parents say in movies. It's better than him talking to me like I'm developmentally delayed, but I won't accept it. I stare at him. The air is so still I can see flecks of dust in the thin rays coming through the kitchen window.

"You said you would tell me what you know, and so far all I've heard are questions."

He sighs. "The best place for you right now is your apartment. I know this whole situation is a lot to take in and I wish you hadn't gotten so tangled up in it. I do. I'll get you to your car, then you can go home. You can call your . . ." He almost says *family*, I can tell. "Call your friends," he says instead, catching himself.

When I imagine my apartment, my stomach feels like a hole the size of Nashville. I picture *alone* and know I'll go crazy waiting.

"No," I say, "no way. You can't just . . . use me for information then dump me off."

"That's not what . . ."

"Are you going to the studio?" We both know Robert Holloway practically lives in the studio on Music Row when he isn't on a tour.

"That's the . . ."

"Robert tricked *me*. And whatever you just put together you only did because of what I just told you. So I'm going to see him now whether you drive me or not. I'll take a cab. Besides, there's no time to take me back to my car . . . unless you want to backtrack across town."

From where I stand, I can see the kitchen clock's face showing nearly six o'clock. Driving across town to where I'm parked only to backtrack to Music Row would take the more than an hour. Marion's boots shift like he is eager enough to run all the way there. He pinches the bridge of his nose, then looks at his watch.

"I'll stay in the car while you go talk to him," I say. I know I almost have him convinced. "I'll wait there."

He looks at me, considering, before glancing at his watch again. "You'll stay in the car *the whole time*. No exceptions."

"The whole time," I say, halfway meaning it.

Rain pelts the kitchen window so suddenly we both turn our heads. I see the bird that was perched on the branch outside fly away.

* * *

Neither of us knows what to say as we drive toward the studio. Once I ask about what he's thinking about Robert, but all he says is, "We'll see."

"How . . . are you now?" he asks after a long moment, apparently trying to make conversation.

I know he's asking about my general mental health, but I don't know what to say under the circumstances. I settle on "Better."

"I always wanted to tell you," he says. "I never had the sense that you went to that concert meaning to hurt anyone."

Part of me is stunned that he's brought this up, though it's what he'd said to Detective Williams earlier, when he thought I couldn't hear. I guess he wants to say it to me too.

"Why *did* you have the knife?" he asks.

"It protected me," I say. "It's how I felt safe. Once, in a foster home—the one I was in before I went inside the closet—I woke to find the dad's hand resting on my chest."

Just thinking about it makes my skin crawl. I can still feel his callouses pressed against my thin T-shirt, his face half lit by the streetlight. I can smell the beer he drank earlier while my hand brushed along the dusty drywall beside the bed, looking for a way out.

"Closest I ever came to hurting anyone was right then. I started carrying a knife after that."

Marion gives me a look that's both sympathetic and angry. "I hate that that happened to you. Just hearing about it makes me want to . . ."

He doesn't finish. I see his temple throbbing. Maybe he understands.

He drives to the studio the same way he had after he picked me up—down side streets and then up an alley that runs between Elliston Place and mid-town. Music Row is where most entertainment businesses are located—record labels, publishing houses, and recording studios sit side by side. Some of the studios are in big buildings, as you would expect, but others are tucked in the backrooms of bungalows. We pass the forty-foot-tall *Musica* statue as we circle the roundabout and turn onto 17th Avenue. He rolls right on a red light so that the car will keep moving, then splashes up an alley toward the studio. When he parks, the car rocks once and gas sloshes somewhere deep inside. The engine goes quiet and rain dots the windshield, blurring the view of the studio's back stairs.

Marion leans against the steering wheel. "This is a mistake. Seriously, stay here."

He sounds like he is half talking to himself and half to me. He gets out and jogs toward the studio, his shoulders hunched, until he disappears around the front of the building.

Alone in the car, I begin to think of all the times I watched the studio from pretty much right where I'm sitting. That version of me seems much younger, less capable, and I wonder what I was even hoping for by catching a glimpse of Owen or Shelly. My distant involvement with them seems like a security blanket that I held onto for too long.

Raindrops on the windshield become jagged streaks. I start to roll down the window for some air when I see the studio's back door opening and Robert Holloway stepping out. He closes it very slowly behind him and runs his hands roughly through his hair. He starts down the back steps, shoulders hunched as he squints up into the rain.

My heart starts to race. Detective Marion went around to the front door. In a few seconds, Robert will get to his car and be gone down the alley. It feels like one of those times that moves fast and slow at the same time because a decision must be made *right now.*

I reach over and press the horn. A loud burst sounds. Over the steering wheel, I see Robert freeze and look around like he is trying to understand what is happening, his shape blurred in the watery dots on the glass. When he starts down the stairs again, I know I can't just watch him leave. I can't do nothing. I have to try.

I get out of the car and run toward him. His eyes catch mine. Robert outweighs me by a hundred pounds and could easily push past me, I know, but I put my hand on the rail and face him. The painted metal, still warm from the afternoon sun, rattles against my palm. I half hear what he says over the rain. ". . . who is back *again,*" that makes me grip the rail harder. He turns to head back up the stairs, but the studio's back door flies open and Detective Marion steps out. Robert looks at Marion, then down at me, just as the clouds open up and rain begins pounding loudly on the metal hoods of cars and trucks.

I gauge the shape of Robert's head and wonder . . . could that have been him in the park? But surely Finch would have recognized *him* if she'd come upon him and Shelly. Would Robert have run from the party to confront them? And if so, why? Would there even have been time?

Marion calls, "Come on back inside, Robert."

Robert looks past me but seems to estimate that I could slow him down enough that Marion would catch him easily. To Marion he says, "You're making a mistake."

But Marion says nothing as he puts his hand square on Robert's back and shoves him inside. A second later, I realize he's pulled Robert's phone from his pocket—he cradles it, shielding it from the rain.

"Hey!" I hear Robert say from inside.

"Go back to the car, Jessie," Marion says before disappearing inside, a screen door slamming behind him. But I didn't come this far to wait in a car.

My cotton shirt sticks to my shoulders and chest as I climb the rest of the stairs and push my way in, where we three stand in a break-room kitchen. A coffee machine sits at the end of the dark countertop with two stacks of white paper coffee cups beside it. No one closes the outer door and the sound of the rain carries inside like very heavy white noise. Puddles spread from each of us across the floor. I start to shiver as the air-conditioning chills my rain-soaked clothes.

"Go back," Marion says to me.

But I'm looking right at Robert. "You lied to me."

Robert looks at me like he is trying to make sense of a dream, the full insanity of the situation washing over his face. The air smells like a mixture of his cologne, coffee, and something sweet and decaying—like a pastry left sitting out too long.

Marion reaches for a towel on the countertop and tosses it to me, but his eyes never leave Robert. He steps forward, backing him into the wall as if pushing him with an invisible force. Seeing the two side by side, I realize how much larger Robert is than Marion, but Marion takes another step forward, holding up Robert's phone, fury in his eyes. "Who were you going to call? Not the police again, I'm sure."

"You're not here as a cop," Robert says. "What the fuck are you two anyway, the dynamic duo? Do the police know *you're* here?" He points at me, his expression a mixture of shock and disgust.

"No one knows we're here, Robert." Marion's voice deepens, back to the way it sounded when he and Detective Williams questioned me. He takes another step closer. "No one at all. Who figured out you were stealing from the James family, Robert? Was it Shelly?"

Robert shakes his head back and forth, very slowly, as his hand shuffles searchingly along the wall. "I don't know what you're talking about."

"Sure, you do. All that memorabilia that started going missing during the last tour. Just a little at first, here and there. A favorite scarf, a handwritten set list. Shelly asked me to look into it, but I could never quite figure it out. She could be forgetful, so it took a while for her to know there was a thief on the tour."

My insides sink. Of course, I think. I'd been so blinded by my own *need* at the time that I couldn't see the items I bought for what they were: stolen property. Instantly, I want to send it all back, get rid of it. I feel like I'm getting further and further from being the person who wanted it to begin with.

Suddenly, Robert jerks himself toward the door. His shoes squeak as he scrambles, slipping forward.

When Marion pulls a pistol from the back of his jeans, he skids to a stop.

Time slows to a halt.

Robert's eyes show panic. He breathes as if heaving himself those few yards took everything he had. "Holy fucking shit, Jason. You're really doing this?"

"Is that why you killed her? You didn't want to go to jail?"

"You losing your fucking mind?" Robert asks, his voice cracking.

I can't tear my gaze away from the gun. Sweat is warm under my arms, mixing with the cool rainwater.

Robert says, "I'm not saying any more in front of *her*. The hell are you doing carting her around anyway? You switch teams? You're not thinking clearly." He taps the base of his palm against the side of his head. "You lovesick? Or just plain nuts? 'Cause I think you've lost your mind."

Lovesick? I don't have time to wonder about what he means before Marion motions toward a sunken room with a white L-shaped couch. He pulls a chair away from the wall.

"Stay here, Jessie. This isn't going to take long."

But I can't wait here while they talk in the other room. I follow them, lingering in the hallway as I take in Owen and Shelly's studio. Along the paneled wood hallways, black-framed gold albums catch the light as if glowing from inside. Behind the couch is a glass wall through which I see a dimly lit room with gray egg-carton-shaped siding. A microphone hangs above a single stool. I sway a little, suddenly dizzy. There are no words for seeing a place where a world was made. I know this is where Owen and Shelly recorded their albums. *The* album I had, when it was *all* I had.

"It all makes too much sense," Marion says, his gun still pointed at Robert. "It wasn't just the memorabilia you were stealing and selling, was it? You found a way to make some dupli-cate VIP passes, sold them yourself. No one would notice, right? But Shelly started to suspect something wasn't right, didn't she? Not just a scarf or a set list here and there, or even all-access passes, but maybe real money too. She told me once she didn't understand why you were linked to their business bank account. So why was that?"

"Shut your fucking mouth," Robert interrupts, his eyes twitchy. "I'm probably the straightest manager in history. Any-thing I took wasn't worth her attention. I never left their house last night. Ask anyone there. Only time I left was to get security, to handle your little friend." Robert looks at me with hate in his eyes.

I bite my lip and look right back.

"Is that so?"

I can't see Marion's eyes from where I sit, but from the way his hands are moving I can tell he's scrolling through Robert's phone in his lap. I see the dull reflection of the overhead light on the gun in his other hand.

"The fuck are you even looking for in my phone?" Robert asks. He sounds so afraid it is making me afraid, and I realize that I don't know what Detective Marion means to do to him.

"Just sit still," Marion says calmly.

"I'll sit still when you tell me where *you* were last night. And where *she* went when she left the party." Robert points at me, his voice breaking with emotions I can't name. Above us, another wave of rain sweeps across the roof, loud enough that it makes me look up.

"Cut the shit. She was only there because you asked her to be. You found yourself a perfect scapegoat to blow the whistle on so you could look like a hero, right?"

My eyes drop to my shoes. A dull ache begins in my stomach for having been so gullible.

"You never used to come to parties at the house, but you showed up *last* night, hobnobbing with Owen's old Nashville crowd, making a show of it to seem less suspicious. You know there's a new album coming out and they were going to go on tour to promote it. Shelly couldn't prove you took any money but she was suspicious of you because her stuff kept disappearing on the last tour. So, you figured you could blame last year's scapegoat one last time. Were you going to hand her something to make it look like she'd stolen it from the house? You figured out who was buying some of what you sold, so you knew that if the cops searched her place, they would find enough there to take any blame off you. Didn't quite work out though, so maybe you asked Shelly if you could talk with her somewhere private, then led her out to the woods . . ."

"I watched Shelly *start her career.* I helped get her from Lower Broadway honky-tonks to the Ryman. I stood by her. I was her protector when she used to sing to empty rooms, or to a few drunk guys yelling for her to shimmy with the microphone stand. I was like a father to her."

"Please. A father who probably gave her pills to keep her distracted while he robbed her, then killed her to save his own skin."

Robert stands and spits on the floor, his lip curled at the sight of Marion's gun. "Now you listen. Shoot me if you have to, but know by *God* that I never laid a hand on Shelly James."

"Sit down, Robert."

Robert drops back onto the couch, his eyes red now. I can tell his world is upside down, and for a second I feel bad for him.

"And I never gave her any *fucking* pills," he says. "I'm a drug dealer, too, now. Right?" He makes the blowing air noise people make when something can't be believed. "She started with those pills to sleep. Started mixing them with alcohol. I'm sure you remember as well as anyone. Probably came from you. That's what I always suspected, anyway."

"Right," Marion says.

"Or maybe you should be talking to her new boyfriend."

Marion goes slightly limp, like he's been punched.

"Who?" is all he asks.

"Someone. I never saw him. She hadn't been seeing him for very long, maybe a month. She hid it, a lot better than you two ever did. I think you wanted people to find out, sometimes. You never bothered to be discreet."

Marion makes a noise with his mouth, but I catch him glance at me quickly. My mind starts to race. *Discreet?*

"What? You don't think people knew? It's a miracle Owen didn't, to be honest. I knew about you two from day one. Last month, I thought she was running out to meet you, but then she told me she didn't want you at events going forward. She asked me to interview new security."

The obviousness of Marion having had some sort of romantic relationship with Shelly hits me. I don't know how I didn't see it as possible, but learning now that it happened, it makes complete sense. My stomach sinks with disappointment—in him, *and* in her—even as my head begins fitting this fact into a picture that is becoming clearer piece by piece.

Now Marion's voice is overly calm, like he's trying to prove he's unaffected by learning Shelly had started another relationship. "You think the guy she started seeing could have . . . ?"

"I don't know. He drove a sports car. A white one. I saw it from a distance once out this back door, heard the engine growl. I may have seen the same car last night near the house."

"May have?" Marion asks.

"Yeah, maybe. I don't know, it's not like I knew to look out for it. That's not my business. But it sounded the same anyway. I forgot to tell the cops that."

Marion stands up and slips the gun into the back of his jeans, then motions toward the door as he comes toward me.

"Let's go," he says. He tosses Robert's phone to the other side of the room where it settles against the wood-paneled wall.

"You've always been a scumbag, Robert. Call whoever you want."

Robert leans back. "I already talked to the cops. They mostly wanted to talk about *you*. But I still don't know where *you* were last night."

What has just happened? One second he was pumping information from Robert, now he's ready to leave? Have I missed something else? Unable to conceal my . . . what? Anger? Disappointment? I squint as we walk toward the back door. We start through the kitchen, still marked with our wet footprints. The rain has stopped and, through the glass, I see hints of steam rising from car roofs in the alleyway.

Robert follows us. "Jason, go home," he says now, almost like they're friends. Like Marion confronting him was nothing personal.

This business is crazy, I heard him say once.

Maybe it is.

No, I *know* for sure it is.

I take one last look at the inside of the studio and picture Owen perched there, the shadow of his hat covering his eyes, as he recorded the verses of "American Moves". Seeing the inside of the studio is like visiting somewhere you always dreamed of just as the world ends. In my head I hear the sound of his cufflink scratching against the wooden front of his guitar, then I open the door. A tiny patch of blue breaks through the clouds overhead, and the outside air smells cleaner than before. Detective Marion moves behind me like he means to be the last one out.

"You better watch your back riding around with your little friend," Robert calls out.

"I'll handle my back, Robert," Marion says. I hear the squeak of his shoes on the floor, the screech of the screen door—then Robert's voice again.

"We had a name for her on the tour, you know, since she came to all the shows."

"Goodbye, Robert."

"We called her the Irregular Regular."

I turn when I hear that, the sudden sadness feeling like a hollowness inside me.

"Somebody made it up. We said it the whole tour. The Irregular Regular. That's your partner now. That's how much she freaked everyone out. She was *such* a psycho, she got a catering job just to get close to Owen and Shelly again. If it wasn't so scary and sad, it'd be . . ."

Marion looks at me while Robert talks. "Just wait out here a second."

The screen door screeches closed as Marion lets it go, then clicks shut. I hear a wooden chair hit the tile, then a thick-sounding thud as Detective Marion punches Robert right in the face. A second later, Marion is back outside again, shaking his right hand. "Let's get out of here," he says.

* * *

Outside, puddles shine everywhere. Through the thick air, I hear Robert moaning something behind us, his voice distorted in a way that tells me Detective Marion broke his nose. I brush my fingertips over my own nose and pinch the bones there as we walk back to the car, my head flooding with adrenaline from everything that just happened.

"Will Robert call the police?" I ask. "About you . . . hitting him?"

"No." He sounds sure. "He knew he was asking for that." I watch the muscle ripple under his shirt as he drops into the car.

His energy is completely different than it was on the way to the studio, when he meant to confront Robert. We drive in the direction of the community health center, back to my car. How much of a relationship did she and Marion have? And who else knew about it? Marion started doing personal security for the James family after he arrested me. He'd proven himself, I understood. He cut his forearm taking the knife away from me and was given seven stitches at the Vanderbilt ER. I saw a picture online showing off the wound. Owen was beside him, looking at the camera. Shelly was on the other side. In the photo, she was looking at Marion.

I wonder if his and Shelly's relationship started the way I imagine: him taking on more and more responsibilities in his off time, meeting Finch and everyone else in their circle. I imagine him being understanding, too, about how much Owen worked. No doubt Shelly and he would be alone for hours at a time. I picture the two of them messaging and talking, more and more and more.

What if she took pictures for him like the one Andre and Malik saw her take?

Could he have fallen in love?

Of course.

"Sorry you had to hear all that," he says. "That was a dead end. Robert may be a dirtbag, but he didn't have anything to do with Shelly getting killed."

"How do you know?" I ask. I'm too curious not to, but unable not to sound cold from what I've learned about him and Shelly.

He winces as he bends his fingers back and forth, evidently sore from punching Robert.

"His phone. I guess he'd just been on it, because it wasn't locked. I looked through his call records. Just like he said, he called the police at seven PM, probably to report you for being at the house. He had to wait from then on for the cops to arrive. Our first call related to Shelly came in at seven twenty, which means she was killed before then, most likely. The crime scene in the park is too far from the house for Robert to have gotten there and back in time. And in any case, no one calls the cops and then commits a crime while waiting for them to show up."

I think this over. The timing sounds about right. But it still doesn't put me at ease.

"What is it?" he asks when he notices my silence.

"You . . . and Shelly."

He nods once, shyly.

"I should have known," I say quietly. "The way she looked at you and you looked at her after what happened at the concert . . . But she's married."

"Yes." Marion sighs. "I told myself that Shelly and Owen's marriage wasn't real, but that was to justify what we were doing because I knew it was wrong. I couldn't stop seeing her."

"Who knew? Aside from Robert."

"I thought no one did, honestly. I caught a few glances from the stage crew, but I always had a legitimate reason to be wherever

I was. I thought maybe Owen suspected near the end, but she told me he didn't. She was sure. Finch never knew; we were careful about that.

"She and I texted back and forth for more than a year, sometimes burner phones she bought and sometimes not. My number comes up on the records again and again. Metro doesn't have the content of all of those texts yet, but they will. And with everything else . . . there's good circumstantial evidence against me. If I was looking at it, I'd suspect me too. I look desperate. And maybe I was. I *am*. No, more than that, I'm *ashamed*. Did I think she was going to leave Owen? That we would be together? Maybe. Another part of me knew it was just a fantasy. Those texts read differently now, but no matter what, I would have never, ever, hurt her."

There is a catch in Detective Marion's voice. His jaw clamps down like he wants to bite back his feelings. "But that's not all. There were photos of Shelly that I saved on my phone, and what she'd written across them was pretty graphic. I'm praying to God they don't leak."

I hear the—*the word for extreme discomfort—anguish* in his voice as he considers photos of Shelly being posted online for anyone to see.

He runs his hands through his hair, making it stand up wildly. The car creaks again. The gas-dust smell hasn't gone anywhere. Maybe he knew they never could be a couple, that there was no way forward, but kept on seeing her anyway. Thinking about something so adult makes me shift in my seat. I've never had a boyfriend. I've never been touched by someone in the right way. I've wondered—after being in the dark, would the romantic part of my life ever be normal?

Love is in every song.

Love makes you do things.

"But it's over?" I ask. After all, he's been off her security for three weeks.

He nods.

"A few weeks ago, she stopped picking up. Then three weeks ago, she sent me a text saying that she couldn't see me anymore. Just like that. I know I should have just walked away, but after a year that seemed insane. I couldn't just show up at the house, so I called and texted. I know Shelly; she can't be alone. I followed her once, and Metro knows that. I left her a voice mail Metro played back to me." He looks at me then, right in the eye. "I said I was willing to do anything to keep her."

He sounds like a stalker.

Neither of us has to say it.

"Could Owen have found out?" I ask. I don't know everything about marriage, but I don't see how Owen could have been functioning as a husband and as a business partner while knowing that Shelly was cheating on him.

Marion bites the inside of his cheek the way I'm learning he does. "Believe me, I've wondered about it a lot in the last days. But the answer is, no, I don't think he knew, and I definitely don't think he killed her. Owen has a temper but he wasn't abusive. I think they were both lonely for a long time. He wanted her to be something she wasn't, and she was so young when she married him that she didn't know who she was in the beginning. No, if Owen had found out, it's more likely he'd want to kill *me*."

"I saw something between the two of them once." I tell Marion the story about the time I saw Owen grab Shelly's arm.

I hear the low-pitched buzz of the old tires on the road for a moment before he eventually says: "I saw a few moments like that, too. I don't want to say it made it easier for me to get close to her, but it probably did. They fought, true. But if I'm looking for a motive, there isn't one. Even if there was insurance, it's not like Owen needs money. She even said they talked about divorcing once Finch was out of the house. Plus, on a practical level, I don't know if Owen was away from people at any point last night. He was busy hosting the party, after all, because Shelly wasn't there."

The way he describes their relationship fits what I saw between the two of them at the Petersons' party: Owen calm but distant, going through the motions as a party guest, while Shelly seemed restless and lost and unhappy—and probably drunk.

I think Marion must be right. Owen was busy all last night, and even if he did somehow slip away, Finch would have recognized her own father. She would have *known*. She would have never gone back home. It has to have been someone else.

I ask very carefully, "Do you think . . . the person she was . . . seeing, was the . . .?"

"Maybe. But I'll tell you what, if it wasn't him, I guarantee you he knows something that will help put everything together. Metro already went through her phone, of course. Her communication is hard to track because half the time Shelly used burner phones for privacy. If anything ever leaked, she didn't want it tied to her number. Seemed shady, but I understood. The one that she was using last night was on the ground beside her. And Metro knows Shelly was sending texts from one of her burner phones *to* a burner phone for the entire last week. But we can't see what was in those messages, at least not yet."

Maybe he knew he and Shelly would never be a couple but kept seeing her anyway. I think about how love was in every one of her songs. I think about how they say love makes you *do things*. Then I remember something.

"Robert told you about the other car he saw."

"Yeah, he said it was a sports car, but that's not much to go on. Shelly lives in Belle Meade. Half the people in 37205 drive sports cars."

I picture the parking lot of the Belle Meade Country Club and know he is right.

"He said it was *white*," I remind him. "I know someone who owns a white P-O-R-S-C-H-E." As I tell Marion it's Brian Peterson, I see sweat form on his forehead.

"You're sure?" he asks, as the car's tires graze the curb on my right.

"One hundred percent."

I tell him about working the Petersons' party and going into the dark garage for Lane Peterson to get the sparkling water for Shelly—feeling my way through the garage to the refrigerator, my fingers touching the letters along the back of the car. The P-O-R-S-C-H-E letters raised up from the creamy paint.

We stop at a red light. A car beside ours is playing music so loudly I feel it through the seat in the backs of my legs. I hear paper crumple as Detective Marion reaches behind me. His hand comes forward with a can of Red Bull that he pops open with one hand. He drinks before grimacing at what I know is warm liquid.

I replay Brian's body language during the party in my mind— the glances he cut toward Shelly, the calm but cool handshake he'd given Owen. And Lane Peterson's nervousness, especially when she asked if I could get the water for Shelly. Lane had wanted Shelly to be steadier, less impulsive, and out of their house as quickly and quietly as possible.

I remember the way the cooks agreed that everyone in Nashville was in love with Shelly—but why would Brian have wanted to hurt her? Did he and Shelly have an argument about whether or not to leave their partners? Did she reject him?

Brian was so composed at his party. Such a family man. Could he have gone that crazy? Driven to a murdering rage by . . . an argument?

I don't know.

But there is another part too—an action that my suspicions can't explain: The man on top of the hill didn't run away. He *chased me*. I wonder if what happened in the park was somehow an accident.

Nine blows to the head, I think. That's no accident.

Marion shakes his head slightly as we start moving again.

"Let's just say that white Porsche belongs to Brian Peterson, and that Shelly left to meet him last night. There would still have to be some proof to justify a search warrant to collect other evidence either from the car or the Petersons' house. Tire tracks could help. The scene was pretty washed out, but you would be amazed what they can find. If they could match his tires to tracks left at the scene, then potentially Metro could get a warrant to search his car and the house. What I really would need—what *the police* would need, I mean—are things they can't currently get. Dirt from the bottoms of Brian's shoes, for example. Sometimes police get lucky and find a car parked in a public place and can get a visual of the tires for a match, then try to make a case for a warrant. In this case, I don't know."

My thoughts spin with everything he just told me. My hands fidget in my lap as my mind tries to keep up, but my gut is churning, and I'm curious about why he is telling me anything at all. But he keeps on talking, maybe more to himself than to me, and I listen intently.

"Metro pinged that phone they got the 911 call from and nothing came back. It might be long gone, but it may just be turned off. If *that phone* was found, in either Brian's car or anywhere in the house, it would be enough to get a search warrant, and maybe enough to make an arrest."

The car slows and Marion pulls into an alleyway that runs beside the mental health center parking lot. I see my car as Marion creeps to a halt. The same trees sway above the same gold roof, but the light reflecting off it now looks dull and different. He adjusts the column shifter and the old car idles heavily.

Marion rubs his eyes like the meeting with Robert took something out of him and points to the road ahead with the bottom of the Red Bull can.

"I've asked enough of you already, so I don't want to ask for anything more, but if you can forget that you've seen me for the next few days, I would appreciate that."

"Forgotten."

I remember how I felt getting into Detective Marion's car, and how quickly everything had changed—the panic over thinking he was attacking me had become a kind of pride for being helpful. For the most part I trust him.

"Where are you going now?" I ask. "You're going to arrest . . ."

"I can't *arrest* anybody right now. I can't even collect evidence." He takes another sip of the warm Red Bull and makes a face like he wants to spit it out. He closes his eyes. "Tell me one more time about the man you saw last night. The man you saw up on the trail."

I know what he wants to know.

"It could have been Brian," I say. "It was dark, but he was tall. He wore a baseball hat I think."

My memory—no one ever seems to think it is accurate, but it is. I *always* remember right.

"Finch told you the man chased her too. Did she describe him?"

I search my memory. "No."

She'd been running away, as fast as she could, from the man who murdered her mother.

Marion makes a fist. "I haven't heard about funeral arrangements yet, but I assume you know there's an impromptu function in Shelly's memory downtown tonight."

I nod, reluctantly. Of course I know about it.

"A lot of people will show up, I'm sure. There will be a stage, a band or two, but the safest place for you is at home. Don't give Williams or anyone in Metro a reason to pick you up, okay?"

I want to say I hadn't planned on going, but my history of decision making is pretty poor. I answer him with a look that says *I understand*. I reach for the door handle again but stop.

"How do I contact you?"

"You don't. I want you to keep talking with your counselor, okay?" He motions toward her office.

"What if I *need* to talk to you? What if I think of something else?"

He nods solemnly when he sees fear in my eyes. I shrink back against the seat as he reaches to the glove box, his shoulder nearly touching me—so close I register his sweat and shampoo smell. He pulls a small black bag from the glove box and empties it, dropping an old flip phone into his lap. I wonder: Was this the phone he used to talk to Shelly?

Marion sees me noticing the bag.

"It's called a faraday bag. It keeps a phone from being tracked. Copper wiring lines the inside, as fine as hair. Most electronic devices—phones, even newer cars—can be pinged, but this is like a black hole that signals can't hit." He leans back and pops open the phone. "Here. What's your number?"

I tell it to him and he punches the keys. My phone buzzes a second later. "It's untraceable," he says, turning off the phone again. He returns it to the bag and then sets the bag back in the glove box. "It's not optimal, but I'll check it, okay? My best advice is to just go home and stay there for now."

Because there's a killer among us.

"Are the police still looking for you?" I ask.

"They have their eyes on me, sure. But most people won't do what it takes to stay hidden," he says. "I know how to not be found."

If anyone else had said it, I might have laughed.

I start out the door, then twist my mouth as I remember I have no idea how much gas I have. I can't remember when I last calculated my mileage.

"What is it?" Marion asks.

"I'm just thinking . . . I don't know how much gas I have." I don't want to tell him about Ken and my job and my last few dollars, but I see in Detective Marion's eyes that he puts it together. He reopens the glove box, finds his wallet, then hands me two twenty-dollar bills. I shake my head but he sets them in my lap.

"Get some gas, something to eat," he says.

I tell him "thank you" as I get out, already folding the bills inside my pocket, like making them smaller will keep them safe. From the parking lot, I watch him pull away, the sound of the old car eventually fading.

I drive back to my apartment with my head full of thoughts. The encounter has left me disoriented enough that if something else crazy happened right then, it might not even register. My throat feels like I'd tried swallowing food before chewing it. The hum of my car tires on the road sounds the way anticipation feels. Learning the extent of Marion's relationship with Shelly surprised me some, but it fit with the other side of Shelly I was starting to understand. I wonder what Marion thought would happen between the two of them. Did he picture her moving out of the mansion and in with him? Did he see Finch in their lives? Did he imagine staying together, having more kids? Or maybe he was love-blind and *made* her into something she wasn't.

Even if I don't like how they became involved, my heart trusts him. I start daydreaming a scenario that might have been his— Marion and Shelly walking hand in hand through the tall grass in an East Tennessee field, Finch nearby. Maybe the three of them would have rented a cabin for a long holiday weekend together.

Did Marion dream about that? About parenthood?

If so, Shelly had ended that dream when she stopped her relationship with Marion.

"Someone was with her," Finch had told me. "A man, standing over her." Shelly had started seeing another man, but she kept who it was a secret.

She went into the woods to meet him, but never came back out.

12

have to have quiet to sort through what just happened. I head to my apartment to be alone. I'm so shaken up I run a red light without noticing, and a horn sounds angrily beside me. I slow down and tell myself to be smarter. As I crest the small hill before reaching my complex, I see three police cars circled in the parking lot. The hedges that line the lot are bleached white by their headlights. The door to my building is propped open, and dark uniforms pass in and out.

I hit the brakes, but not quickly enough, and my car rocks over the lip of the road. A tall cop turns around as my headlights splash over the scene, his head pivoting like a crane's. I know it's Detective Williams just by the way he stands.

Light explodes as I begin to turn the wheel—flashing police blue, so bright it reflects off every surface. A siren chirps so loudly I jump in my seat. Detective Williams's hands are resting on his hips. His face is in shadow, but I picture his satisfied expression—a look that says he's been waiting for me. He holds up his hand like he's saying *halt*, then points to the empty space where he wants me to park.

I've come home to a trap that I somehow baited myself. I've driven right into it. Someone called the police, but who? Robert? Of course, I think.

I consider the distance back to the road with a quick glance in the rearview mirror. I wonder for half a second if the cars parked at the end of the row would block me from turning around—from gunning it. But I see clearly there is no way out. Time starts to slow down again.

Williams moves behind my car. His eyes look hungry, like those of a starving person finally being offered a meal. Two other officers bound down the apartment steps toward us. Some of my neighbors appear on their porches, watching everything unfold. A girl in a long-sleeved shirt wraps her arms around her waist. Her boyfriend looks on grimly beside her, his arm around her shoulder. I see him bend down to her, whispering something in her ear.

"Go ahead and turn off your car, Ms. Duval. I need you to step out of the vehicle and leave your keys inside," Williams says.

I realize what is happening is not the ending of a story but the start of another story entirely. And I have no idea where it will go. I ache to return to a week ago, even two days ago. I know I could stop everything bad from happening. I could and I *would*. But now I have to listen to Detective Williams. A small part of me holds on to the hope that I can somehow explain everything to him, that maybe he will want to hear about what I've learned. It's a wish I'm not ready to give up on entirely.

I get out, my shoes slipping on the wet pavement.

"Ms. Duval, we're executing a search warrant into your residence at this time. Come with me."

Another police car pulls into the lot. I blink the headlights away, shaking it out of my vision while Detective Williams follows me up the steps. In the hallway everything is the same— same dusty smell, same flickering light overhead—except everything feels like we are in a movie now. Like we're on a screen being watched by an audience that is somewhere else.

The front door of my apartment is open. From inside a radio crackles. My lungs seem to press into my ribs as pressure builds in my chest. Every light in the apartment seems to be turned on. The shadow of someone moves across the kitchen wall. I want to rush forward to see, but Detective Williams's presence is like a dragging anchor behind me.

At the door, I see my fears are justified. Five policemen are inside. Only one looks up as we enter. The others go about their jobs, busily picking apart my space. One crouches under my sink like a plumber, his flashlight making the clear plastic bottles around him glow.

Part of me is furious at this intrusion, but I know I can't show it—not now. *Act normal*, I tell myself, *as normal as possible. You will get your chance to explain everything.* Maybe Detective Marion will show up and help untangle this mess.

The vacuum lines on my carpet are a blur of their dark footprints. I understand the police mean to find evidence against me, but it looks like what they really want is to destroy as many of my things as possible. They're wearing uniforms, but I feel like I am being robbed. *The word for when you can't protect yourself* . . . The *helplessness* is the worst part. I want to shout for them to stop, to scratch at their clothes, to call for help, but I can do nothing except watch.

Detective Williams pulls one of my chairs away from the kitchen table. It screeches across the linoleum. "Have a seat here, Ms. Duval," he says in the same horrible, patronizing tone he used earlier, then goes into my bedroom to speak to whoever is in there.

I try not to watch the man under my sink as I wonder if the police know where Detective Marion is. If they want to know if I've seen him, what will I tell them? Or about confronting Robert at the studio? I try to breathe in the way Ms. Parsons showed me, but my lungs feel like they've shrunk. When I inhale, they can't hold any air. My head buzzes with *wanting*—to run again, for things to make *sense*. My thoughts are like angry, fighting things, clawing their way on top of one another.

Detective Williams is asking someone, "You sure?" He sounds like he has stifled a laugh. Maybe this is just business for him, just another day at work.

A second later, he emerges from my bedroom holding a crowbar. He walks with such purpose that I know where he means to go. I flash back to yesterday morning—him, me, and Detective Marion sitting around this very table. Me trying to keep my eyes off the bottom drawer of my dresser. Now he looks down at the very same thing, smacking the crowbar against his palm.

"Last chance to open this up for us," he tells me, then winks.

"Stop," I say. "Please."

Williams hesitates. He tests the edge of the crowbar against his thumb as the officer looking under my sink shifts forward and looks up, his neck an accordion of wrinkles.

I need to tell them about Brian Peterson, but my head is a mess. Where would I begin?

"There's something else, something I know," I manage to say.

Williams shakes his head.

"I'm sure you *do* know a thing or two. You can give a statement later. The only thing now is whether you want to open this drawer or watch me pry it open. Your choice."

I twist the soles of my shoes on my kitchen floor and dig my fingernails into the knees of my jeans. Not wanting to open the drawer isn't about the restraining order. I'm already in trouble. The only reason charges haven't been pressed already is the police have been too busy to bother—maybe that is about to change.

No, wanting to keep the drawer locked is about having things that are mine. Only mine. Possessions. Privacy. A safe place.

A dream.

Unless you have one, you can't explain wanting to protect it. Sometimes, I wonder if I am the only one on earth with a private world.

Williams widens his eyes at me, waits one more moment. Then he shrugs and begins to kneel.

"I'll open it," I say.

I walk across the living room, my shoes adding more prints to the marked-all-over carpet. My space feels ruined already, but keeping things a certain way doesn't really matter anymore. Williams glances at the officer standing in the kitchen like he's just won some kind of bet while I reach inside the shade of my floor lamp, my fingers finding the space between folded fabric and the plastic piece, and pull out a key—shiny and silver and small. It looks strange as I hold it in my hand, almost like I am seeing it for the first time. It's warm in my palm from the heat of the lightbulb.

Inside I feel like I'm falling, collapsing, as Williams makes space for me. I feel a surge in my throat, like both a cough and a sob, as I slip the key into the lock. Another officer comes up beside Williams. Then another.

I pull open the drawer and step away. I go to my seat at the table as Williams begins to go through what I've kept to myself— James memorabilia sits on top, all there now for him to see. Even having it risks breaking the court order, I know. Ticket stubs. A program. Photos of Shelly I'd taken and printed at the library. There is a copy of Shelly's high school yearbook I ordered on eBay. Bags of the confetti dropped during their shows. One of Owen's guitar picks in another bag.

I spent too much of my state stipend on it. I can't help it, I want to say. I guess I could tell the police that most of it came from Robert, but would that matter to Williams? I can feel that it won't. His drive to arrest me feels so focused.

Williams jerks his head back and hollers, "Somebody take a few pictures of this. And I'm going to need some evidence bags."

One of the cops steps forward with a camera. Then, a flash, blinding me.

Another cop comes forward and hands Williams a set of large tweezers and a stack of Ziplock Piece by piece, he lifts and examines my things. He looks at me, just once, and quickly shakes his head. Then he goes back to sorting through the drawer the way kids sort candy at Halloween. He's found what he was looking for. Hiding it only made it worse. He seems to believe he is holding confirmation in his hands.

Another flash.

My stomach turns over as I watch.

Williams reaches into the drawer and picks up the Discman. I had it wrapped in a soft cotton cloth to protect it from scratches and dust. A shudder goes through my body. All I can think is: *What if he drops it?* I could buy a new one, but it would never be the same. My legs are tight like I mean to spring forward. My hands grip the bottom of the chair.

Williams squints at it and removes the cloth, drops it on the carpet where it partly covers the round black tip of his shoe. "Huh," is what he says, like he is puzzled by a relic. Maybe that's what it is to him.

But what he holds in his hands kept me alive for thirteen months. He doesn't understand that what he's holding is a world.

I think I may throw up across the table when he pops open the cover and peers inside. "Please," I say, out loud.

Williams turns his back to me, holds the Discman to his ear, and shakes it.

"No, please," I beg. "I have to have that."

The other officers look at me, then exchange glances.

"Sometimes, there are little compartments in these things," he tells the others. He pulls out Shelly's CD and drops it onto the floor beside the cloth, then digs his thumbnail into the spring-loaded battery cover.

I shut my eyes in a long blink, a reminder not to feel sorry for myself. Finch and Owen lost much, much more. Shelly James actually lost her life. But I can't watch Williams anymore. I set my head down on the table over my folded arms.

I will not cry in front of these men, I think.

A second later, a different cop rushes in. I feel the table tremble from his footsteps and prop my chin on my arm, looking up. He whispers something to Detective Williams, who looks confused and asks, "Really?"

They both look at me. In that second, the room's air pressure drops, the way it does right before a thunderstorm. When another cop comes over, I hear Williams tell him clearly, ". . . likely recovered the murder weapon."

No.

I shake my head. That's not possible.

I wasn't present when Shelly James was killed. I have no idea what weapon killed Shelly James. I couldn't possibly have it.

But they are sure I do.

The look on Detective Williams's face tells me everything I need to know about his intentions now. He has a drawer filled with evidence, a suspect he can place at the scene of the crime, and now a murder weapon. I am not guilty, but it sure as hell looks like I am—even to me.

His handcuffs jangle as he takes them from his belt. The cop beside him rests his hand on the butt of his gun.

"Jessie, stand up for me."

I try to talk but my throat feels airless and dry. Did I hear right? Why else would Williams be about to arrest me?

"Turn around," he says, "and spread your feet apart. Put your hands together behind your back."

He is about to touch me.

"Let me . . . put them on," I try, finally finding the words. I hold my hands out in front of me. I don't want to go, but it will be better this way.

"Turn," he barks. "Now."

Beside me, the hallway light flickers. The room spins a little like a rolling screen on an old TV.

A hand suddenly grabs my shoulder from behind. Electricity shoots through my body from the suddenness of the touch. As I jerk upward, the back of my skull connects with the bridge of the cop's nose.

After that, everything happens very fast.

Drops of blood splatter all over my kitchen floor. The cop I've hit starts to shout as his shoe smears them horribly. Williams's eyes widen as he lunges forward, searching for my wrists. I can't think, don't think, knock over the chair I've been sitting in as I turn, the top beam catching Williams's shin. He jumps back, wincing.

"Somebody fucking grab her," he screams.

Two more cops rush out of my bedroom, but I'm already out the front door. I run into the hall, ducking under the arms of another cop who tries to block my way. I fling open the hallway door and tear down the steps, into the night.

I've officially lost my mind.

You can't run from police, I know. At least not for long. I have no idea where I mean to go, or how to get away. I am not Detective Marion, able to "lay low" until I can crack the case. Wherever *he* is, he suddenly is of no concern to the police. I am now *the* suspect.

My legs turn, my feet landing one ahead of the other, a reflex that keeps firing. I tell myself I can figure out where I'm going later. I just breathe and go as voices shout behind me, yelling my name, telling me to stop. An engine starts and blue lights begin to move. I cut across the road without looking, a car screeching to a stop inches from me, its horn blaring, its driver furious. The thick night air stings the back of my throat. I grip the top of the wooden fence, my hands knocking loose dust and debris that's settled there from the trees above. The board bends where I plant my foot but holds my weight as I throw my other leg over the top.

I see the bounce of approaching flashlights during the second I'm poised on top. I hear the commanding call of men's voices telling me to stop immediately, to go no farther. But I do the opposite—I let go and fall backward, my hair whipping around my cheeks. The ground is a jolt against my back that shakes my whole body, forcing the air from my chest.

I roll once, and for a second my legs feel numb. I gasp, but can't breathe. I force myself to roll onto my stomach, where I push myself up onto my elbows, then onto my hands. I heave myself forward, my head light from moving without oxygen. I pray my breathing will come back quickly. Already I hear boots scraping against wood, the police at the fence, trying to scale it—unable to find traction enough to let them get over the top.

Gravity seems to shove at my back, forcing me down the small hill into a parking lot, then toward a sidewalk. I brush myself off as I go, staggering, the world spinning as I manage to draw in tiny breaths.

I recognize the street in front of me, though I've never approached it from this side. Ahead is the bus stop where I bounced from one foot to the other to stay warm the winter before I saved enough for my car, where each morning I pulled my sleeves over my frozen hands.

I glance behind me—they still have not cleared the fence. The bus shelter is thirty feet away, then twenty, and is empty. I hurry to it as the bus rounds the corner with its sad-sounding acceleration and blinding, near eye-level lights. The air brakes cry out just as I reach the shelter. I keep my eyes down and climb aboard as the door swings open. I brush clumps of dirt from my shirt as I take my seat and then disappear down the dark road, hoping like hell there will be time before I'm arrested to do what I know I have to do.

* * *

I change buses to get to where I'm going, and the second is slightly more crowded than the first. This time the driver gives me a long, disapproving look as I board and make my way to an empty seat near the back. Any other day riding the bus might have been a chance to sit quietly and think, but now I keep looking up at the rearview mirror, catching the driver's gaze twice. *Stop*, I tell myself, *eyes down, between your shoes*. Because there is no going dim—not here, not now. The driver might not be able to place me fully, but he recognizes me, at least partially. I see a searching intensity in his eyes.

But my mind can't fully process him. Too much of it is trying to figure out how the *murder weapon* was found in my apartment. Just when I thought I was starting to understand where I fit into the story, the structure had crumbled again.

What kind of weapon was it? Neither cop said. Did Williams plant it somehow? I don't think so—he seemed satisfied when its discovery was announced, but a little surprised too.

Outside, a police car goes screaming past, headed in the other direction, its red-and-blue lights on, siren shrieking until it fades. Is it headed toward my neighborhood? There are probably all kinds of ways to find me—police techniques I could never begin to guess. My tongue's tip finds my chipped tooth as I picture Marion and his faraday bag and think of how he described staying hidden. He'd said most people weren't "willing" to do what it took.

I will be, I know.

I am.

At my stop, I get off at a measured pace, then trot up the sidewalk toward the store I mean to go to, its cursive sign red and aglow. I pull my phone from my back pocket, pausing for a second to appreciate the miracle of it still being in my possession—somehow it managed to stay in place during my escape over the fence. The screen is a spiderweb of cracks, but lights up when I touch it. I find Detective Marion's number as the store's glass door whooshes open.

The cool air-conditioning chills the sweat on my skin. Soft rock plays as I step into the fluorescent light. I press the phone to my ear and listen to the call ringing, picturing his phone tucked away in the little bag he showed me—maybe still in the glove box of his car. As I move into the first aisle I pass a clerk and switch the phone to my other hand to shield my face. When the call goes to voice mail, I curse under my breath, then turn into another aisle. I pick a pine needle from my sleeve as I scan the shelves. I don't know where to find what I am looking for, but there is no way to ask. *Think, pay attention. Stay calm and look.*

A second later, the phone rings in my hand, making me jump a little. During the pause between rings, I realize I'd partly given up hope of reaching him. I answer in a whisper, "Detective?"

"Hello?" he asks. "You called?"

"Yes," I say . . . *the word for having a style and a strategy,* trying to ask my question tactfully. "You mentioned collecting evidence before—samples and tire prints. If you could do that rubbing on a tire, what would you use?"

"Um," he begins, tiredly. I picture his hand half-covering a confused expression on his face. We parted ways less than an hour earlier.

"For the tire, you'd just need a picture to start. Shoes, you'd be scraping bits of dried mud, soil. The analysts look for a match to place them at the crime scene. Why? Did you remember something? About the car?"

This is going to be easier than I'd thought. No real rubbing on the tire.

I know how to handle the physical evidence—I just watched the police with my things. I turn down the aisle where the Ziploc bags are kept, aware now of the black-domed store cameras recording me from above.

"Are . . . you there?" he asks. "Listen, promise me you aren't going to that memorial event tonight. It would be so easy for people to get the wrong idea. Officers know to look for you and won't hesitate to pick you up, and I don't want you to spend any more time in jail. Okay?" He sounds like he's walking now. I hear street sounds in the background.

He and I aren't much alike—no, we are hardly *anything* alike. There are about a hundred reasons for us not to trust each other, but we're helping each other despite them. My head finally puts words to how I feel about Detective Marion: he is kind to me because that's the kind of person he is.

"I promise," I say. "I don't want to get arrested again. I don't need another chipped tooth."

He laughs a little. The sound brings me a few seconds of happiness.

"I'm sorry about that. You were lighter than I thought and I had to get you to the ground."

It's no biggie, I want to say. It's not like you locked me in a closet for a year.

"Sometime . . ." he begins, then hesitates. "Sometime, I'd like to get that fixed for you."

I don't know how to respond. If he only knew, that chip is the least of my worries at the moment.

"Have you found anything?" I ask. "Of Brian's?"

"No. I drove by hoping I'd get lucky with the car parked out-side. But, no, collecting evidence isn't going to be easy. And apparently now there's added security at their house. Either Brian Peterson truly thinks a killer is on the loose and is afraid for his family, or he's over-correcting. He's trying to make it look like he's on the right side of this thing by acting like they're in danger, too."

This thing.

This thing that ended Shelly's life and swirled ours together. My mind wanders to what she must have looked like lying on the ground, lifeless—an image I still can't fit together with the ener-getic, charismatic woman who ran across stages all her life.

I shake the thought from my head. "Can you meet me at the Belle Meade Walgreens in an hour?"

I hear him sigh.

"I'm lost, Jessie. Mind telling me what's going on?"

He doesn't know that Williams has searched my apartment. This is good. I pray he doesn't hear anything in the next hour about the fact that I've run.

"Can you? Something I want to give you in person," I say. It's slightly misleading, but necessary.

There's a pause during which I picture him checking the time.

"The one on Harding?" he asks, finally.

I tell him yes, then hang up.

Marion said he couldn't gather evidence. But I can. I know how to get in and out of a house, and how to be invisible while I do it. I only have one chance to find the evidence that will solve Shelly's murder and prove my innocence.

I buy the Ziploc bags and a set of tweezers from a sleepy-eyed clerk with one eye on her phone. On the TV screen behind her, I see a shot of a crowd with a ticker along the bottom that reads: *Shelly James Memorial*. The camera cuts to a shot of Municipal Auditorium, where people have already begun to gather, the sky behind them yellowed by the streetlights. Some are holding candles, a few others carrying signs. One sign is held by a woman whose hair looks like Shelly's. It reads: MISS YOU ALWAYS. Another says, SEE YOU IN HEAVEN, SHELLY JAMES.

The fine print on the ticker says: *Doors open at 7PM, the service begins at 8*. I check the time on my phone, then take a left out the door and cross the street into the Petersons' neighborhood.

13

The Petersons' neighborhood feels quieter than it did a week ago even though it looks the same—like a fog of no-talking and no-music has settled over everything. Tree branches droop sadly, and no wind plays through their branches.

I pass the streets in the same order as when I'd come for the party: Aspen, Dogwood, Live Oak. The names impressed me before, but now they make me think of fake advertising, of lies, of chaos below a perfect surface. I can't help but think: *a person who lives among these idyllic names could be very, very dangerous.* A chill runs through me. Ken told us about Brian Peterson's business tactics. I don't know why I didn't listen more closely. No, I know why I didn't listen. I *wanted* to believe in the Petersons' perfect family. Just like I wanted to believe the James family was perfect. That wanting made me ignore the obvious. I feel a weird resentment for the person I was nine days earlier, for being so naïve. Now, I play a different part—same place, new goal. I know I can find evidence that will show Brian went into the woods last night.

If Brian was seeing Shelly, what would have pushed him to kill her? Did he go into the woods intending to? Or had she told him something that sent him into a rage? Had she planned to come out with their affair? If so, why would she be going to such lengths to keep their meeting a secret? I wonder if her judgment was clouded by pills. I wonder if he knew about her taking them, as Owen clearly did. One thing was for sure—if Brian was in the woods with Shelly when she died, he knew more details about what happened than I did.

I walk to the end of the Petersons' street and wait until I see their black SUV pass, presumably heading for the memorial. I count three shapes inside, and my heart pounds the way it used to before a James show. I remind myself that what I'm about to do is for the right reasons—I don't like turning dim to go where I shouldn't, but now I have to. I grind my teeth. My back is hot with sweat.

I want to listen to an Owen and Shelly James song, but I can't. I am alone now.

I circle around back, into the driveway of a house directly behind the Petersons' that is under construction. A dumpster heaped with scrap metal and plywood sits in the side yard. All the windows are dark. The Petersons' roof is just over the fence, steep and gray against the almost-black sky. I cut through their neighbors' backyard, then slip under a fence, the wood is wet and soft against my fingers. A guard wearing a black uniform is sitting on the Petersons' back step biting his thumbnail. Extra security, just like Marion said.

I cross the back lawn to the side porch, staying in the shadows. A dog barks in the distance. Another answers. I freeze and wait for them to stop. Not being seen requires moving very slowly and being exquisitely patient. I let out my breath and stay still until the dogs are quiet, then wait—maybe two minutes—until the guard looks the other way. I slip up the driveway along the side of the house, lift the planter, and find the key just where I know it will be from my last time here. I wipe my hands on the sides of my jeans, unlock the back door, and step inside.

Inside the house, I face a soundless world. Only a week has passed since the Petersons' party, but it feels like much longer. The air smells *rich*, like faint cologne. Clean as heaven on the pages of a magazine. I've never belonged in a place like this, but alone now I feel especially alien. I slip my shoes off and set them beside the door, then leave the key inside the left one so I'll remember to put it back when I leave.

I cradle my collection materials against my stomach, the plastic warm against my palm. Through the back window, I can see the side of the guard's head, his hair clipped scalp-short, his expression so blank he can only be daydreaming.

I unbox the tweezers. I'll go from room to room and pick up what is needed. I'll label each sample, one by one. Maybe I'll get lucky, I think, and find the other phone. No matter where that was found, it could surely be traced to Brian. And surely, if an anonymous call can influence an entire investigation, evidence can be dropped off anonymously too. Maybe Marion can do that, I think. I'll have to leave that part up to him. Maybe I can find enough to make them question Brian.

I know my plan is not a particularly good one, but neither is walking away, or going to jail. I have to try something.

I look again at the framed family photographs I was so impressed by a week ago. The perfect family. There they are skiing. There are their heads tossed back in laughter. There they are visiting the campus of Sean's expensive soon-to-be college. The photos look different the second time, knowing what I think I do about Brian. When I look closer, they look like framed lies.

I decide to document the tire tread first. If I get caught in the garage, I reason, I can at least find more than one way out. I move through the kitchen silently—rolling my feet heel to toe, heel to toe, resting my weight on the outside of each foot.

I think of Lane Peterson's voice as she sent me down to fetch water for Shelly. *"Ms. James might like something else to drink besides wine."* If Brian and Shelly were involved, did Lane know? And if so, when had she found out? Maybe that night. I remember the murmurs about Shelly's behavior I'd heard. I wasn't the only one who sensed that something was off.

I leave the door to the garage slightly open for when I come back up, the metal strike plates millimeters apart. Inside it is what *most* people would call pitch-dark, but around the doors are seams of faint light—enough to see by once my eyes adjust.

I heard once that jazz musicians leave out some notes on purpose so a listener's mind has to fill them in to hear the full song. Seeing in the dark is like that. I see just enough to know where things are—parts, shapes—and my mind fills in the rest. I've been here before, so I know which car is parked where. When the Petersons left, I saw them go by in their SUV, so I figure the P-O-R-S-C-H-E will still be closest to the kitchen door. My fingertips trace along the back bumper until I find the letters' familiar ridges.

The cement floor is hard against my knee when I go to the rear tire, kneel, and take my phone from my pocket. The screen is shattered but lights up, the battery still with some charge. The tiny ridges in the cracked screen brush against my thumb as I breathe in the smell of dry grass and dust. I find the camera setting, touch the lightning-bolt icon for the flash, point it at the tire, and close my eyes tight. I know the photo takes because my eyelids light up red. I do this three more times, each photo at a slightly different angle so there is no mistaking the tire. Then I stand and take photos of the back of the car for context. When I send these to Marion, I want there to be no mistake about whose tire I've photographed.

I go back up the steps and close the door, holding the knob as it turns back into place so there will be no loud click, no sound at all.

I remind myself not to hurry. Hurrying makes noise.

Next, upstairs. There is only one way up and thus one way out short of breaking a window, which I know I won't have time to do should a security guard rush me. The thought of being trapped there makes my stomach tighten as I lean against a door frame in the kitchen and look for the guard. He is still on the patio, sitting in the same position, his face now lit by his phone. Past him, a firefly lights up in fluorescent yellow—just a quick wink as it hovers over the backyard. Then another, like they're talking to each other. But the guard seems not to notice. His head stays still, aimed at his phone, the ripple of his double chin lit from below.

I get close enough as I move through the kitchen that I could make him turn with a whisper, but I stay silent, a shadow within a shadow. I pass the hallway where I overheard Owen and Shelly's conversation, then pivot on the first stair on the ball of my foot, using the heavy banister to start up toward the bedrooms.

Finding my way through this part of the house requires more guesswork. The hallway at the top of the stairs leads to three doors on each side. In the first room on my left I see a stack of boxes beside the door, clothes draped over the bed. This is Sean's room, I realize. He's obviously packing for his move to college in a few days.

The bedroom on the opposite side of the hallway has a four-poster bed. The furniture looks antique—more for appearance than for daily use—and the bedspread is tucked in so tidily, I figure the room must be for guests. Even the air there seems still.

I continue moving forward, rolling my feet heel-to-toe along the runner. The hardwood floor is old enough that any pressure creates noise no matter how careful I am, and I wince each time I hear myself. One creak is loud enough that I stop and I hold my breath. I look behind me, hoping not to see the security guard's shape coming up the stairs. Good thing he is on his phone, I think, hoping I can count on him being distracted a little longer. After maybe a minute, my foot finds a different board, and I start forward again.

The next door on the left is closed. I turn the knob slowly until it gives way, then push the door open an inch at a time. It is the Petersons' bedroom—everything in its place, like a set from a movie. I haven't felt guilty about being inside their house, but seeing the bedroom seems . . . *The word for when something is yours alone* . . . Being among their things seems so *personal.* Stepping through the door feels like breaking into church. I have to remind myself of what is at stake.

I find the closet and pop open the sample bags. I scrape the bottoms of three of Brian's athletic shoes—sort of like the way I've seen on TV shows, and sort of the way I saw police taking evidence from my place—then seal the bags back up and put them in my pocket.

I exhale.

Now is when I have to be most careful, because what I want more than anything is to run. But I have to leave silently—out the back, remembering to put the key back in its place before I make my way through the backyard. In the hallway, I hear only the steady sound of my own breathing.

But then I hear another sound.

A downstairs door is closing.

I hold still, my whole body trying to unhear the noise, my heart crashing like waves. Its whoosh fills my ears. A light flicks on somewhere below, and the stairwell becomes slightly brighter. The banister now casts a steep diagonal shadow onto the wall. I hear the jangle of keys dropping onto a hard surface, then footsteps.

Shit.

Shit, shit, shit.

I duck into Sean's room, where I steady myself against a stack of boxes, my heart hammering so hard that my hands vibrate with each beat.

What time is it? Why are they home so soon?

Fragments of speech echo up the stairwell. I recognize each voice immediately.

Brian Peterson says, ". . . Abso*lute*ly let's go out." His normally deep, authoritative voice sounds drained of energy.

Then Lane replies, ". . . don't feel like cooking some big thing."

They have only stopped off home, I understand, just as I hear the pounding of footsteps on the stairs. I look around. My feet feel planted, or like they're glued to the floor. If it's Brian and Lane talking downstairs, I know exactly whose steps I'm hearing. In a few seconds, his door will swing open and he and I will be face to face.

There's no way out—it's just like I was afraid it might happen. My eyes search the stacks of boxes, the loose tissue paper on top wafting in the breeze of a slowly turning fan. The window would take too long to open, and the fall from the second story would be at least twenty feet. I'd risk breaking my legs.

A thump vibrates through the hallway—a footfall at the top of the stairs heavy enough that the framed photo on the wall rattles slightly.

There's only one place to go.

I slip into Sean's closet, then pull the door toward me without closing it all the way. Every muscle in my body tenses.

I am a ghost, haunting the house.

The door to Sean's room bursts open, and I hear a rumble and then the springy bounce of a body dropping onto a bed.

Slowly, I tell myself. *Breathe slowly.*

When Ms. Parsons taught me coping skills, I'm sure she never imagined I would use them like this.

Through the door slats, I watch Sean kick off a shoe with the toe of his other foot.

His mother's voice comes from downstairs, "Sean, we're leaving in a few minutes, okay?"

He shouts back, "Okay, Mom." His voice is so loud it seems impossible—some kind of punishment for me having kept so quiet a minute before. My heart races as I watch Sean being so casual in the very place I'd just been. Soft cotton sleeves brush against my cheeks and arms, the smell of his clothes is all around me. They smell like a guy wears them, and like detergent, and a little like plastic because they are all pretty new. I keep breathing as slowly as I can, with no idea what I will do if he opens the door. I hear the rip of tape unsticking, then the scratch of cardboard on cardboard.

My head spins as I realize what is about to happen: I'm having a panic attack. The confinement is too much. His being in the room, his physical closeness, traps me inside, and I feel my head grow light as breath leaves my body. As if on cue, sweat forms on my forehead. My hands begin to go numb, so I tense and release them to encourage blood flow there.

I can't gasp or make a sound, because if I do it will finish me. I'll surely go back to jail and whoever killed Shelly will be free. And yet every part of my body wants to quickly draw in air—to hyperventilate—to get oxygen back into my blood.

Oh, Ms. Parsons, when you taught me how to handle panic attacks, you never imagined a situation like this.

Outside the closet door, I hear Sean opening drawers and slamming them shut. He mutters something to himself, distractedly.

I hear Ms. Parsons's voice telling me, "Breathe," and I force myself to do it the way she showed me—in, very slowly to a count of four, until my lungs are uncomfortably full, then holding that breath for two seconds before letting it out again to another count of four.

Repeat.

Remember—this will pass. I tell myself that panic is just a temporary feeling, not a permanent state. It rolls in like a wave and will roll away again. I go through the breathing sequence again, as silently as I can. I pray that Sean won't hear me. And that he won't open the door. If he does, I'm caught. I've never been more vulnerable.

Stop. Redirect your thoughts.

I tell myself I could fight my way out of this house if it came down to it. I know how to hit. I could get out, away.

I draw another breath. I count as I let it in, hold it, and let it out. I ground myself by focusing on the texture of fabric—one of his shirt sleeves.

The spinning is less. My muscles grow less rigid.

And eventually, my heart rate begins to slow. Gradually my lungs feel fuller.

It's only then I can listen.

Sean mutters the word "T-shirt." Then a second later, I hear him say, "Fuck."

"Hey," he whispers, "I told you don't text that shit."

I realize he is speaking into his phone.

"Don't be *sorry*, just don't fucking do it, okay?" he says before his voice softens. "We did go, not like it was my idea or anything. I think my mom had some kind of FOMO. But it was so crowded, it was nuts. We bounced after like fifteen minutes."

His mattress springs whine as he falls onto his bed again. I rest against the back of the closet, praying that he won't see me.

"Whatever, just don't text me about it. Of course it was fucked up. How could me being there *not* be fucked up? I literally fucked her the day before."

My breathing stops.

What?

Lane calls from downstairs, "Sean?"

"Coming," he shouts, before switching back to his phone voice. "Dude, don't ask me that. It's not like she is . . . or *was* Finch's actual mom. Who wouldn't want to fuck Shelly James? You saw her."

A pause. My heart is pounding so hard my ribs begin to ache.

Is he the man who chased after me? Why would he have done that?

His voice drops to a whisper as he keeps talking, and I stop being able to hear clearly what he's saying. He means to keep his parents from eavesdropping, I realize.

I strain to hear, but can pick up only fragments of what he whispers.

". . . Got rid of my shoes and clothes from last night, so no dirt or whatever in the woods connects back to me. I vacuumed the car before my dad was up this morning and I'll run it through a car wash . . . that car is usually immaculate . . . phone she gave me, I broke in half. They have no idea . . . nobody is going to suspect, we were just family friends or whatever. The other can't come out. I'll keep up appearances until I leave."

". . . girl gets wiped off the face of the earth."

He stands up and moves to a place where I can't see him. "Keep any of that shit out of my texts. No messages. I'm serious. No Insta, Snap, nothing. I'll see you later." He coughs again, loudly, theatrically. "We're going to dinner somewhere. Then . . . Finch."

Breathe.

"Where she always goes. The Paramount Grille. They don't bother carding anyone in that back room."

From downstairs: "Sean!"

"I gotta go. Later."

I watch him pick his shoes up from the floor. He moves in front of the closet door. Then he stops.

He looks right at me.

Or seems to.

I draw a tiny gasp of a breath.

I see his shape—his head, neck, shoulders. Even if I hadn't just heard what I had, that would be enough to know it was him I'd seen.

He pushes the closet door until it clicks shut, and everything turns pitch-black.

I hear his footsteps again, this time moving away from me.

Downstairs there are voices, softer. Then a door closing. He must not have seen me. Otherwise I'd be getting hauled out of here in handcuffs.

Breathe. Just a little longer.

On the floor around me are the sample bags I've dropped. I can feel the slight weight of them on the tops of my shoes. My legs are shaking so violently that my knees knock together.

What did I just hear?

14

The second I hear the downstairs door close, I fling open the closet door so hard it bounces against a box. I catch the door as I fall forward, the hard floor jolting my hands. The breath I've been holding escapes, and I gasp in another. Every muscle in my body is coiled but I tell myself I have to wait—just a minute—until I'm sure they've really gone. Their security guard is still downstairs, still watching—maybe even more closely than before. My elbows sink into the soft rug at the foot of Sean's bed as I pant for air.

It wasn't Brian Peterson who was involved with Shelly.

It was Sean.

He'd been in the woods with her last night and now was covering his tracks. Maybe one of them tried to break off the relationship. Maybe they fought. Maybe the fight went too far.

My head is swimming and my insides churning with nausea. I retch, then hold back the sourness of what I might have thrown up. I'd promised myself I would never go back into a space like that. Once I did, part of me thought I'd never get back out again.

Breathe.

Every memory I have of them is changed: Shelly asking about Sean at the Petersons' party—even drunk, her voice had sounded a little more than curious. Because she wasn't asking as Finch's mother.

I think of how the cooks had laughed about Shelly's "obsession" with being young. And of Detective Marion saying Shelly had stopped wanting to see him, all of a sudden, a few weeks before she was killed. Now I understand who the person was she'd started seeing instead.

Robert Holloway had seen Brian's car, except it wasn't Brian who was driving it. Detective Marion was so blind with envy he could never have guessed.

Everything fits.

Except for my part in it. *How was the murder weapon in my possession?*

I can't make sense of that fact now. The last phrase I heard Sean say keeps ringing in my mind. *". . . girl gets wiped off the face of the earth."*

He was the man Fitch had seen standing over her mother. He'd chased her, the only witness, through the woods. I picture the scratches I'd seen on her arms.

I have to warn her.

You have to go. Now.

I move down the middle of the stairs heel-toe, heel-toe, watching as the security guard stands still as a statue. The air still smells a little like Sean's cologne, and somehow also like Lane. And like flowers. It feels warmer inside, the family's movement having disrupted the stillness of the air. I tiptoe to the back of the house and find my shoes still sitting beside the back door where I left them, the key still tucked inside. It is a miracle they weren't seen.

I'm slipping them on when I hear a door close. When I look up, the shadow of the guard in the black uniform moves toward me across the hall. In a second he'll be close enough to grab me. I'll be trapped behind him in the kitchen, I know, unless I move now. It takes half a second for me to know what to do—then instinct takes over. My hands move quickly, like a reflex, slipping the key out of the double-sided deadbolt and flinging the door open.

"Hey!" he shouts. I hear a thunder of heavy boots charge in my direction. I pass through the door, and when my feet touch the driveway, I slam the door closed behind me. I slip the key into the other side of the lock and turn it just as the knob rattles. In the precious second it takes for him to realize I've locked him in, I drop both keys—the tinny sound of metal against cement—and run.

I've nearly crossed the backyard when floodlights pop on—a jolt of white light all around, like frozen lightning across the sky. I hear a door slam open behind me as I crash into the bushes. He calls out in frustration, because he's too late. I hop another fence, dart through another yard, and am gone.

* * *

I run—tree-named street signs flying past in backwards order. It feels like someone is watching from each house I pass, each lawn a tangle of shadows stretching toward a lantern-lit door. My first instinct is to call the police, to say what I've found out—but how can I tell how I know?

I'm not just afraid. I'm petrified.

For myself, and for Finch.

* * *

Just like he promised, Marion is waiting in the Walgreens parking lot when I return, sitting in the same car that he'd picked me up in earlier. The engine starts as I approach. As the lights go on, I shield my eyes and climb into the passenger seat beside him.

"You want to tell me what this is about? I was starting to worry about you."

I'm very out of breath. I try to slow down, but it's no use. "Can you drive me somewhere?" I ask him.

He looks at me for a second. "Where?"

"Please," I say.

He steps on the gas and the car lurches forward.

"Hill West Shopping Center," I tell him. It's close to the Paramount Grille, but far enough away that he won't be able to track me directly there. He hits his blinker as we turn out of the parking lot. "I have to tell you something important," I say. "But it may . . . be hard to hear."

"Let's start with why we're meeting here," he says. "I could have come to your apartment. This looks sketchy." His chin dips. "And it occurred to me that we're not far from the Petersons' place."

He waits for me to respond, but I don't.

"What's at Hill West?" he asks.

"If I tell you that I did something I shouldn't have, do you have to arrest me?"

"It depends," he answers.

"*Do* you or *don't* you?"

The car slows. "Did you remember something about last night?"

I can't go back to jail. I have to set things right—warn Finch, and then disappear. To where, I don't know, but I'll worry about that after.

"It was Sean Peterson who was involved with Shelly, not Brian," I blurt out. "I don't know for how long, but it was him who met her in the park. I think he was the man I saw on top of the hill. He was the one who chased Finch when she saw him there. He chased me too before I picked her up and got away."

He looks at me until a car horn honks and headlights flash across the windshield before setting his eyes back on the road. "*Sean*? The son? The one going to college? What makes you think all this?"

"I . . . overheard him."

"Overheard *when*?" he asks, like he's trying to sound incredulous, but his voice breaks because he knows already what I'm saying is true. The truth of it fits with something he'd sensed before now.

I point at the turn I want him to take. "Take a right up here."

I watch his throat bob as it swallows. I find my phone and text the photos I took of the Porsche tires to his number. His hands grip the wheel while I open my shopping bag. "I couldn't find the phone. I took samples off Brian's shoes, but only the tires matter now. I just sent the photos to you. I'm sure they'll match what was in the park."

He glances down at the Ziploc bags I set beside him. His breathing speeds up. "If you went into that house, it's breaking and entering. Even if you're right, even if they match, they wouldn't hold up in court because of how you got them."

"You . . . have to figure that part out. You said you know how to get around things. Another right," I say.

He turns. "What's *at* Hill West?" he asks.

But I can't say, I know he'll follow, try to stop me. I can't risk that now. I can already see the shopping-center lights, glowing butter-yellow against the dark sky. The Paramount Grille is just on the other side of the hill.

"Take these." I motion toward the bags. "Just one more thing I need to do. A little farther up here." I point.

"I'm taking you to the police, Jessie. We'll talk to them together. You'll tell them what you know. I'll sit right beside you."

He still hasn't heard about me running.

As we ease to a stop, my hand is already on the door handle.

"They were already at my apartment. I . . . had to get away from them. You can tell them what you need to about me," I say. "Thank you, Detective."

Then I'm out the door.

I'm on the sidewalk, crossing an alleyway as he's yelling out my name.

* * *

The streets are busy with the rush of passing traffic. Ahead of me, I see a bright green sign lit up against the gray-orange night sky, and the name written in cursive there clicks in my head—it's the place Sean mentioned. As I walk, I notice a woman across the parking lot leading her two kids away from me. In her eyes I see . . . *the word for when you've seen someone before* . . . a look of *recognition*. Am I imagining it, or is she hurrying her kids along because she knows who I am? I can't tell. I check the time on my phone and step against the side of a column, where I can see the entrance Finch would be coming through. The seconds seem like hours as I try to keep still.

The parking area beside the restaurant has only a few cars, none of which look like something Finch would drive. Two teenage girls stand beside the front door as if they are waiting for someone to arrive.

The hair on the back of my neck stands up when I think of Shelly's SUV brushing past me just one night ago. Now, I'm following her daughter. The daughter everyone, even Detective Marion, assumes I envy.

I *have* envied her perfect life, her luck in being adopted into a perfect family. Is she aware of her luck, or has she not considered it much? I wonder why she would go out with friends so soon after what happened, but I realize that of *course* she wants to. She probably wants to think about *anything* aside from her mother being gone. And naturally, she wants to see Sean.

And she has no idea.

How did she not recognize him?

I hope he isn't waiting inside, wearing that same forced smile I saw him welcome her with at his graduation party. She didn't know who she was dealing with that night—and neither did Owen or Shelly. Neither did I.

I know Sean will arrive soon, but I don't see the Porsche anywhere, or either of the SUVs from the Petersons' garage. Is he aware that Robert saw him? Is Brian aware of his and Shelly's affair? Is Lane? What must it take for their lives to look so perfect? Perfection calls for attention to every single detail. It requires discipline and calculation, like the fine movements of a knife against a cutting board.

I watch a few cars come and go, and then a set of red taillights appears—small, low to the ground. A bright green Mini Cooper. The girls beside the door seem to notice the car too. One drops her phone into the purse she's carrying.

I swallow. I know it's probably Finch arriving. I squint, trying to peer through the tinted windows as she slows down. I pray she's alone, but I can't tell. I can see the dark tombstone-shaped headrests, but nothing more. I may have only one chance to warn her before my time runs out.

As she gets out of her car, I try to put my words together, to organize what I need to communicate to her.

Your boyfriend is a murderer. He murdered your mother. The man you saw standing over her body was him. He chased you, wanting to kill you too.

". . . girl gets wiped off the face of the earth."
I clear my throat.

I don't know how I'll talk, but I have to. Her life may depend on it.

She closes her car door with a soft push and looks around, rubbing the back of her neck like it's sore. She waves at two girls standing near the restaurant's front door, who both wave back. We're close enough that when the restaurant's front door opens, I hear the sounds from inside—a girl's quick laugh, a guitar solo everyone knows. I jog out into the lot, between two cars, speeding up so that I see her—and so she sees me.

I clear my throat.

"Fin . . . ," I start, then halt as my throat catches. I shake my hands out nervously, and try again, "Hi."

She jumps a little.

I raise my hands to my mouth like I am stifling a cough. "I'm sorry," I say through my fingers. "I didn't mean to startle you."

Finch's eyes widen before she looks side to side, then toward her friends by the door.

From the corner of my eye, I see her friends stop. They look at each other. I steady myself to not lose my nerve. I keep rubbing my fingers and thumb together like Ms. Parsons showed me to stay in the moment. "It's just me, I'm alone. I have to tell you something."

But she looks confused. "What are *you* doing here?" she asks, sounding frightened.

"It's about last night," I stammer. "You're not safe. Your mom . . . and Sean."

Finch steps back, wobbling, reaching for a car's sideview mirror to keep herself from falling. Neon from the restaurant window shines in her eyes. It's amazing how much she looks like

Shelly James, I think in a flash. Or how much Shelly had looked like her.

"Wait, *what*?" Her voice rises. "Stop. Okay? *Stop*! You're that *stalker* girl."

Something is wrong. I've misunderstood the situation.

"You're *not safe*," I tell her again, searching for the right words. The more nervous I get, the harder talking becomes. My head fills with a noise that makes it hard to hear my own thoughts.

Finch steps back again, and I stop cold.

She looks at me like she has never seen me before.

It makes me doubt, for the first time, if I really picked her up from the side of the road last night.

I step back again, trying to understand her expression. Finch James seems to be looking at a complete stranger.

"You're that stalker girl," she says again, even louder the second time, glancing to where her friends are standing.

They start toward her again. One is looking at her phone but drops it to her side. The other steps off the curb and calls out, "Finch?"

I stop rubbing my thumb and forefinger together. I meant to do the right thing, but I can see that coming here was a mistake. Finch's eyes glisten like she might burst into tears. I know I need to run.

"What are you doing here?" she screams, her voice carrying like a shot across the parking lot. "Someone help me!"

More people rush toward us like a flock of shadows. I shake my head as I raise my hands.

"No, no, no. I just want you to be safe. Sean Peterson . . ."

But Finch is screaming, "Help! Oh my God, help! What the fuck!"

She slips as she tries to turn, landing on her knee, crying out from the pain. Then her friend from the doorway is at her side, her hand under Finch's arm. When Finch looks over her shoulder at me, her expression has changed so much that she looks like an entirely different person.

Across the parking lot, a boy yells out her name. Her friend helps her stand up, and I watch as she merges into a group. I see a finger point at me. I step back again, my shoes rippling neon-lit puddles. When I see a phone light up, I turn to run.

I feel kids watching as my feelings chase each other like ghosts inside my chest, swirling and fighting. Why is Finch so afraid of me? Doesn't she know, after I found her on the side of the road, that I would never hurt her? Last night, she'd seemed so thankful after she climbed into my car. But now she didn't seem to remember that at all.

Did I dream all of it?

When I told Detectives Marion and Williams I'd seen Finch, they'd both said that was impossible. But I *was* sure, until just now.

I know she was real. I drove her to the police station.

There's something I don't understand—invisible but painful, like a sharp rock inside a shoe. A small fact that explains everything.

Maybe she's confused, I tell myself. Maybe something's happened to her memory.

Or maybe something's happened to mine. Even as I replay the sequence from last night over and over—my being recognized at the party, asked to wait, walking to my car, seeing the man on the hill, finding Finch along the road—I know there is a part of the story I'm not seeing.

There has to be.

When I turn to walk away, two police cars enter the parking lot.

I cut through the space between the restaurant and the shopping center, then hop a guardrail. I feel the blacktop under my shoes, then grass. In the distance, a siren begins to wail. Old sets of curtains and vertical blinds in shop windows shimmer in the blue light. I sprint around a corner, then cross another parking lot before jumping over a ditch. Cool, muddy water splashes over my ankles, soaking my shoes and the bottoms of my jeans. I follow the ditch, then cut up through another lot. From there, I cross through a drainpipe so big a car could drive through it. Each step is a heavy splash. I kick away clumps of leaves as I move into the dark. I follow the sound of the water through the end of the tunnel, then push open a drain—wet metal slipping against my hands, my shoulders struggling with the weight. I try to stand but fall down an embankment, rolling down the hill until I stop at the edge. The rush of water has turned to a powerful flow. My body is beaten, the starts of bruises already forming under my wet shirt.

In front of me is the rush of the Cumberland River, swollen and muddy from the recent rain. I catch the flicker of a flashlight on the wet drain behind me just as I dive into the water.

15

Most people won't do what it takes to stay hidden. Detective Marion had said that. Did he do what it took? Will I?

I can't see through the gray-brown water. Reflex forces me to breathe, at least to try, but water fills my mouth, my lungs. It tastes a little like metal. The river is full from the rain the days before. It pulls like it wants to swallow me. I push to the surface and gasp for air as I try to blink the water from my eyes. My arms flap under me like a dog's paws, hands sweeping beneath me, like I'm dragging myself through outer space. I have only a basic idea of how to swim, so my struggling only manages to keep me afloat as the current drags me away.

I have the thought that if I live, I'll be very, very cold once the shock wears off.

A branch scrapes my shoulder as it floats past. A small wave slams into me, forcing my head under water again. Chilly as it is, the water burns the inside of my nose. I draw another breath when I come up and search the surface for any straight line that could be the riverbank. I see only water, rushing soundlessly in every direction, little waves rising into angry peaks. I don't know how far the river has taken me, but I do know I will drown if I stay in it. A part of me would rather die than face the police. But a stronger part won't let me give up.

When I finally spot concrete, I focus on the shoreline and paddle with my arms toward the bank as the river begins to curve. I move toward a steady light like it's a star I want to catch with my hand, like I'm reaching for a firefly that's frozen in place.

Rocks slam my knee, scraping upward along my right thigh. I bite my lip to push away the pain. I want to scream, but somehow stretch my foot forward to halt my momentum. My shoe knocks against something else that is jagged and hard. A cinder block, maybe. Getting out will be a scraping mess that could cut me to shreds, but what choice do I have? I reach for branches, brambles— whatever I can grasp and hold onto as the current pulls at me.

I wedge my foot onto something sturdy, take hold of the corner of a rock, and haul myself up. Over the seawall, I see that the light I followed belongs to a back porch. Bugs circle listlessly around the bare bulb. I move my hand again until it finds another rock I can pull myself onto. I find another, and another, until I fall forward into grass, where a big-sounding dog howls at me from behind a fence. It's deep-voiced and uncertain—a dog that doesn't know me.

I turn my head toward the chipped white fence slats and shush it because I know I have to move. I run between two houses, the stars bright pinpoints above. When I come onto the street, I see that I'm in a neighborhood that is completely unfamiliar to me even though it's just across the river from where I've been. The dog barks on, a steady voice asking for *attention, attention*. Behind me, I hear the swoosh of a sliding door open, and I make my way onto the quiet street, my shoes sloshing with every step.

I cut between two more houses and find myself in an alley. The cars a few blocks away sound like sweeping brooms. My knee aches meanly, but I won't look at it—not yet. I may need to stop if it's bad, and I *can't* stop, even though I don't know where I'm headed. When I hear the *thwack-thwack* of a helicopter, I look up and see the hazy edge of a search light.

Go.

Who can help me? Detective Marion would have to aid in my arrest. Ms. Parsons would open her door, but she has *professional responsibilities*. She would have to act appropriately because I am a person running from the police. Thoughts press against the back of my mind—thoughts that I have no time to think about now. How could the police have found the murder weapon in my apartment? *Was that even true?*

It has to be. Detective Williams hasn't liked me from the beginning, but I heard the other officer whisper it to *him*. They wouldn't *all* be working against me, creating a story. *The word for when people work together against you* . . . I know better than to think their finding a murder weapon in my place is a *conspiracy*.

But what *is* the weapon? I ran away before I heard.

I know how that looks.

Off the main street is a hardware store. A camera, black and round, hangs beneath the eaves, pointing toward the rear door but not the dumpsters out back. I crouch beneath an overhang, my shirt and jeans soaked. Lucky it's summer, I think. Three months earlier I might have frozen to death. I go as dim as I can, even though I'm trailing a puddle behind me with every step.

I know already what I mean to do here.

Before I went into the dark, I lived with a foster kid named Hannah who taught me things about being on the street and running away. She had done it plenty of times. It has been so many years since she told me, but I tell myself: *remember,*

remember. Hannah could make a shelter, and start a fire by short-circuiting a battery, then build it up using dry leaves and twigs.

She taught me to sleep away from insect nests and places prone to flooding. She'd slept under houses in crawl spaces for half a year before getting caught.

"I got sloppy," Hannah told me, lying awake one night, full of advice. She'd been arrested for shoplifting a few days earlier. "I thought living off the land was impossible, but I got water from plant leaves using plastic bags, once. Finding water in a city like Nashville is actually easy." She could find her way from the position of the sun during the day, then at night by finding the North Star. I think that if she could do it, I can, too. At least until I can make a plan.

I push aside the fear nestled in my stomach. I wait for the traffic at the intersection to clear, then walk through shadows along the hardware store's perimeter fence. The rusty dumpster door cuts into my hand as I try to slide it to one side, but I tuck my hair behind my ear and yank it the rest of the way open. Inside, cardboard pieces lie piled in a heap. I pull out three long panels and fold them under my arm. At the fence line, I slip the cardboard underneath, then hop over, skidding down the embankment to the railroad tracks. Like a hobo, I think, turning east, traveling on foot. My wet skin feels like the same temperature as the night air, like I am disappearing into it. As my arms tire, I shift the cardboard onto my back and carry it like a beetle.

After a while, I realize I don't hear the helicopter anymore.

I walk a few miles, trying to keep my feet going. I want something to eat—anything. I think of the food I've prepared for parties and the spreads I've imagined must be backstage on Owen and Shelly's tours—trays of sushi and sandwiches, arranged in neat rows. Then later, the waste. The rubble-gray trash bags spilling over plastic bins, straining to contain it all.

Maybe I will . . . what? Go somewhere?

As I pass under a road, I hear the swishing of tires from the overpass. I move through the overgrowth of an empty lot, rain-heavy branches brushing my bare arms. I hop another fence, dirtying the front of my shirt, then move through a clearing behind a large house. A cricket hymn welcomes me. Somewhere in the distance a car alarm sounds. In my mind I beg it to quiet down. There's no telling the time. The hour is *don't get caught.*

I circle behind the house. Its windows are dark. I hope it's the right age—mid-century, which Hannah had told me was best, built with an entry to a ventilation space. The air-conditioning unit hums like a giant insect. Thirst begins to hurt, so I find a smooth rock in the garden, wipe it against the hem of my T-shirt, and pop it onto my tongue. I close my eyes at the relief of spit returning to my mouth. I glance back at the tracks of my shoes through the wet grass, then push apart the laurels in the landscaping. I find a little door just where I'd hoped on the side of the house, made of plywood, cream paint chipped from years of weather. I slide the latch left, hunch down, and toss the cardboard into the dark. When I pull the door closed behind me, the blackness is nearly absolute.

The dark knows me as well as I know it.

I take my clothes off except for my underwear and lay them under me. My wet skin prickles as the air touches it. I rest my hand on my chest, where my heart is hammering. Finally, quiet— a chance to think, though everything is insane.

I've found a tiny space of no-danger for a moment, but I have nothing: no money, no car. My phone is who-knows-where. Emptiness burns my stomach like I will never feel full again, but hunger is a strange kind of strength, one more thing to prove you can endure.

There is so much to figure out. Too much to understand.

Could I have killed Shelly and not remembered?

No.

I *know* I didn't. But I have to wait until there is proof. Or I have to prove it myself. I have to find a way to tell the police about Sean.

Then I remember something else about last night—Finch had said my name.

When I picked her up in my car, she said, "You . . . you're Jessie Duval."

I'm embarrassed to think it, but it was as though my name wasn't even a name until she said it. They were two words that didn't seem like they should come from Finch's mouth, but also they were the best sounds I'd ever heard. I swallowed the feeling of wanting her to say my name again, to be known by her as a real person with a name.

She had said it, I'm sure. So then, she knew about me.

I think about that as I try not to close my eyes, but my body needs to rest.

I fall into a dreamless nothing for I don't know how long.

*   *   *

I draw in a gasp when I wake that pulls me up onto my elbows. I've slept a little, maybe. Light frames the small door I came through and wind whistles lazily between the slim gaps. The play of dust motes in the air makes it look like I'm underwater, and a train whistle calls me from the world of sleep, like a fragment of a dream. The air conditioner rumbles as it switches on, but above me the house is silent. Surely, I think, I would hear footsteps if someone were awake.

And then I hear them: car doors closing outside, the squawk of a radio. Voices talking back and forth. I roll onto my stomach and put my clothes back on, as they have mostly dried. Grit from the dirt on them chafes my skin. The button of my jeans presses into my stomach.

Sound reverberates through the crawl space: it is a fist pounding on the tiny door so hard that the motes shift in the air. I want to believe I'm still dreaming. But when the door flies open, hands grasp at my wrists, dragging me into the light.

And I fight.

I scratch and yell, "Don't touch me, don't touch me!" Two try to hold me, even while they look away. The world is so bright it's like I've gone blind.

Through my thrashing, I hear them talking about me.

"Is there a blanket or something?" someone asks.

"The hell is she doing?"

"The hell *are* you doing, miss?"

I try to bite the one who asks me that. I can't help it. I am, as Ms. Parsons would say, *totally overstimulated*. It is *a self-protective reflex*.

Then another voice tells me: "You have the right to remain silent. Anything you say can and will be used against you in a court of law. You have the right to an attorney. If you cannot afford an attorney, one will be appointed to you."

Handcuffs pull my arms back at an angle that lights my shoulders on fire. I'm shoved into a car, my face pressed against warm vinyl. Everything turns sideways before the world begins to move, the sky accelerating. My stomach drops, a sinking that will never stop. I try to sit up and realize I can't. I am fully restrained.

* * *

At the station, the sun is warm on my face as three dark uniforms lead me up a ramp. Worn concrete feels slick beneath my shoes.

"You're going to like this a lot more if you just relax some please," a voice says. "Make this easy on everyone?"

I do struggle less—I know it is no use fighting my arrest now.

Green light shines under my fingers as they are rolled over a scanner.

"Look! Here!" a voice shouts.

They take my picture, and there is a flash so bright I see veins inside my eyelids. They look like the bare branches of a tree.

"Hold her still."

A prick stings the back of my arm.

Then comes complete darkness.

* * *

I wake in a small cell. A cot with a green blanket is attached to the wall, but I lie curled up on the cement floor. I hear people's voices, sometimes close and sometimes farther away, but mostly I block them out. I go inside myself, and I stay there. What I knew before, everything I built—my apartment, my job, my visits with Ms. Parsons—that's over now.

That life has ended. That me is dead.

The police think I am Shelly's killer. If I am to blame, I don't understand how. I am in jail and a killer is free. I can't see all of the events of the last two nights—it's as if a curtain is hiding the part of a stage where the action in a play goes on beyond my view.

Jail is a place of *extremes*. When the lights come on, they are very bright. When they go out, the cells become very dark. Sometimes, there are sudden loud noises all around—even yelling—like an accident happening over and over. Banging, slamming. But when those sounds stop, there are moments of extreme quiet. Silences so full they're like buzzing insects you can never swat away.

When I am taken to the cafeteria, I don't stay long. I feel eyes on me. I hear people talking. Someone yells, "This bitch killed Shelly James," and I keep my head down. I know better than to talk. Hands shove me down, the ground unforgiving against my hands and knees. Another shove comes, then more yelling. Some names I don't remember, and then spit.

This is the world now, I know. I'm trapped again.

After that trip to the cafeteria, I'm switched to a different cell. Instead of taking me out, they bring food to me—which I mostly don't eat.

"You'll be safer this way," a voice tells me. "By yourself for the time being."

Time becomes distorted, but everything is structured—when food comes, when voices start, and when they stop. The lights switch on, then off. Sometimes I sleep and other times I can't tell if I am asleep or not. I'm somewhere in between.

One morning, a lawyer from the public defender's office comes to talk to me. The painted cinder blocks feel cold and damp through my shirt when I sit up and lean against them.

He introduces himself and tells me, "I'm here to offer you representation." The overhead light shines through his stack of blonde curls as he pushes his glasses up his nose. "I can help you with the hearing process. You had an attorney help you before, right?"

"I want to talk to my social worker, Ms. Parsons."

The public defender clears his throat. "That's not going to be possible. Amanda Parsons is on a list of people not allowed to contact you."

I sit up straighter. "Why?"

"Because of the circumstances of when you ran away," he says. "The state considers what you did evading arrest. They're trying to decide whether or not she assisted you."

I thought life couldn't get worse, but the idea that I might have gotten Ms. Parsons in trouble seals up my lungs.

"No," I tell him. "She didn't."

He blinks at my words, holds up his hand. "The police are just making sure, Ms. Duval. They're trying to figure out how you spent the day before they found you. They know that you went to her office."

I press my palms into the floor to keep the world from spinning. "She had nothing to do with me running," I say. I can't see how she would have gotten in trouble for just meeting with me, but the past week has been so full of misunderstandings that I can't believe anyone is safe. I just know I would say anything to keep her out of this.

When I look up again, the public defender is saying my name, waving a hand back and forth. He stands, telling me he will come back soon, maybe in a day or so. As the door closes, I run my finger along the concrete edge between the wall and the floor, the edge of my fingernail scraping along the rough texture.

Maybe the man on top of the hill looked like Sean Peterson, but he could have been anyone. Only one other possibility makes sense: that I went into the woods on the night of Shelly's party. That I killed Shelly James. And that I somehow just don't remember doing it.

That's what everyone seems to think, and there is evidence to prove it.

I know it's not true, but I can't figure out what happened instead.

* * *

Later I'm taken to a room with a kind of metal desk that doesn't move. There's a mirror on my left. From TV shows I know people are on the other side, watching me, but I see only my reflection in the blank glass. Me, on my own jumbo TV.

An overhead light buzzes above me. It blurs everything to a haze, like the smear made by an old eraser on school paper. I wonder if they know about me and dark and sudden light. Maybe they mean to intimidate me. Or maybe questioning is like this for everyone.

The door opens and a man comes in who I've never seen before. He's bald, maybe in his early forties. He wears a blood-red tie. His expression says he knows I'm guilty. He just has to get me to say it.

He closes the door and begins to pace around the room. My eyes follow him, but my head hangs low.

"Ms. Duval, I'm Detective Allen. We haven't met before, but I have a few questions. Very simple. Okay?"

My palms leave sweat condensation on the metal table. Because of the light, I can hardly look at him.

"Okay?" he asks again, meanly. There is a hurriedness to the questioning that makes me even more nervous. I think to ask for my public defender, but I want out of this room as quickly as possible. I want to make it clear, if asked, that Ms. Parsons didn't help me in any way. Then I need to go back to the darker, quieter space. I nod.

"You're aware the murder weapon was found in your possession. Correct?"

"I'm aware they found . . . what they thought. I don't know."

He leans over the table. "Did you take the murder weapon away from Percy Warner Park last Saturday evening?"

"I never had a weapon. *Any* weapon."

"The object."

Blunt trauma to the head, I remember.

"I left my car in the gravel lot before the party," I tell the detective. "When I came back, I drove away. I didn't take anything from the park." I try looking up again. "What *is* the object?"

He ignores me. "How did the murder weapon come to be in your possession if you didn't take it?"

I try to find words. "Come to be in . . ."

"How did you *get the object*?" he asks.

"I don't even know what the object is."

"How did you?"

"*What* object?" I shout.

The detective steps back. Everyone always steps back whenever I finally let myself get angry.

"The jagged piece of limestone that was in your possession. There were traces of Ms. James's skin and blood on it. Did you take it from the park?"

"*No!*"

"Then how did you get it?"

Round and round. The questions make me feel crazy, feel like I'm falling into hell—and there is no way out. Thinking of skin and blood—Shelly's—on a piece of rock makes me want to throw up. My eyes feel salty and hot. I wrap my arms around my stomach and start to cry, unable to hold back now. The chair screeches across the cement as I push away from the table.

"Now, I'm going to ask you *again*." The detective steps closer. "I'm going to ask you one more time." He raises his hand. I look up a little more, shaking my head, because I can see already what he means to do. His hand moves toward my shoulder.

I stand. "Don't," I say. "No, don't." Sometimes all I want is not to be touched—as simple as that. I try to warn people, I really do.

"How. Did. You. Get . . ."

The second his hand touches me, my hand goes around his wrist. His eyes widen when I stomp on his foot. He cries out, struggling toward the door, but I am already behind him, turning his arm. My left elbow connects with the back of his skull, a crack that echoes off the close walls. I shove him hard against the side of the metal table and hear his head crack again.

When the door flies open, I'm surrounded by voices and dark shirts. The sting of electricity surges through my body, so strong it becomes everything. All my fear and confusion is erased by the pain. Just before I pass out, I catch the detective's angry eyes, his lip curled so that his teeth show.

Everything turns black again.

16

When I open my eyes, it's dark again. Somehow, I hear music, as if the wind has carried it from some far-off place.

Maybe I'm awake. Maybe I'm still dreaming.

My thoughts wander, as they did in the dark before, to Shelly.

I see you, your heart beating so fast that your whole body trembles as you speed down the road. How long since your heart ached this way—so powerfully it hurt? People might say you're being deceitful. Unfaithful. Sinful. But what do they know?

They don't know.

Maybe being in front of twelve thousand fans, their lips synced with yours—maybe even that doesn't compare to the feeling you're running toward. This is what you wrote songs about. You think: if this isn't love, there's no such thing. You have to follow it.

Maybe you think that if you died tonight, you would die happy.

You pull in to a gravel lot that is empty except for some old car and skid to a stop. Will people at the party notice you're gone? Maybe. Probably. Maybe you'll make something up.

Or maybe you won't.

Maybe you want to get caught. A laugh rises in your throat like a bubble in champagne.

The turn signals of your Mercedes strobe yellow as you lock the doors with a chirp. Then the trees fade into shadowy brushstrokes. It is the edge of dark just now, and you start up the trail, the song of cricket bows all around. By the top of the first hill, your forehead is already slick with sweat. When you pause to catch your breath, a twig snaps behind you. You turn, but dusk blurs the trail into the overgrowth on either side. Maybe the snap came from another trail. Or from an animal.

The air is so thick it stings your lungs. Something sweet blooms. Jasmine, most vivid at night, a flower that opens for moonlight.

Nashvillians have discussed this heat like they've been carrying on a rumor. Your makeup has run, and you wonder how you will look when you go back, but your heart feels like you've taken one of your pills. Seeing him somehow slows your pulse, but also makes you feel like you're flying. Like a bird, or an angel.

You keep on, the sky's edge pink with the last of the Tennessee sunset, far from the distant lights of Lower Broadway. A hundred people move here every day to try to make it the way you did. You wish them luck.

A gust rises at the top of the next hill, turning the backs of your arms to gooseflesh. Two rows of streetlights glow rose-gold in the new dark, running like an aisle leading to a stage. You hear a footfall behind you, a gentle cracking.

You say his name into the dark, but hear no response. You tell yourself you imagined the noise and come to the bench where you plan to meet. Your finger traces the splintery grooves of initials carved into the wood and the serpentine curvature of a heart. Maybe you want to cut your initials there too, but you wonder: Will this last? Despite everything? It has become the most wonderful, hazy dream, from which you never want to wake. Your fingertip circles the frayed wood until a splinter bites and you pull it away, stung.

Maybe you check your phone, then swing your feet like a child on a swing pretending to fly. But something makes the hair on the back of your neck stand up. You want to swallow but can't. Your head swirls with thoughts, distracted, but your body knows the electricity of danger right away. Another gust of wind blurs the streetlights.

When movement comes, it is so sudden you stand up. It takes your breath away. Your heel catches on a root as you stagger sideways and fall—a shockwave as you land on your bottom, the brush gnawing your fingertips. Moisture from the soil rises through your jeans and you feel the warmth of blood on your palm.

You say, "Please wait." You say, "Oh my God!" It comes out of you as a scream as your left shoe knocks loose, the ground tearing away your sock. You push yourself backward over the rocky soil. Dirt streaks your cheek when you wipe your hand over your face.

You say, "Please. Stop looking at me that way."

Overhead, clouds like vermillion cotton pull apart, revealing the moon between soft shreds.

You don't ask why.

You know why.

When the blows begin to fall, your head crackles with pain. Such pain.

You turn your face to look one last time.

Your eyes widen, then close forever.

I'm talking to Shelly James.

She is beside me in my cell. Her perfume smells like orange blossoms, the same as it did outside her dressing room. Am I looking at a ghost? Am I dead? The cell seems exactly the same as it had earlier. If I'm dreaming, it is the most real dream I've ever had. Water drips from the leaky faucet, and voices echo faintly from somewhere unknowable. The air feels warm and still.

She's close enough that I could touch her if I reached forward. She's so familiar that I'm not afraid. The mattress shifts as
she sits gently on the end of my bed. The faint light catches the
sleeve of her cotton dress. It's the color of a bluebird.

"Are you here?" I ask.

I can tell she's smiling, even in the dark. "I am, but I'm not,"
she says.

I start to sit up, but the ache in my head is a force pushing me
back onto my elbows. I must have hit my head on the table or
ground after the taser hit me, I realize. I must have been knocked
out. "I didn't kill you," I tell her. I've been wanting to say this.

"Of course not." Her voice is like honey, so gentle it seems to
soften the concrete around me.

A year in the dark I spent with her voice.

I blink hard, searching for words. "You met someone . . . in
the woods. I saw you. It was Sean?"

Shelly doesn't answer.

"You were having an affair with him," I say. I can't hide the
disappointment in my voice. My hands are fists atop the thin
blanket.

She sighs. "It's a story. Do you want to hear it?"

Yes.

"I grew up not far from here, our family was very poor. Not
as bad off as you, but enough that kids teased us, pretty much all
the time. My father ran off. My sisters, Mom, and I, we had to
make do with very little. Mom was always away, and my oldest
sister went to work at sixteen. You know what that's like in a mill
town?" Tears gleam in her eyes in the faint light. "We stole food.
I stole food. I'm not proud of that, but what could I do? I listened
to the sound of traffic from the highway at night, learning every

note on the fret-board of a guitar my uncle stole from someone. Again and again until I knew how to play."

I think of the way my neighbors practice night and day, repeating the melodies over and over like they're searching for something. I picture Shelly practicing like that.

"Owen was already a celebrity, but when he met me I was nobody. I played state fairs, pool halls. I ate fast food in a van for two years. I slept on floors, using rolled up magazines for pillows. Early one morning when I was twenty-one, the van skidded off the road, everyone inside nearly died." She touches a tiny star-shaped scar on her cheek. "I looked in the mirror after I got stitches. I wanted to quit. But I couldn't go back to what I'd come from.

"When Owen and I got married, I thought I'd never need to worry again, thought I'd never be lonely. But he worked. Constantly *worked*. More each year it seemed. I told him, we've made it, we don't have to push so hard. But no success was ever enough, even though I knew we could live anywhere we wanted to, drive any kind of car, send Finch to the best schools.

"He never really *got* me. He was a millionaire, but drove a '78 Ford truck that shot steam from the hood because he was used to it. Once, I went to go look at a property. Owen said I was acting different, full of myself. I told him, 'I *am* different. I have three million dollars in my pocket now.'" She laughs shyly, teases her hair with her fingers, then inhales as if about to hold her breath. "I told him, 'I can do whatever I want.'

"I guess eventually he lost interest in me. We'd been together for a decade. It happens. After we adopted Finch, we drifted even farther apart. That's not an excuse, but nothing was ever the same. We had separate lives. And I needed to *live*. I needed to *feel*. I spent money. I traveled." She looks at me and lowers her voice. "I did other things I shouldn't have."

"You saw . . . Detective Marion," I say. "And Sean."

She makes a motion with her chin that I think is a nod. "Just so you know, I took no pleasure in betraying anyone, or in sneaking around like we did."

My stomach sinks, even if I'm only dreaming, or talking with a ghost. I picture Sean, standing so confidently in his backyard, waiting for Finch to arrive. Shelly didn't want him because he was Finch's boyfriend—she wanted him despite it.

I also try to picture her and Detective Marion as a couple. He got caught up in the fantasy part of her—that was clear. But maybe she allowed him to keep seeing her in that idealized way. Did she ever let her guard down with him, like she is with me now?

There are things I want to thank her for, so many things, despite everything. Phrases in her lyrics, bits of her songs, that maybe only I would have noticed. There are also so many things I need to ask.

There are things only Shelly and I will ever know.

"Did Sean . . ."

From the other end of the hall comes the creak of a door opening, then the echo of it slamming shut.

She sits up straight when she hears the sound, and sniffs like she's just been woken up. I feel the mattress shift as she stands up, her motion bringing the orange blossom perfume back into the air. She smooths her hands over her dress. "Someone's coming," she tells me.

I'm saying the word "wait" when the overhead light pops on—so suddenly I close my eyes.

When I open them again, I'm alone in my cell.

When the cell door opens, it sounds like the roar of a metal lion. I force myself to sit on the bed and bring my knees up to my chest. The guard blocks most of the light from the hallway. He looks at me curiously, the way people do when they know what happened when I was young, but his mouth is pinched tight. He looks at whatever he is holding, then tosses it into my lap and steps back.

"This came," he says.

I wave a little as the door creaks closed again. He could have thrown it away, I know.

The handwriting on the package is familiar, but I can't place it. I slide my finger inside the rough paper and pull away the tape. The second I open it, I know exactly who it's from. Four small packages fall into my lap—two of strawberry Pop-Tarts, two of orange peanut butter crackers. Neat, contained food. I smile for the first time in a week. *Ms. Parsons.* There may never be a way to show her how much her thoughtfulness means.

I lay three of the packages on the shelf beside my bed, then sit on the floor again and eat the first of the Pop-Tarts very slowly. Crumbs scatter everywhere—green and pink stars on the dark floor. For just a minute, I don't even mind.

Later, the public defender returns. He looks neater, like he's cut his hair, but he wears the same beige-cream-colored shirt as before. It feels like we're alone even as voices echo all around us—sounds bouncing off concrete, off metal. The jail is so sturdy, it traps sound too.

The attorney winces when he comes close enough to see my eye, which is purple from being slammed into the desk after I was tasered. He makes a kind of inhaling sound—his lips tightening into an O.

The cool concrete feels good against the backs of my legs, so I stay seated on the floor.

"I heard about yesterday," he says, as he lowers himself to sit on my bunk. "And I'm sorry that happened. That's why I offered to represent you the day before. Sometimes a neutral party can keep things calm. I should have been there."

I see his point.

He crosses his feet under him. His shoes are covered with white streaks and scuffs. The sole of the left one flaps where it comes apart from the rest of the shoe.

"I'm still willing to be your attorney," he tells me, almost like he is joking. "I mean, the offer still stands."

I straighten my back against the wall. I don't want to talk to him, or anyone, but I also don't want a repeat of yesterday either. I know I'm in deep trouble. And I need some answers.

"I have a question," I say.

The lawyer looks up, hopefully.

"If it stays . . . between us."

"Of course." He looks at the bars, as if to make sure no one is coming. He rubs his hands together a little. "Absolutely, it does. Attorney-client privilege still stands, if this means that you're agreeing for me to represent you."

He pulls a yellow legal pad from the briefcase he brought with him and sets it on his lap. He opens a pen with a click that echoes through my cell.

"The detective said something that can't be right," I say. "He said there was an object used like a weapon. He said it came from the crime scene but that they found it in my apartment. That can't be true."

"You're talking about the rock they recovered. It had Ms. James's DNA on it. I saw the crime-lab report. Why do you say it's impossible that you had it?"

I am not normal in a lot of ways, but I'm not the kind of cra.
that makes up stuff or loses important memories. I have n
memory of the trail where Shelly James was killed. And no one
had handed me a bloody piece of limestone. That, I would have
remembered. I'm innocent. I try not to glare as I answer him.
"Because I didn't go near Shelly James in the park, and I didn't
leave there with anything. And no one has been in my apartment
between then and now . . ."

Find the right words.

The throbbing in my head from hitting the table doesn't help
any.

". . . except for the detectives."

I want to *not* say Detective Marion's name, but I'm sure
everyone knows who interrogated me the first time anyway.

He starts shaking his head before I can go on. He moves the
pen around the pad as if he's doodling a shape. "The rock wasn't
in your apartment, Ms. Duval. It was found under the passenger
seat of your car."

17

The attorney starts talking again but I just look back at him in a daze. I'm confirming his impression of me—that I'm too weird, too far gone, to defend. That I may not be able to help myself even though my life is at stake. He's right. I am gone, in a way—my thoughts are stuck on what he said.

They found that rock that struck Shelly James *inside my car*.

I *knew* it wasn't possible for it to be in my apartment. I *knew* I hadn't brought it inside, and the only other people who came there were Detectives Marion and Williams. Neither of them would have carried it in, and they were both in my sight the whole time they questioned me. Maybe it would have been possible for someone to break in and hide it there, but that explanation started to stretch even what I could imagine.

Until this morning, I had wondered if I had been set up somehow. I wondered: Would Detective Williams have planted it to clear Marion? No cop wants to see another cop found guilty. But no, I'd heard about the murder weapon being found just as Williams did.

The attorney repeats my name a few times again before he stands to leave, his voice swallowed up by the hallway voices, slamming doors, and laughter around the jail.

Where has my car been? And who has been inside it?

Then I realize something that turns my blood cold.

I clench my hands into fists as I sit on the jail floor, pounding the ground with each realization until the backs of my hands begin to ache.

My attorney's almost to the door.

"Wait!" I run to the door to catch him.

He turns around, looking at me with a half-impatient, half-surprised expression. "Did you remember something else?"

"I want to talk to Owen James."

He scratches the side of his head while giving me a we-don't-have-time-for-this look. "You're serious?"

I understand why he's asking. After all, I have a history of having very bad boundaries with the James family. Why should any one of them want to meet with me, considering the evidence? But the *answer* has clicked in my head, and I need to tell someone. "Of course I'm serious. I understand what happened now."

His head cocks slightly as he walks back toward where he was sitting. He grips the bunk rail and stays standing. "These are the first truly coherent words you've said since I offered to represent you. If you recall something about that night, I suggest you tell me. I'm the one trying to help you, and I can't let my client just . . ."

But I cut him off by shaking my head, no. After being tricked by Robert Holloway into believing Owen and Shelly wanted to "set things right" with me, and Finch acting like she'd never met me before, I've had enough. "It's only Owen I'll tell," I say. "He deserves an explanation too."

"Ms. Duval," he begins.

"My mind is made up."

One advantage of being seen as unusual is that normal people don't know how far to push.

He lets out a long, whistling sigh. "As your attorney, I advise you that you're not in a position to dictate terms. Even if I did communicate to the court that you would prefer to talk with Owen James directly, the chances of the kind of meeting you're talking about are very small."

We look at each other for a few seconds.

"What I'm saying is it won't happen," he says.

"I'm saying . . . you haven't asked."

"Are you looking to make a confession? Because, if so, we should start talking about what you're about to admit. There are ways to go about . . ."

"I'm not admitting anything. I did nothing wrong that night."

"You don't have the right to ask for that sort of meeting."

"I have more right to it than you understand," I tell him.

We go back and forth for a while, him talking past me, trying to explain why what I'm asking for isn't appropriate. He leaves, eventually, shaking his head, but not before agreeing to submit a request. I know he's trying to help, and I appreciate that. What he doesn't understand is that I don't care if what I'm asking for is appropriate or not.

*　*　*

I pace from one side of the cell to the other, thinking, thinking.

No one would understand if I told them the cell feels big. So big and open and bright. I know it wouldn't seem that way to other people, but the size feels like a . . . *the word for something God gives you: blessing.* The length of the cell is a *blessing.*

Shadows shift across the floor, time stretching forward. A tray appears. My insides feel empty but also like food doesn't

belong there. I force myself to eat a roll, to wash down the pa⬛
bites with warm water that tastes like dish soap. There are noise⬛
but I hardly hear them.

Maybe I close my eyes. Maybe I sleep, I don't know. A day
passes that way.

* * *

The cell door opens again, waking me, and I sit up. At the door,
the police officers stand two by two. When it rolls open, they
enter slowly. None of them wants to come near me.

"Ms. Duval, you have a visitor. You're going to need to come
with us. You'll need to be cuffed."

One of the officers holds a taser. I want to tell him he won't
need it, but instead I just rest my head against the cinder-block
wall, sticky from my sweat mixing with the humid air. Being
touched, even cuffed, isn't as bad when I know when it's coming.
I put my hands behind my back and hear the metal zip and feel
the cold against my skin.

We walk down the hall to the room where I was the day
before. Same table, same buzzing lights, same mirror. I wonder
if the detective who questioned me then is watching from
behind it. I look at my reflection—my right eye is slightly less
swollen than it was this morning. Though my vision is still a
little blurry, at least the eye opens now. When I sit, the police
lock my hands behind me to the chair with a long chain.

Then they all leave, and for a few seconds I'm alone.

The door opens and the same detective from the day before,
Detective Allen, walks in. His eye is slightly bruised and what
looks like a white piece of tape covers the bridge of his nose.
Today, he talks to me more calmly but still close enough that I
can smell his citrusy aftershave.

"Behind that glass is a team of people watching—the detec-
ves working the case, as well as the state attorney. I want you to
know that this scenario is extremely unconventional, but since
Mr. James has agreed to it—against the advice of his attorney, I
might add—we will allow a short face-to-face meeting. The state
understands that because of the circumstances earlier in your
life you may require a special arrangement in order to make a
statement. Mr. James, in particular, wants to proceed with the
investigation as efficiently as possible. But please hear me when I
tell you any reckless behavior on your part will end the meeting
immediately. Do you understand?"

I nod.

He gestures toward the glass before returning to the door
through which he entered. "You have five minutes," he says, then
leaves. I'm by myself again, but I don't feel alone because I can
sense that I'm being watched.

After a minute or so, I hear footsteps in the hallway and see
the door handle turn. Owen James opens the door and walks in.
His boot heels click on the concrete. He is no ghost. He stands
across from me wearing a dark gray button-down shirt and blue
jeans.

I stand up so quickly the handcuffs connecting me to the
chair bite into my wrists, but if there is pain, I can't feel it.
Owen and I look at each other for a second—him just standing
there, frozen—like we're each the last person the other expected
to see. His eyes are red and lined with tired grooves. He moves
with his usual stage-practiced grace until he pulls the chair
away from the desk and begins to sit down. Then, he practically collapses onto the chair, his legs seeming to buckle
beneath him. He tugs at his collar as he looks at me, his gaze
heavy with exhaustion.

"Hi, Jessie, I'm Owen," Owen James rests his hand on his c̶ and looks at me as if to make sure I know what he's saying. H̶ shoulders relax when he seems to understand that I do. Seeing̶ him makes me wonder—just for a second—if I've dreamt every-thing that happened, starting with the Petersons' party. The hope-ful thought fills my lungs, and my chest seems to reach up toward the ceiling. *Is Shelly alive? Has all this been some fantasy?*

But Owen's expression dispels any doubt that Shelly is gone. Reality returns—I'm in jail, and may be for the rest of my life. I'm believed to be a killer. I glance at our reflections in the glass and swallow, or try to.

"Good to meet you," he says. The metal chair he sits in creaks a little.

There were always two Shellys—the rebellious entertainer she showed everyone and the vulnerable person underneath try-ing to keep up with her own persona. But there is only one Owen I understand just then. He's the exact same on stage and off, and interacting with him is thrillingly real.

He points over my shoulder. "I'm sorry about the handcuffs. I asked that they leave them off, but Metro and my lawyer wouldn't consider letting us talk unless you have them on."

I feel the double cut in the flesh of my wrists—pink lines already beginning to swell.

"It's okay," I manage to say.

"No, it's really not, but I reckon it'll have to do for right now. They said you wanted to tell me about what you saw on Saturday night."

"I do," I say slowly, gathering my nerves, "but it may be hard to hear."

Owen examines his fingernail before looking up at me and nodding, solemnly. "Go ahead," he says.

I take a deep breath before I begin. I imagine that the mirror a movie screen and that Owen and I are in a movie together. I picture Detective Allen watching, and Detective Williams's glare. It's the part of the movie when I'm supposed to own up to what I've done. Except in this movie it's the other way round—instead of confessing, I'm about to tell Owen things I know but he doesn't. I will have no trouble finding the right words. I know exactly what to say.

"It's a long story," I start, "but I know we don't have much time so I'll tell it quickly. You knew . . . I used to follow your tour?"

"Yes, I know."

"I had a strange childhood. I was confused about life for a while. I had . . . I wanted to be a part of what you and Ms. James were doing. I never meant to hurt anyone, or to frighten anyone, even though it may have seemed like it sometimes."

"I believe you about that," he says, evenly. "I've heard about your childhood. And for what it's worth, I'm sorry."

I keep on, aware of the audience behind the glass, and of the dwindling time. *Five minutes*, Detective Allen had said. Now, I had less.

"I was arrested at your show in Nashville, but I started a new life after I got out of jail. I started working as a caterer and focusing on living a good life. I didn't want to bother you or your family anymore. The weekend before last, the company I worked for catered the Petersons' party. I didn't know your family would be there, and I was scared. I tried to stay out of the way. Ms. James saw me once, but I managed to get away."

"When the lights went out, that was you," Owen says, the corner of his mouth showing—very slightly—a shadow of a smile. "Right?"

"That's right. I turned them off. I wanted to stay out of trouble because I wasn't supposed to be close to your family, so I slipped away."

"You were scared," he says calmly, like he's forgiven me.

I nod. "But you hired us for your party the next weekend, and your manager, Robert Holloway, found me at my work after everyone else was gone. I said I wouldn't go, but he told me that you and Ms. James felt bad about my arrest and wanted to set things right with me, that you admired hard work and we would all have our photo taken together when I worked at your party—it would be a happy ending. He said it would be good publicity with the album coming out."

Owen's face clouds over with confusion. He cuts a quick glance at the mirror.

My thoughts flash back to the cases of wine, the smirk on Robert's face, the sound of the music coming from inside the house, and the flickering light reflected in the swimming pool.

"He was actually stealing from you and Ms. James, some of it valuable, but he wanted to look like a hero—like he'd caught me trespassing and protected you. He wanted me to be caught at the house so it would look like I was the one taking it. I learned later that Ms. James had suspected him of taking things as far back as last summer's tour, and that he had access to a bank account of yours. But that's another story. Robert didn't know what was about to happen to Ms. James Saturday night."

Owen's jaw clinches. "He asked you specifically to come to our party? Even though you intended to not go?"

"Yes," I say.

His exhausted eyes brighten with understanding. "Go on," he says.

"Of course, I wanted what Robert was saying to be true. So I believed him and agreed to work the party. I saw Ms. James on my way to your house. She passed me in her SUV, then walked into the woods. After Robert called the police to tell them I was there, I was scared and ran to my car. In the dark, I saw someone on the same trail Ms. James had gone up—the shape of a man. I know now I was seeing Sean Peterson. They were having an affair. He had gone to meet her."

Owen doesn't move a muscle, his face perfectly still.

"But you knew already. You found out right before the party."

He doesn't respond, so I keep going with my story.

"Finch told me that you and Shelly had fought earlier. You were fighting because you found out about the affair. Shelly left just before the party, that was when I saw her. When I left the party, Sean saw me coming toward my car. He ran after me, so I drove away. A few minutes later I nearly ran into Finch on the road. She said there was a man too. She said she'd run away from him. I asked her to get in my car, and she did. She sat right in the passenger seat. I wondered if the person chasing her was the same person I'd seen. But she didn't actually see a man in the woods. Finch made that up. I didn't understand that until yesterday."

I hear Owen's chair creak and I look up. He puts his hands in his pockets. "Finch was at a friend's house," he says.

I glance at the glass, then back at Owen. I see his pulse throbbing in his neck.

"She actually made that up too. Finch wanted more than anything for her family to stay together, but she knew everything was about to end, right?"

"That's not . . ." he mumbles, then stops.

"She was angry, and she chased Shelly to the park to confront her."

"Finch was at a friend's house since earlier that afternoon," Owen says, changing direction. I picture a car slowing at a dead end and turning around. "She never got in your car that night."

"You know that isn't true," I say. "And so do I. I believed every word Finch told me that night, and I didn't understand until yesterday how the murder weapon ended up in my car. See, when I thought back, I realized I never actually watched her go inside the police station. I was afraid—the police had been called on me. And I was scared because of what Finch was saying. I drove away before I could see her open the police station door. But Finch left something behind when she got out—the limestone rock she'd used to hit Ms. James. I didn't see that she had it—it was so dark and pouring rain. She must have quietly slipped it underneath the passenger seat of my car. It stayed there until the police found it."

Owen rubs his temples, irritated. "You're just making things up now."

"I'm not making anything up. A minute ago you wanted to hear the truth, and I'm telling it to you." I think of Detective Marion when I go on: "Check the times in her phone records. Friends sometimes cover for each other. When I went to warn Finch about Sean, she had to act like she'd never seen me. Her friends were watching. She had to keep her story straight that she hadn't seen me the night before. She started screaming for help." I look right into Owen's eyes. "At the time, I didn't understand why she acted like I meant to harm her."

He stares at me blankly before standing up, glaring at the mirror. He begins to shout, "You don't know what you're . . ."

There's a knock on the door, then Detective Allen and a man in a dark blue suit enter. Owen's nostrils are flaring, but his voice softens back to how it sounded a minute earlier. "I'm . . . sorry you were involved in what happened," he says.

The man in the blue suit squeezes Owen's shoulder. None of them look at me as they leave the room. The door stays open, and I watch as Owen runs his hands through his hair. The man in the blue suit speaks very quickly. Detective Allen folds his arms over his chest.

Then the door is pulled closed, and I'm alone in the blinding lights.

18

'm led back to my cell and am alone again for a while.

A meal arrives, and I eat it. A little time passes. I drift off to sleep, and dream.

I'm standing in front of a newspaper recycling bin, a stack of old editions in my arms, conflicted because I'm destroying history. But somehow I know that what I'm destroying will actually be transformed. I open the lid and find a snake coiled inside, defensive and ready to strike. Its fangs gleam, slick with venom. When the lid slams closed with a bang, I step back, wondering as my heart pounds: *Am I safe?*

Then, I wake up.

Later, my lawyer returns. He seems in a rush this time—chewing and then hurriedly crunching a mint. He talks into a phone while typing onto a tablet. I raise my hand but he's looking upward, like he's trying to remember something by reading it off the ceiling.

"Sir?" I ask. I've forgotten his name.

"Oh, hi." He smiles, almost like he's just realized we are sitting in the same space. "I'm trying to get you released."

I pause as this sinks in.

"Suffice it to say that meeting with Owen James may have gone just as you planned, but it was definitely not what he or his attorney expected. You're now being held in connection to a crime that someone else has now been arrested for."

My hands begin to tremble with relief. My eyes look heavenward. But at the same time my chest begins to ache. I don't want to be in jail, but there's no joy in Finch being arrested. I never wanted any of this to be true. My throat feels tight as I ask him, "So, I'm going to be let out?"

"I'm trying to see if the state wants to press any other charges—which they may. But they also *may not*, you know, considering your, you know."

He means my history as a kid. He sounds shy as he mentions it, and he sounds young. He looks at his phone and squints, then lowers it and looks up at me. He says, "From what I understand, Finch James has confessed to the murder."

*   *   *

The next day, I am led into a room with little tables where visitors sit on one side and prisoners on the other. A guard is stationed at each side of the door. The room smells like hairspray and perfume and everyone speaks in a voice just above a whisper. The echoes caught between the hard walls sound the way I imagine a beach's tide would, only softer.

When I see Ms. Parsons sitting stiffly with her hands in her lap, I realize she looks completely out of place but I recognize her expression. It's the same as when we first met, when she first heard the details of what had gone on when I was a kid—before and during my living in the dark. To my eyes, she has a warm glow around her. I feel bad that she has had to come to a room like this to see me.

She chews her bottom lip as I sit across from her.

"Jessie," she says, "Your eye."

"It'll . . . it's okay. In the case, Fin . . ."

Ms. Parsons nods. "Yes, Finch was arrested."

It has to be true. Ms. Parsons wouldn't lie.

"What you said in your meeting with Owen James changed the whole investigation. When you told him Shelly was with the Petersons' son, Sean, the police had to look more closely at Finch. Up to then, they hadn't had a motive, and she had an alibi. She was questioned again after you spoke to Owen. Her story didn't fit what she'd said before, apparently. They searched your car again and found a strand of her hair. There was no other explanation for that except that you had picked her up like you said. She said she wanted to talk to her father and to the family attorney."

I take a breath as what she says washes over me.

"Your lawyer told me that the state isn't going to pursue charges against you. But there may be a hearing that sets different terms of your probation."

I glance at the people sitting at the other tables and feel a strange guilt that I may be leaving soon but they won't. I ask Ms. Parsons, "You and I will still be able to work together?"

"Probably even more than before."

There aren't many good things about what happened, but this is one.

*   *   *

How could she?

That's what anyone who knew the James family asks about Finch as the true story comes to light. How could a girl kill her own mother? After Shelly and Owen adopted her, took her into their home, and made her a part of their family? How could she be so cruel? The question is already a whisper around Nashville, I'm sure.

"She wasn't cruel," I say to Ms. Parsons, a week later. "She was afraid."

I understand her fear.

I've seen a bumper sticker that says: *It's never too late to have a happy childhood.* That's really nonsense. Sometimes the chance to have had a family when you're growing up has passed.

"When I think about what it must have been like for Finch to be given what she always wanted, then watch Shelly try to throw it away, my heart breaks for her," I tell Ms. Parsons.

No, Finch wasn't cruel—she got angry and lost control. She tried for years to keep the family together—I know because I heard her myself when I was eavesdropping outside a dressing room. I could hear the desperation in her voice, even then. I think of her protectiveness when she thought Andre and Malik were taking pictures behind her home.

Ms. Parsons rubs the arm of her chair. Her throat moves as she swallows. "Finch sat beside you that night, right after she'd left the woods," she says, and looks at me like, *How do you feel about Finch considering that?*

Would I have handled things differently if I'd been in her shoes? If I'd been given what I'd dreamed about, then watched as it was destroyed from the inside out?

Maybe.

Yes.

I can live without.

But most people can't.

*   *   *

Two months have passed since everything happened, but I still call Detective Marion, Detective Marion. He tells me I don't have to, that I can call him Jason, but I keep on, and now he smiles when I say it. He says he doesn't mind being formal and that it actually feels good to be reminded he was a detective because he's working at a desk for a few months. It's a kind of punishment for having run away. He says he doesn't mind the pace of the work for the time being and that he feels lucky to still have a job.

Detective Marion and I text almost every day and get together a few times a week. Today, we're meeting at a diner near where I live that smells like baked bread and burnt butter and coffee. He sits on one side of the booth and I sit on the other. The waitress pours coffee and smiles at him. He stirs sugar into his coffee with an old-looking spoon that clinks against the sides of the cup. The edge of it reflects a little of the pink in the neon sign that says OPEN.

"I kind of like this," he says, meaning me and him sitting together.

"It's nice," I say. Sometimes, when I'm with Detective Marion, I smile until my face feels sore. I don't want to tell him that I've never been taken out to breakfast before, but I think he can tell, as I probably act confused about how to do everything.

He sips his coffee, makes a too-hot face, then blows a little on the surface.

"I mean, a person can't live on strawberry Pop-Tarts alone."

Actually, they can, I think, but I know what he means.

I wonder about everything from earlier this summer, sometimes a little too much. We hardly ever talk about what happened. I want to put that time behind me, but I also have a thousand questions. Today, I need to ask just a few.

Detective Marion keeps his voice low when I bring it up. "Ask away, I guess. I'll tell you what I can. I wasn't there, of course, so I can only tell you what I've heard."

I ask about when they started to suspect Finch.

"What your counselor told you was right. Finch wasn't a suspect before your conversation with Owen," he says. "The detectives listening in believed your story enough to trick her a little. Detective Allen asked her if she'd noticed any scratches on your uniform when you picked her up on the side of the road. She started to tell him, then remembered she wasn't supposed to have seen you. It unraveled pretty quickly from there on. The police scheduled another interview. Their family attorney was present, of course. Owen was in denial, or maybe he felt guilty about his part in Finch's rage. He made the mistake that night of telling Finch, not only that his relationship with Shelly was ending, but exactly why. Losing her family and her boyfriend all at once was more than she could take."

"And the man on top of the hill?"

"That was Sean, you were right. He probably looks just like his father at that distance, so at a glance, in the dark, it would have been hard to tell. He was the one who made the anonymous call about Shelly. He saw you drive away and called the police on the phone Shelly and he used to communicate, then destroyed it immediately afterward. When the police found her burner phone, the numbers matched the one he had used."

When I imagine Sean being questioned, I hear a catch in his voice, like he's on the verge of crying. I know he likes to act tough, so I picture him hiding it with a cough. I imagine him telling the police that the relationship went further than he had intended. I wonder what he and Shelly felt for each other, even if their relationship was wrong.

I can't help but think of Owen—the unbelievable enormity of his loss. No wonder he was in denial about Finch's role. Who could absorb that kind of shock?

A while after we've ordered, the waitress comes by and sets two plates on the table. Detective Marion's has eggs and bacon and grits. Mine has three pancakes and four strips of bacon. I've never had so much food on my own plate. He thanks the waitress and puts his paper napkin in his lap. I do the same with mine.

"I've been meaning to ask you something," he says. "Do you remember me saying that I wanted to help get your tooth fixed? The one that chipped at the concert?"

The word for doing something without thinking about it . . . Instinctively, I find the chipped place with the tip of my tongue.

"Yes, but you really don't have to. It wasn't your fault. I'm used to it now."

That isn't true, exactly, I'm not sure I would ever get used to it, but I don't want him to feel bad. The chip is always there, as a reminder. It can be hard to forgive yourself when you do something bad, the thing you regret most.

He taps the spoon on the side of his cup and sets it on the napkin.

"I know that," he says. "I'm not offering because I have to. I want to help get it fixed because it feels right."

I don't know what to say. His offering reminds me of Ms. Parsons and the *overtime session* feeling, except that she is my counselor and Detective Marion is my I-don't-know-what.

My friend.

I watch the waitress pass by and smile at him again.

"I set up an appointment for you with my dentist two weeks from today. He'll have to touch your mouth, though. There's really no way around that. But he said the work probably wouldn't take long and that it would be no big deal."

Detective Marion is wrong, though. His help is actually a very big deal.

"You can think about it, Jessie."

"No," I say, swallowing. "I don't have to."

*　*　*

I need to do something else that makes my heart speed up in a different way. It feels like a risk, although I tell myself I'm really just accepting an invitation. I find my phone, which was returned to me in the same barely functional condition in which it had been found, and scroll my finger carefully over the cracked screen until I find Malik's number.

I type and erase the beginning of a message several times.

Hi Malik, it's Jessie . . .

Malik, I'm out of jail and . . .

Sorry it's taken so long to get back to you . . .

But then I stop typing, take a deep breath, and begin a call. I pace my tiny porch as I listen to it ring, taking in slow, deep breaths of air freshened by the summer rain. The ring sounds distant somehow, like an echo in a cave. I decide I've missed my chance and that I won't leave a voice mail, when he answers.

"Jessie?" he asks cautiously, like he's not sure it's really me calling.

I clear my throat. I find my voice.

"Hi," I say, "It's me."

"I thought I might not hear from you again. I'm so glad you called."

"I was wondering . . . if you still want to have coffee."

The word for wanting to do or have something very much; I wonder if he hears the *eagerness* in my voice.

A small, yellow bird lands on the railing, right beside me, the very moment he says, "Yes."

*　*　*

Light.

Everything is so bright I see red when I close my eyes. Above me, the light moves close to my face, then holds in place. I lie nearly flat, my heart pounding because there is so much light and because I know I am about to be touched. My stomach feels sick, but not completely *kitchen cabinet.* I tell myself a good thing is happening. I draw in a breath until my lungs are full. When I let it out, I feel calmer.

Detective Marion's voice is at my shoulder. The dentist has allowed him to sit beside me because Marion told him I don't like being touched. He knows the right distance to stay from me.

"Jessie, there's going to be a tiny pain in your gum that will only last a second. Then you won't feel anything. Right, doc?"

"That's right, just keep your mouth open nice and wide for me, okay?" the voice above me says. He leans over me, blocking part of the light.

I nod "okay". A drop of sweat from under my arm feels cold as it runs down my side. I close my eyes and try to hold still as the pain stings my mouth—sharp but fast, like Detective Marion said. With both hands, I grip the sides of the chair.

"You're doing great, Jessie," Detective Marion says.

From the corner of my eye, I can see the tiny scar I put on his forearm, thin and milky, like a spiderweb. The cut is completely healed, and the mark is barely visible, unless you know just where to look. What I do next must be a reflex, another instinct. It's nothing I've ever done before, but it feels right. I reach my hand toward Detective Marion, meaning for him to hold it. It hangs in the air for a second. I imagine him hesitating. And then I feel his fingers against mine, his rough skin and gentle squeeze. "Jessie, you okay?"

I squeeze his hand a little tighter, then make a thumbs-up.

"We're almost done now," the voice above me says. "Not too bad, right?"

"You're doing great, Jessie," says Detective Marion.

And I am.

I'm doing great.

ACKNOWLEDGMENTS

I would like to thank my editors Chelsey Emmelhainz and Melissa Rechter. Creating this book has been a team effort, and it was vastly improved by your thoughtful guidance. Thank you.

Many thanks to my agent, Rachel Ekstrom Courage. I continue to be indebted to you for your wisdom and support. Your enthusiasm for this project has been invaluable along the way.

Thank you also to my family and friends for their encouragement and advice (and patience) at various times while I was working and fretting about this book.